UNIVERSE 15

UNIVERSE 15

Edited by TERRY CARR

DOUBLEDAY & COMPANY, INC.
GARDEN CITY, NEW YORK
1985

Library of Congress Cataloging in Publication Data
Main entry under title:
Universe 15.
Contents: Mercurial/Kim Stanley Robinson—
Paladin of the lost hour/Harlan Ellison—Giraffe
Tuesday/Juleen Brantingham—[etc.]
1. Science fiction, American.   I. Carr, Terry.
II. Title: Universe fifteen.
PS648.S3U537   1985   813'.0876'08
ISBN: 0-385-19890-6
Library of Congress Catalog Card Number 85-4346

CONTENTS

UNIVERSE 15

Science fiction stories that project the problems of crime detection into the future have proven over the decades to be a favorite form for writers and readers alike. (Isaac Asimov's novels about Lije Baley—most recently The Robots of Dawn—*are perhaps the classics of this type, though Larry Niven, John Varley, and many others have produced excellent stories in this vein.) The combination of genres is a natural one, because both sf and detective fiction strongly appeal to the intellect.*

Now Kim Stanley Robinson gives us a tale of murder on Mercury, with delightful characters and well-considered science. (Despite references at the beginning to other cases solved by his protagonists, "Mercurial" is the only story Robinson has actually written in this "series"—so far.)

Kim Stanley Robinson's stories have been featured in the past several volumes of Universe, *and his first two novels,* The Wild Shore *and* Icehenge, *greatly increased his reputation in 1984.*

MERCURIAL

KIM STANLEY ROBINSON

"She rules all of Oz," said Dorothy, "and so she rules your city and you, because you are in the Winkie Country, which is part of the Land of Oz."

"It may be," returned the High Coco-Lorum, "for we do not study geography and have never inquired whether we live in the Land of Oz or not. And any Ruler who rules us from a distance, and unknown to us, is welcome to the job."

—L. Frank Baum, *The Lost Princess of Oz*

I am not, despite the appearances, fond of crime detection. In the past, it is true, I occasionally accompanied my friend Freya Grindavik as she solved her cases, and admittedly this watsoning gave me some good material for the little tales I have written for the not-very-discriminating markets on Mars and Titan. But after the Case of the Golden Sphere of the Lion of Mercury, in which I ended up hanged by the feet from the clear dome of Terminator, two hundred meters above the rooftops of the city,

my native lack of enthusiasm rose to the fore. And following the unfortunate Adventure of the Vulcan Accelerator, when Freya's arch-foe Jan
Johannsen tied us to a pile of hay under a large magnifying glass in a
survival tent, there to await Mercury's fierce dawn, I put my foot down:
no more detecting. That, so to speak, was the last straw.

So when I agreed to accompany Freya to the Solday party of Heidi van
Seegeren, it was against my better judgment. But Freya assured me there
would be no business involved; and despite the obvious excesses, I enjoy a
Solday party as much as the next esthete. So when she came by my villa, I
was ready.

"Make haste," she said. "We're late, and I must be before Heidi's
Monet when the Great Gates are opened. I adore that painting."

"Your infatuation is no secret," I said, panting as I trailed her through
the crowded streets of the city. Freya, as those of you who have read my
earlier tales know, is two and a half meters tall, and broad-shouldered; she
barged through the shoals of Solday celebrants rather like a whale, and I,
pilot fish-like, dodged in her wake. She led me through a group of Grays,
who with carpetbeaters were busy pounding rugs saturated with yellow
dust. As I coughed and brushed off my fine burgundy suit, I said, "My
feeling is that you have taken me to view that antique canvas once or
twice too often."

She looked at me sternly. "As you will see, on Solday it transcends even
its usual beauty. You look like a bee drowning in pollen, Nathaniel."

"Whose fault is that?" I demanded, brushing my suit fastidiously.

We came to the gate in the wall surrounding Van Seegeren's town villa,
and Freya banged on it loudly. The gate was opened by a scowling man.
He was nearly a meter shorter than Freya, and had a balding head that
bulged rather like the dome of the city. In a mincing voice he said,
"Invitations?"

"What's this?" said Freya. "We have permanent invitations from
Heidi."

"I'm sorry," the man said coolly. "Ms. Van Seegeren has decided her
Solday parties have gotten overcrowded, and this time she sent out invitations, and instructed me to let in only those who have them."

"Then there has been a mistake," Freya declared. "Get Heidi on the
intercom, and she will instruct you to let me in. I am Freya Grindavik, and
this is Nathaniel Sebastian."

"I'm sorry," the man said, quite unapologetically. "Every person turned away says the same thing, and Ms. Van Seegeren prefers not to be disturbed so frequently."

"She'll be more disturbed to hear we've been held up." Freya shifted toward the man. "And who might you be?"

"I am Sandor Musgrave, Ms. Van Seegeren's private secretary."

"How come I've never met you?"

"Ms. Van Seegeren hired me two months ago," Musgrave said, and stepped back so he could look Freya in the eye without straining his neck. "That is immaterial, however—"

"I've been Heidi's friend for over forty years," Freya said slowly, once again shifting forward to lean over the man. "And I would wager she values her friends more than her secretaries."

Musgrave stepped back indignantly. "I'm sorry!" he snapped. "I have my orders! Good day!"

But alas for him, Freya was now standing well in the gateway, and she seemed uninclined to move; she merely cocked her head at him. Musgrave comprehended his problem, and his mouth twitched uncertainly.

The impasse was broken when Van Seegeren's maid Lucinda arrived from the street. "Oh, hello, Freya, Nathaniel. What are you doing out here?"

"This new Malvolio of yours is barring our entrance," Freya said.

"Oh, Musgrave," said Lucinda. "Let these two in, or the boss will be mad."

Musgrave retreated with a deep scowl. "I've studied the ancients, Ms. Grindavik," he said sullenly. "You need not insult me."

"Malvolio was a tragic character," Freya assured him. "Read Charles Lamb's essay concerning the matter."

"I certainly will," Musgrave said stiffly, and hurried to the villa, giving us a last poisonous look.

"Of course, Lamb's father," Freya said absently, staring after the man, "was a house servant. Lucinda, who is that?"

Lucinda rolled her eyes. "The boss hired him to restore some of her paintings, and get the records in order. I wish she hadn't."

The bell in the gate sounded. "I've got it, Musgrave," Lucinda shouted at the villa. She opened the gate, revealing the artist Harvey Washburn.

"So you do," said Harvey, blinking. He was high again; a bottle of the White Brother hung from his hand. "Freya! Nathaniel! Happy Solday to you—have a drink?"

We refused the offer, and then followed Harvey around the side of the villa, exchanging a glance. I felt sorry for Harvey. Most of Mercury's great collectors came to Harvey's showings, but they dissected his every brush-stroke for influences, and told him what he *should* be painting, and then among themselves they called his work amateurish and unoriginal, and never bought a single canvas. I was never surprised to see him drinking.

We rounded the side of the big villa and stepped onto the white stone patio, which was made of a giant slab of England's Dover cliffs, cut out and transported to Mercury entire. Malvolio Musgrave had spoken the truth about Heidi reducing the size of her Solday party: where often the patio had been jammed, there were now fewer than a dozen people. I spotted George Butler, Heidi's friend and rival art collector, and Arnold Ohman, the art dealer who had obtained for many of Mercury's collectors their ancient masterpieces from Earth. As I greeted them Freya led us all across the patio to the back wall of the villa, which was also fronted with white slabs of the Dover cliffs. There, all alone, hung Claude Monet's *Rouen Cathedral—Sun Effect.* "Look at it, Nathaniel!" Freya com-manded me. "Isn't it beautiful?"

I looked at it. Now you must understand that, as owner of the Gallery Orientale, and by deepest personal esthetic conviction, I am a connoisseur of Chinese art, a style in which a dozen artfully spontaneous brushstrokes can serve to delineate a mountain or two, several trees, a small village and its inhabitants, and perhaps some birds. Given my predilection, you will not be surprised to learn that to look at the antique rectangle of color that Freya so admired was to risk damaging my eyes. Thick scumbled layers of grainy paint scarcely revealed the cathedral of the title, which wavered under a blast of light so intense that I doubted Mercury's midday could compete with it. Small blobs of every color served to represent both the indistinct stone and a pebbly sky; both were composed of combinations principally of white, yellow, and purple, though as I say every other color made an appearance.

"Stunning," I said, with a severe squint. "Are you sure this Monet wasn't a bit nearsighted?"

Freya glared at me, ignoring Butler's chuckles. "I suppose your com-ment might have been funny the first time you made it. To children, anyway."

"But I heard it was actually *true*," I said, shielding my eyes with one hand. "Monet *was* nearsighted, and so, like Goya, his vision affected his painting—"

"I should hope so," Harvey said solemnly.

"—so all he could see were those blobs of color; isn't that sad?"

Freya shook her head. "You won't get a rise out of me today, Nathaniel. You'll have to think up your dinner conversation by yourself."

Momentarily stopped by this riposte, I retired with Arnold Ohman to Heidi's patio bar. After dialing drinks from the bartender we sat on the blocks of Dover cliffs that made up the patio's low outer wall. We toasted Solday, and contemplated the clouds of yellow talc that swirled over the orange tile rooftops below us. For those of you who have never visited it, Terminator is an oval city. The forward half of the city is flat, and projects out under the clear dome. The rear half of the oval is terraced, and rises to the tall Dawn Wall which supports the upper rim of the dome, and shields the city from the perpetually rising sun. The Great Gates of Terminator are near the top of the Dawn Wall, and when they are opened shafts of Sol's overwhelming light spear through the city's air, illuminating everything in a yellow brilliance. Heidi van Seegeren's villa was about halfway up the terraced slope; we looked upon gray stone walls, orange tile roofs, and the dusty vines and lemon trees of the terrace gardens that dotted the city. Outside the dome the twelve big tracks of the city extended off to the horizon, circling the planet like a slender silver wedding band. It was a fine view, and I lifted my glass remembering that Claude Monet wasn't there to paint it. For sometimes, if you ask me, reality is enough.

Ohman downed his drink in one swallow. Rumor had it that he was borrowing heavily to finance one of his big Terran purchases; it was whispered he was planning to buy the closed portion of the Louvre—or the Renaissance room of the Vatican museum—or Amsterdam's Van Gogh collection. But rumors like that circulated around Arnold continuously. He was that kind of dealer. It was unlikely any of them were true; still, his silence seemed to reveal a certain tension.

"Look at the way Freya is soaking in that painting you got for Heidi," I said, to lift his spirits. Freya's face was within centimeters of the canvas, where she could examine it blob by blob; the people behind her could see nothing but her white-blond hair. Ohman smiled at the sight. He had brought the Monet back from his most recent Terran expedition, and apparently it had been a great struggle to obtain it. Both the English family that owned it and the British government had had to be paid enormous sums to secure its release, and only the fact that Mercury was universally considered humanity's greatest art museum had cleared the matter with the courts. It had been one of Arnold's finest hours.

Now he said, "Maybe we should pull her away a bit, so that others can see."

"If both of us tug on her it may work," I said. We stood and went to her side. Harvey Washburn, looking flushed and frazzled, joined us, and we convinced Freya to share the glory. Ohman and Butler conferred over something, and entered the villa through the big French doors that led into the concert room. Inside, Heidi's orchestra rolled up and down the scales of Moussorgsky's *Hut of Baba Yaga.* That meant it was close to the time when the Great Gates would open (Heidi always gets inside information about this).

Sure enough, as Moussorgsky's composition burst from *The Hut of Baba Yaga* into *The Great Gates of Kiev*, two splinters of white light split the air under the dome. Shouts and fanfares rose everywhere, nearly drowning the amplified sound of our orchestra. Slowly the Great Gates opened, and as they did the shafts of light grew to thick buttery gold bars of air. By their rich, nearly blinding glare, Heidi van Seegeren made her first entrance from her villa, timing her steps to the exaggerated Maazel *ritard* that her conductor Hiu employed every Solday when *Pictures at an Exhibition* was performed. This *ritard* shifted the music from the merely grandiose to the utterly bombastical, and it took Heidi over a minute to cross her own narrow patio; but I suppose it was not entirely silly, given the ritual nature of the moment, and the flood of light that was making the air appear a thick, quite tangible gel. What with the light, and the uproar created by the keening Grays and the many orchestras in the neighborhood, each playing their own overture or fanfare (the *Coriolan* came from one side of us, the *1812* from the other), it was a complex and I might even say *noisy* esthetic moment, and the last thing I needed was to take another look at the Monet monstrosity, but Freya would not have it otherwise.

"You've never seen it when the Great Gates are opened," she said. "That was the whole point in bringing you here today."

"I see." Actually I barely saw anything; as Freya had guided me by the arm to the painting I had accidentally looked directly at the incandescent yellow bars of sunlight and brilliant blue afterimages bounced in my sight.

I heard rather than saw Harvey Washburn join us. Many blinks later I was able to join the others in devoting my attention to the big canvas.

Well. The Monet positively *glowed* in the dense, lambent air; it gave off light like a lamp, vibrating with a palpable energy of its own. At the sight of it even I was impressed.

"Yes," I admitted to Freya and Harvey, "I can see how precisely he placed all those little chunks of color, and I can see how sharp and solid the cathedral is under all that goo, but it's like Solday, you know, it's a heightened effect. The result is garish, really; it's too much."

"But this is a painting of midday," Harvey said. "And as you can see, midday can get pretty garish."

"But this is Terminator! The Grays have put a lot of talc in the air to make it look this way!"

"So what?" Freya demanded impatiently. "Stop thinking so much, Nathaniel. Just *look* at it. *See* it. Isn't it beautiful? Haven't you felt things look that way sometimes, seeing stone in sunlight?"

"Well . . ." And, since I am a strictly honest person, if I had said anything at all I would have had to admit that it did have a power about it. It drew the eye; it poured light onto us as surely as the beams of sunlight extending from the gates in the Dawn Wall to the curved side of the clear dome.

"Well?" Freya demanded.

"Well yes," I said. "Yes I see that cathedral front—I feel it. But there must have been quite a heat wave in old Rouen. It's as if Monet had seen Terminator on Solday, the painting fits so well with this light."

"No," Freya said, but her left eye was squinted, a sign she was thinking.

Harvey said, "We make the conditions of light in Terminator, and so it is an act of the imagination, like this painting. You shouldn't be surprised if there are similarities. We value this light because the old masters created it on their canvases."

I shook my head, and indicated the brassy bedlam around us. "No. I believe we made this one up ourselves."

Freya and Harvey laughed, with the giddiness that Solday inspires.

Suddenly a loud screech came from inside the villa. Freya hurried across the patio into the music room, and I followed her. Both of us, however, had forgotten the arrangements that Heidi made on Soldays to cast the brilliant light throughout her home, and as we ran past the silenced orchestra into a hallway we were blasted by light from a big mirror carefully placed in the villa's central atrium. Screams still echoed from somewhere inside, but we could only stumble blindly through bright pulsing afterimages, retinal Monets if you will, while unidentified persons bowled into us, and mirrors crashed to the floor. And the atrium was raised, so that occasional steps up in the hallway tripped us.

"Murder!" someone cried. "Murder! There he goes!" And with that a whole group of us were off down the halls like hounds—blind hounds— baying after unknown prey. A figure leaped from behind a mirror glaring white, and Freya and I tackled it just inside the atrium.

When my vision swam back I saw it was George Butler. "What's going on?" he asked, very politely for a man who had just been jumped on by Freya Grindavik.

"Don't ask us," Freya said irritably.

"Murder!" shrieked Lucinda, from the hallway that led from the atrium directly back to the patio. We jumped up and crowded into the hallway. Just beyond a mirror shattered into many pieces lay a man's body; apparently he had been crawling toward the patio when he collapsed, and one arm and finger extended ahead of him, still pointing to the patio. Freya approached, gingerly turned the body's head. "It's that Musgrave fellow," she said, blinking to clear her sight. "He's dead, all right. Struck on the head with the mirror there, no doubt."

Heidi van Seegeren joined us. "What's going on?"

"That was my question," George Butler said.

Freya explained the situation to her.

"Call the police," Heidi said to Lucinda. "And I suppose no one should leave."

I sighed.

And so crime detection ensnared me once again. I helped Freya by circulating on the patio, calming the shocked and nervous guests. "Um, excuse me, very sorry to inform you, yes, sorry—hard to believe, yes— somebody had it in for the secretary Musgrave, it appears"—all the while watching to see if anyone would jump, or turn pale, or start to run when I told them. Then, of course, I had to lead gently to the idea that everyone had gone from guest to suspect, soon to be questioned by Freya and the police. "No, no, of *course* you're not suspected of anything, farthest thing from our minds, it's just that Freya wants to know if there's anything you saw that would help," and so on. Then I had to do the difficult scheduling of Freya's interviews, at the same time I was supposed to keep an eye out for anything suspicious.

Oh, the watson does the dirty work, all right. No wonder we always look dense when the detective unveils the solutions; we never have the time even to get the facts straight, much less meditate on their meaning. All I got that day were fragments: Lucinda whispered to me that Musgrave had worked for George Butler before Heidi hired him. Harvey Washburn told me that Musgrave had once been an artist, and that he had only recently moved to Mercury from Earth; this was his first Solday. That didn't give him much time to be hired by Butler, fired, and then hired by Van Seegeren. But was that of significance?

Late in the day I spoke with one of the police officers handling the case. She was relieved to have the help of Freya Grindavik; Terminator's police force is small, and often relies on the help of the city's famous detective for the more difficult cases. The officer gave me a general outline of what they had learned: Lucinda had heard a shout for help, had stepped into the atrium and seen a bloodied figure crawling down the hallway toward the patio. She had screamed and run for help, but only in the hallway was clear vision possible, and she had quickly gotten lost. After that, chaos; everyone at the party had a different tale of confusion.

Following that conversation I had nothing more to do, so I got all the sequestered guests coffee, and helped pick up some of the broken hall mirrors, and passed some time prowling Heidi's villa, getting down on my hands and knees with the police robots to inspect a stain or two.

When Freya was finished with her interrogations, she promised Heidi and the police that she would see the case to its end—at least provisionally: "I only do this for entertainment," she told them irritably. "I'll stay with it as long as it entertains me. And I shall entertain myself with it."

"That's all right," said the police, who had heard this before. "Just so long as you'll take the case." Freya nodded, and we left.

The Solday celebration was long since over; the Great Gates were closed, and once again through the dome shone the black sky. I said to Freya, "Did you hear about Musgrave working for Butler? And how he came from Earth just recently?" For you see, once on the scent I am committed to seeing a case solved.

"Please, Nathaniel," Freya said. "I heard all of that and more. Musgrave stole the concept of Harvey Washburn's first series of paintings, he blackmailed both Butler and our host Heidi to obtain his jobs from them

—or so I deduce, from their protestations, and from certain facts concerning their recent questionable merger that I am privy to. And he tried to assault Lucinda, who is engaged to the cook Delaurence—" She let out a long sigh. "Motives are everywhere."

Bemused, I said, "It seems this Musgrave was a thoroughly despicable sort."

"Yes. An habitual blackmailer."

"Nothing *suggests* itself to you?"

"No. Not only that, but it seems almost every person at the party had a good alibi for the moment of the murder! Oh, I don't know why I agree to solve these things. Here I am committed to this head-bashing, and my best clue is something that *you* suggested."

"I wasn't aware that I had suggested anything!"

"There is a fresh perspective to ignorance that can be very helpful."

"So it *is* important that Musgrave just arrived from Earth?"

She laughed. "Let's stop in the Plaza Dubrovnik and get something to eat. I'm starving."

Almost three weeks passed without a word from Freya, and I began to suspect that she was ignoring the case. Freya has no real sense of right and wrong, you see; she regards her cases as games, to be tossed aside if they prove too taxing. More than once she has cheerfully admitted defeat, and blithely forgotten any promises she may have made. She is *not* a moral person.

So I dropped by her home near Plaza Dubrovnik one evening, to rouse her from her irresponsible indifference. When she answered the door there were paint smudges on her face and hands.

"Freya," I scolded her. "How could you take up an entirely new hobby when there is a *case* to be solved?"

"Generously I allow you entrance after such a false accusation," she said. "But you will have to eat your words."

She led me downstairs to her basement laboratory, which extended the entire length and breadth of her villa. There on a big white-topped table lay Heidi van Seegeren's Monet, looking like the three-dimensional geologic map of some minerally blessed country.

"What's this?" I exclaimed. "Why is this here?"

"I believe it is a fake," she said shortly, returning to a computer console.

"Wait a moment!" I cried. On the table around the painting were rolls of recording chart paper, lab notebooks, and what looked like black-and-white photos of the painting. "What do you mean?"

After tapping at the console she turned to me. "I mean I believe it's a fake!"

"But I thought art forgery was extinct. It is too easy to discover a fake."

"Ha!" She waved a finger at me angrily. "You pick a bad time to say so. It is a common opinion, of course, but not necessarily true."

I regarded the canvas more closely. "What makes you think this a fake? I thought it was judged a masterpiece of its period."

"Something you said first caused me to question it," she said. "You mentioned that the painting seemed to have been created by an artist familiar with the light of Terminator. This seemed true to me, and it caused me to reflect that one of the classic signs of a fake was anachronistic sensibility—that is to say, the forger injects into his vision of the past some element of his time that is so much a part of his sensibility that he cannot perceive it. Thus the Victorians faked Renaissance faces with a sentimentality that only they could not immediately see."

"I see." I nodded sagely. "It did seem that cathedral had been struck with Solday light, didn't it."

"Yes. The trouble is, I have been able to find no sign of forgery in the physical properties of the painting." She shook her head. "And after three weeks of uninterrupted chemical analysis, that is beginning to worry me."

"But Freya," I said, as something occurred to me. "Does all this have a bearing on the Musgrave murder?"

"I think so," she replied. "And if not, it is certainly more interesting. But I believe it does."

I nodded. "So what, exactly, have you found?"

She smiled ironically. "You truly want to know? Well. The best test for anachronisms is the polonium 210, radium 226 equilibrium—"

"Please, Freya. No jargon."

"Jargon!" She raised an eyebrow to scorn me. "There is no such thing. Intelligence is like mold in a petri dish—as it eats ever deeper into the agar of reality, language has to expand with it to describe what has been digested. Each specialty provides the new vocabulary for its area of feeding, and gets accused of fabricating jargon by those who know no better. I'm surprised to hear such nonsense from you. Or perhaps not."

"Very well," I said, hands up. "Still, you must communicate your meaning to me."

"I shall. First I analyzed the canvas. The material and its weave match the characteristics of the canvas made by the factory outside Paris that provided Monet throughout the painting of the Rouen cathedral series. Both the fabric and the glue appear very old, though there is no precise dating technique for them. And there was no trace of solvents that might have been used to strip paint off a genuine canvas of the period.

"I then turned to the paint. Follow so far?" she asked sharply. "Paint?"

"You may proceed without further sarcasm, unless unable to control yourself."

"The palette of an artist as famous as Monet has been studied in detail, so that we know he preferred cadmium yellow to chromium yellow or Naples yellow, that he tended to use Prussian blue rather than cobalt blue, and so on." She tapped the flecks of blue at the base of the cathedral. "Prussian blue."

"You've taken paint off the canvas?"

"How else test it? But I took very small samples, I assure you. Whatever the truth concerning the work, it remains a masterpiece, and I would not mar it. Besides, most of my tests were on the white paint, of which there is a great quantity, as you can see."

I leaned over to stare more closely at the canvas. "Why the white paint?"

"Because lead white is one of the best dating tools we have. The manufacturing methods used to make it changed frequently around Monet's time, and each change in method altered the chemical composition of the paint. After 1870, for instance, the cheaper zinc white was used to adulterate lead white, so there should be over one percent zinc in Monet's lead white."

"And is that what you found?"

"Yes. The atomic absorption spectrum showed—" She dug around in the pile of chart paper on the table. "Well, take my word for it—"

"I will."

"Nearly twelve percent. And the silver content for late-nineteenth-century lead white should be around four parts per million, the copper content about sixty parts per million. So it is with this paint. There is no insoluble antimony component, as there would be if the paint had been manufactured after 1940. The X-ray diffraction pattern"—she unrolled a length of chart paper and showed me where three sharp peaks in a row had been penned by the machine—"is exactly right, and there is the proper balance of polonium 210 and radium 226. That's very important, by the way, because when lead white is manufactured the radioactive balance of some of its elements is upset, and it takes a good three hundred years for them to decay back to equilibrium. And this paint is indeed back to that equilibrium."

"So the paints are Monet's," I concluded. "Doesn't that prove the work authentic?"

"Perhaps," Freya admitted. "But as I was doing all this analysis, it occurred to me that a modern forger has just as much information concerning Monet's palette as I do. With a modern laboratory it would be possible to *use such information as a recipe*, so to speak, and then to synthesize paints that would match the recipe exactly. Even the radioactively decayed lead white could be arranged, by avoiding the procedures that disrupt the radioactive balance in the first place!"

"Wouldn't that be terrifically complicated?"

Freya stared at me. "*Obviously*, Nathaniel, we are dealing with a very, very meticulous faker here. But how else could it be done, in this day and age? Why else do it at all? The complete faker must take care to anticipate every test available, and then in a modern laboratory create the appropriate results for every one of them. It's admirable!"

"Assuming there ever was such a forger," I said dubiously. "It seems to me that what you have actually done here is prove the painting genuine."

"I don't think so."

"But even with these paints made by recipe, as you call them, the faker would still have to paint the painting!"

"Exactly. Conceive the painting, and execute it. It becomes very impressive, I confess." She walked around the table to look at the work from the correct angle. "I do believe this is one of the *best* of the Rouen cathedral series—astonishing, that a forger would be capable of it."

"That brings up another matter," I said. "Doesn't this work have a five-hundred-year-old pedigree? How could a whole history have been provided for it?"

"Good question. But I believe I have discovered the way. Let's go upstairs—you interrupted my preparations for lunch, and I'm hungry."

I followed her to her extensive kitchen, and sat in the window nook that overlooked the tile rooftops of the lower city while she finished chopping up the vegetables for a large salad.

"Do you know this painting's history?" Freya asked, looking up from a dissected head of lettuce.

I shook my head. "Up until now the thing has not been of overwhelming interest to me."

"A confession of faulty esthetics. The work was photographed at the original exhibit in 1895, Durand-Ruel photo 5828 L8451. All of the information appended to the photo fits our painting—same name, size, signature location. Then for a century it disappeared. Odd. But it turned out to have been in the estate of an Evans family, in Aylesbury, England. When the family had some conservation work done on one corner it returned to public knowledge, and was photographed for a dozen books of the twenty-first and twenty-second centuries. After that it slipped back into obscurity, but it is as well documented as any of the series belonging to private estates."

"Exactly my point," I said. "How could such a history be forged?"

As Freya mixed the salad she smiled. "I sat and thought about that for quite some time myself. But consider it freshly, Nathaniel. How do we know what we know of the past?"

"Well," I said, somewhat at a loss. "From data banks, I suppose. And books—documents—historians—"

"From historians!" She laughed. She provided us both with bowls, and sat across from me. As I filled mine she said, "So we want to know something of the past. We go to our library and sit at its terminal. We call up general reference works, or a bibliographical index, and we choose, if we want, books that we would like to have in our hands. We type in the appropriate code, our printer prints up the appropriate book, and the volume slides out of the computer into our waiting grasp." She paused to fork down several mouthfuls of salad. "So we learn about the past using computer programs. And a clever programmer, you see, can change a program. It would be possible to *insert* extra pages into these old books on Monet, and thus add the forged painting to the record of the past."

I paused, a cherry tomato hovering before my mouth. "But—"

"I searched for an original of *any* of these books containing photos of our painting," Freya said. "I called all over Mercury, and to several incunabulists in libraries on Earth—you wouldn't believe the phone bill I've run up. But the original printings of these art volumes were very small, and although first editions probably remain *somewhere*, they are not to be found. Certainly there are no first editions of these books on Mercury, and none immediately locatable on Earth. It began to seem a very unlikely coincidence, as if these volumes contained pictures of our painting precisely because they existed only in the data banks, and thus could be altered without discovery."

She attended to her salad, and we finished eating in silence. All the while my mind was spinning furiously, and when we were done I said, "What about the original exhibit photo?"

She nodded, pleased with me. "That, apparently, is genuine. But the Durand-Ruel photos include four or five of paintings that have never been seen since. In that sense the Rouen cathedral series is a good one for a faker; from the first it has never been clear how many cathedrals Monet painted. The usual number given is thirty-two, but there are more in the Durand-Ruel list, and a faker could examine the list and use one of the lost items as a prescription for his fake. Providing a later history with the aid of these obscure art books would result in a fairly complete pedigree."

"But could such an addition to the data banks be made?"

"It would be easiest done on Earth," Freya said. "But there is no close security guarding the banks containing old art books. No one expects them to be tampered with."

"It's astonishing," I said with a wave of my fork, "it is baroque, it is *byzantine* in its ingenuity!"

"Yes," she said. "Beautiful, in a way."

"However," I pointed out to her, "you have no proof—only this perhaps overly complex theory. You have found no first edition of a book to confirm that the computer-generated volumes add Heidi's painting, and you have found no physical anachronism in the painting itself."

Gloomily she clicked her fork against her empty salad bowl, then rose to refill it. "It is a problem," she admitted. "Also, I have been working on the assumption that Sandor Musgrave discovered evidence of the forgery. But *I* can't find it."

Never let it be said that Nathaniel Sebastian has not performed a vital role in Freya Grindavik's great feats of detection. I was the first to notice the anachronism of sensibility in Heidi's painting; and now I had a truly inspired idea. "He was pointing to the patio!" I exclaimed. "Musgrave, in his last moment, struggled to point to the patio!"

"I had observed that," Freya said, unimpressed.

"But Heidi's patio—you know—it is formed out of blocks of the Dover cliffs! And thus Musgrave indicated *England!* Is it not possible? The Monet was owned by Englishmen until Heidi purchased it—perhaps Musgrave meant to convey that the original owners were the forgers!"

Freya's mouth hung open in surprise, and her left eye was squinted shut. I leaped from the window nook in triumph. "I've solved it! I've solved a mystery at last."

Freya looked up at me and laughed.

"Come now, Freya, you must admit I have given you the vital clue."

She stood up, suddenly all business. "Yes, yes, indeed you have. Now out with you Nathaniel; I have work to do."

"So I did give you the vital clue?" I asked. "Musgrave was indicating the English owners?"

As she ushered me to her door Freya laughed. "As a detective your intuition is matched only by your confidence. Now leave me to work, and I will be in contact with you soon, I assure you." And with that she urged me into the street, and I was left to consider the case alone.

Freya was true to her word, and only two days after our crucial luncheon she knocked on the door of my town villa. "Come along," she said. "I've asked Arnold Ohman for an appointment; I want to ask him some questions about the Evans family. The city is passing the Monet museum, however, and he asked us to meet him out there."

I readied myself quickly, and we proceeded to North Station. We arrived just in time to step across the gap between the two platforms, and then we were on the motionless deck of one of the outlying stations that Terminator is always passing. There we rented a car and sped west, paralleling the dozen massive cylindrical rails over which the city slides. Soon we had left Terminator behind, and when we were seventy or eighty kilometers onto the nightside of Mercury we turned to the north, to Monet Crater.

Terminator's tracks lie very close to the thirtieth degree of latitude, in the northern hemisphere, and Monet Crater is not far from them. We crossed Endeavor Rupes rapidly, and passed between craters named after the great artists, writers, and composers of Earth's glorious past: traversing a low pass between Holbein and Gluck, looking down at Melville and the double crater of Rodin. "I think I understand why a modern artist on Mercury might turn to forgery," Freya said. "We are dwarfed by the past as we are by this landscape."

"But it is still a crime," I insisted. "If it were done often, we would not be able to distinguish the authentic from the fake."

Freya did not reply.

I drove our car up a short rise, and we entered the submercurial garage of the Monet museum, which is set deep in the southern rim of the immense crater named after the artist. One long wall of the museum is a window facing out over the crater floor, so that the central knot of peaks is visible, and the curving inner wall of the crater defines the horizon in the murky distance. Shutters slid down to protect these windows from the heat of Mercury's long day, but now they were open and the black wasteland of the planet formed a strange backdrop to the colorful paintings that filled the long rooms of the museum.

There were many Monet originals there, but the canvases of the Rouen cathedral series were almost all reproductions, set in one long gallery. As Freya and I searched for Arnold we also viewed them.

"You see, they're not just various moments of a single day," Freya said.

"Not unless it was a very strange day for weather." The three reproductions before us all depicted foggy days: two bluish and underwater-looking, the third a bright burning-off of yellow noontime fog. Obviously these were from a different day than the ones across the room, where a cool clear morning gave way to a midday that looked as if the sun were just a few feet above the cathedral. The museum had classified the series in color groups: "Blue Group," "White Group," "Yellow Group," and so on. To my mind that system was stupid—it told you nothing you couldn't immediately see. I myself classified them according to weather. There was a clear day that got very hot; a clear winter day, the air chill and pure; a foggy day; and a day when a rainstorm had grown and then broken.

When I told Freya of my system she applauded it. "So Heidi's painting goes from the king of the White Group to the hottest moment of the hot day."

"Exactly. It's the most extreme in terms of sunlight blasting the stone into motes of color."

"And thus the forger extends Monet's own thinking, you see," she said, a bit absently. "But I *don't* see Arnold, and I think we have visited every room."

"Could he be late?"

"We are already quite late ourselves. I wonder if he has gone back."

"It seems unlikely," I said.

Purposefully we toured the museum one more time, and I ignored the color-splashed canvases standing before the dark crater, to search closely in all the various turns of the galleries. No Arnold.

"Come along," Freya said. "I suspect he stayed in Terminator, and now I want to speak with him more than ever."

So we returned to the garage, got back in our car, and drove out onto Mercury's bare, baked surface once again. Half an hour later we had Terminator's tracks in sight. They stretched before us from horizon to horizon, twelve fat silvery cylinders set five meters above the ground on narrow pylons. To the east, rolling over the flank of Velázquez Crater so slowly that we could not perceive its movement without close attention, came the city itself, a giant clear half-egg filled with the colors of rooftops, gardens, and the gray stone of the buildings crowding the terraced Dawn Wall.

"We'll have to go west to the next station," I said. Then I saw something, up on the city track nearest us: spread-eagled over the top of the big cylinder was a human form in a light green daysuit. I stopped the car. "Look!"

Freya peered out her window. "We'd better go investigate."

We struggled quickly into the car's emergency daysuits, clamped on the helmets, and slipped through the car's lock onto the ground. A ladder led us up the nearest cylinder pylon and through a tunnel in the cylinder itself. Once on top we could stand safely on the broad hump of the rail.

The figure we had seen was only thirty meters away from us, and we hurried to it.

It was Arnold, spread in cruciform fashion over the cylinder's top, secured in place by three large suction plates that had been cuffed to his wrists and ankles, and then stuck to the cylinder. Arnold turned from his contemplation of the slowly approaching city, and looked at us wide-eyed through his faceplate. Freya reached down and turned on his helmet intercom.

"—am I glad to see you!" Arnold cried, voice harsh. "These plates won't move!"

"Tied to the tracks, eh?" Freya said.

"Yes!"

"Who put you here?"

"I don't know! I went out to meet you at the Monet museum, and the last thing I remember I was in the garage there. When I came to, I was here."

"Does your head hurt?" I inquired.

"Yes. Like I was gassed, though, not hit. But—the city—it just came over the horizon a short time ago. Perhaps we could dispense with discussion until I am freed?"

"Relax," Freya said, nudging one of the plates with her boot. "Are you sure you don't know who did this, Arnold?"

"Of course! That's what I just said! Please, Freya, can't we talk after I get loose?"

"In a hurry, Arnold?" Freya asked.

"*Of course.*"

"No need to be too worried," I assured him. "If we can't free you the cowcatchers will be out to pry you loose." I tried lifting a plate, but could not move it. "Surely they will find a way—it's their job, after all."

"True," Arnold said.

"Usually true," said Freya. "Arnold is probably not aware that the cowcatchers have become rather unreliable recently. Some weeks ago a murderer tied his victim to a track just as you have been, Arnold, and then somehow disengaged the cowcatchers' sensors. The unfortunate victim was shaved into molecules by one of the sleeves of the city. It was kept quiet to avoid any attempted repetitions, but since then the cowcatchers' sensors have continued to function erratically, and two or three suicides have been entirely too successful."

"Perhaps this isn't the best moment to tell us about this," I suggested to Freya.

Arnold choked over what I took to be his agreement.

"Well," Freya said, "I thought I should make the situation clear. Now listen, Arnold. We need to talk."

"*Please,*" Arnold said. "Free me first, *then* talk."

"No, no—"

"But Terminator is only a kilometer away!"

"Your perspective from that angle is deceptive," Freya told him. "The city is at least three kilometers away."

"More like two," I said, as I could now make out individual rooftops under the Dawn Wall. In fact the city glowed like a big glass lamp, and illuminated the entire landscape with a faint green radiance.

"And at three point four kilometers an hour," Freya said, "that gives us almost an hour, doesn't it. So listen to me, Arnold. The Monet cathedral that you sold to Heidi is a fake."

"What?" Arnold cried. "It certainly is not! And I insist this isn't the time—"

"It is a fake. Now I want you to tell me the truth, or I will leave you here to test the cowcatchers." She leaned over to stare down at Arnold face to face. "I know who painted the fake, as well."

Helplessly Arnold stared up at her.

"He put you on the track here, didn't he."

Arnold squeezed his eyes shut, nodded slowly. "I think so."

"So if you want to be let up, you must swear to me that you will abide by my plan for dealing with this forger. You *will* follow my instructions, understand?"

"I understand."

"Do you agree?"

"I agree," Arnold said, forcing the words out. "Now let me up!"

"All right." Freya straightened.

"How are we going to do it?" I asked.

Freya shrugged. "I don't know."

At this Arnold howled, he shouted recriminations, he began to wax hysterical—

"Shut up!" Freya exclaimed. "You're beginning to sound like a man who has made too many brightside crossings. These suction plates are little different from children's darts." She leaned down, grasped a plate, pulled up with all of her considerable strength. No movement. "Hmm," she said thoughtfully.

"Freya," Arnold said.

"One moment," she replied, and walked back down the hump of the cylinder to the ladder tunnel, there to disappear down it.

"She's left me," Arnold groaned. "Left me to be crushed."

"I don't think so," I said. "No doubt she has gone to the car to retrieve some useful implement." I kicked heartily at the plate holding Arnold's feet to the cylinder, and even managed to slide it a few centimeters down the curve, which had the effect of making Arnold suddenly taller. But other than that I made no progress.

When Freya returned she carried a bar bent at one end. "Crowbar," she explained to us.

"But where did you get it?"

"From the car's tool chest, naturally. Here." She stepped over Arnold. "If we just insinuate this end of it under your cuffs, I believe we'll have enough leverage to do the trick. The cylinder being curved, the plates' grasp should be weakened . . . about here." She jammed the short end of the bar under the edge of the footplates' cuff, and pulled on the upper end of it. Over the intercom, breathless silence; her fair cheeks reddened; then suddenly Arnold's legs flew up and over his head, leaving his arms twisted and his neck at an awkward angle. At the same time Freya staggered off the cylinder, performed a neat somersault and landed on her feet, on the ground below us. While she made her way back up to us I tried to ease the weight on Arnold's neck, but by his squeaks of distress I judged he was still uncomfortable. Freya rejoined us, and quickly wedged her crowbar under Arnold's right wrist cuff, and freed it. That left Arnold hanging down the side of the cylinder by his left wrist; but with one hard crank Freya popped that plate free as well, and Arnold disappeared. By leaning over we could just see him, collapsed in a heap on the ground. "Are you all right?" Freya asked. He groaned for an answer.

I looked up and saw that Terminator was nearly upon us. Almost involuntarily I proceeded to the ladder tunnel; Freya followed me, and we descended to the ground. "Disturbing not to be able to trust the cowcatchers," I remarked as my heartbeat slowed.

"Nathaniel," Freya said, looking exasperated. "I made all that up, you know that."

"Ah. Yes, of course."

As we rejoined Arnold he was just struggling to a seated position. "My ankle," he said. Then the green wash of light from Terminator disappeared, as did the night sky; the city slid over us, and we were encased in a gloom interrupted by an occasional running light. All twelve of the city's big tracks had disappeared, swallowed by the sleeves in the city's broad metallic foundation. Only the open slots that allowed passage over the pylons showed where the sleeves were; for a moment in the darkness it seemed we stood between two worlds held apart by a field of pylons.

Meanwhile the city slid over us soundlessly, propelled by the expansion of the tracks themselves. You see, the alloy composing the tracks is capable of withstanding the 425 degree Centigrade heat of the Mercurial day, but the cylinders do expand just a bit in this heat. Here in the terminator is the forward edge of the cylinders' expansion, and the smooth-sided sleeves above us at that moment fit so snugly over the cylinders that as the cylinders expand, the city is pushed forward toward the cooler, thinner railing to the west; and so the city is propelled by the sun, while never being fully exposed to it. The motive force is so strong, in fact, that resistance to it arranged in the sleeves generates the enormous reserves of energy that Terminator has sold so successfully to the rest of civilization.

Though I had understood this mechanism for decades, I had never before observed it from this angle, and despite the fact that I was somewhat uneasy to be standing under our fair city, I was also fascinated to see its broad, knobby silver underside gliding majestically westward. For a long time I did nothing but stare at it.

"We'd better get to the car," Freya said. "The sun will be up very soon after the city passes, and then we'll be in trouble."

Since Arnold was still cuffed to the plates, and had at least a sprained ankle, walking with him slung between us was a slow process. While we were at it the Dawn Wall passed over us, and suddenly the twelve tracks and the stars between them were visible again. "Now we'd better hurry," said Freya. Above us the very top of the Dawn Wall flared a brilliant white; sunlight was striking that surface, only two hundred meters above us. Dawn was not far away. In the glare of reflected light we could see the heavily tireprinted ground under the cylinders perfectly, and for a while our eyes were nearly overwhelmed. "Look!" Freya cried, shielding her eyes with one hand and pointing up at the sun-washed slope of the city wall with the other. "It's the inspiration for our Monet, don't you think?"

Despite our haste, the great Rouen cathedral of Mercury pulled away from us. "This won't do," Freya said. "Only a bit more to the car, but we have to hurry. Here, Arnold, let me carry you—" and she ran, carrying Arnold piggyback, the rest of the way to the car. As we maneuvered him through the lock, a tongue of the sun's corona licked briefly over the horizon, blinding us. I felt scorched; my throat was dry. We were now at the dawn edge of the terminator zone, and east-facing slopes burned white while west-facing slopes were still a perfect black, creating a chaotic patchwork that was utterly disorienting. We rolled into the car after Arnold, and quickly drove west, passing the city, returning to the night zone, and arriving at a station where we could make the transfer into the city again. Freya laughed at my expression as we crossed the gap. "Well, Nathaniel," she said, "home again."

The very next day Freya arranged for those concerned with the case to assemble on Heidi's patio again. Four police officials were there, and one took notes. The painting of the cathedral of Rouen was back in its place on the villa wall; George Butler and Harvey Washburn stood before it, while Arnold Ohman and Heidi paced by the patio's edge. Lucinda and Delaurence, the cook, watched from behind the patio bar.

Freya called us to order. She was wearing a severe blue dress, and her white-blond hair was drawn into a tight braid that fell down her back. Sternly she said, "I will suggest to you an explanation for the death of Sandor Musgrave. All of you except for the police and Mr. Sebastian were to one extent or another suspected of killing him, so I know this will be of great interest to you."

Naturally there was an uneasy stir among those listening.

"Several of you had reason to hate Musgrave, or to fear him. The man was a blackmailer by profession, and on Earth he had obtained evidence of illegalities in the merger Heidi and George made five years ago, that gave him leverage over both of you. This and motives for the rest of you were well established during the initial investigation, and we need not recapitulate the details.

"It is also true, however, that subsequent investigations have confirmed that all of you had alibis for the moment when Musgrave was struck down. Lucinda and Delaurence were together in the kitchen until Lucinda left to investigate the shout she heard; this was confirmed by caterers hired for the Solday party. Heidi left the patio shortly before Musgrave was found, but she was consulting with Hiu and the orchestra during the time in question. George Butler went into the house with Arnold Ohman, but they were together for most of the time they were inside. Eventually George left to go to the bathroom, but luckily for him the orchestra's first clarinetist was there to confirm his presence. And fortunately for Mr. Ohman, I myself could see him from the patio, standing in the hallway until the very moment when Lucinda screamed.

"So you see—" Freya paused, eyed us one by one, ran a finger along the frame of the big painting. "The problem took on a new aspect. It became clear that, while many had a motive to kill Musgrave, no one had the opportunity. This caused me to reconsider. How, exactly, had Musgrave been killed? He was struck on the head by the frame of one of Heidi's hall mirrors. Though several mirrors were broken in the melee following Lucinda's screams, we know the one that struck Musgrave; it was at the bend in the hallway leading from the atrium to the patio. And it was only a couple of meters away from a step down in the hallway."

Freya took a large house plan from a table and set it before the policeman. "Sandor Musgrave, you will recall, was new to Mercury. He had never seen a Solday celebration. When the Great Gates opened and the reflected light filled this villa, my suggestion is that he was overwhelmed by fright. Lucinda heard him cry for help—perhaps he thought the house was burning down. He panicked, rushed out of the study, and blindly began to run for the patio. Unable to see the step down or the mirror, he must have pitched forward, and his left temple struck the frame with a fatal blow. He crawled a few steps farther, then collapsed and died."

Heidi stepped forward. "So Musgrave died by accident?"

"This is my theory. And it explains how it was that no one had the opportunity to kill him. In fact, no one did kill him." She turned to the police. "I trust you will follow up on this suggestion?"

"Yes," said the one taking notes. "Death declared accidental by consulting investigator. Proceed from there." He exchanged glances with his colleagues. "We are satisfied this explains the facts of the case."

Heidi surveyed the silent group. "To tell you the truth, I am very relieved." She turned to Delaurence. "Let's open the bar. It would be morbid to celebrate an accidental death, but here we can say we are celebrating the absence of a murder."

The others gave a small cheer of relief, and we surrounded the bartender.

A few days later Freya asked me to accompany her to North Station. "I need your assistance."

"Very well," I said. "Are you leaving Terminator?"

"Seeing someone off."

When we entered the station's big waiting room, she inspected the crowd, then cried, "Arnold!" and crossed the room to him. Arnold saw her and grimaced. "Oh, Arnold," she said, and leaned over to kiss him on each cheek. "I'm very proud of you."

Arnold shook his head, and greeted me mournfully. "You're a hard woman, Freya," he told her. "Stop behaving so cheerfully; you make me sick. You know perfectly well this is exile of the worst sort."

"But Arnold," Freya said, "Mercury is not the whole of civilization. In fact it could be considered culturally dead, an immense museum to the past that has no real life at all."

"Which is why you choose to live here, I'm sure," he said bitterly.

"Well of course it does have some pleasures. But the really vital centers of any civilization are on the frontier, Arnold, and that's where you're going."

Arnold looked completely disgusted.

"But Arnold," I said. "Where are you going?"

"Pluto," he said curtly.

"*Pluto?*" I exclaimed. "But whatever for? What will you do there?"

He shrugged. "Dig ditches, I suppose."

Freya laughed. "You certainly will not." She addressed me: "Arnold has decided, very boldly I might add, to abandon his safe career as a dealer here on Mercury, to become a real artist on the frontier."

"But *why?*"

Freya wagged a finger at Arnold. "You must write us often."

Arnold made a strangled growl. "Damn you, Freya. I refuse. I refuse to go."

"You don't have that option," Freya said. "Remember the chalk, Arnold. The chalk was your signature."

Arnold hung his head, defeated. The city interfaced with the spaceport station. "It isn't fair," Arnold said. "What am I going to do out on those barbaric outworlds?"

"You're going to live," Freya said sternly. "You're going to live and you're going to paint. No more hiding. Understand?"

I, at any rate, was beginning to.

"You should be thanking me profusely," Freya went on, "but I'll concede you're upset and wait for gratitude by mail." She put a hand on Arnold's shoulder, and pushed him affectionately toward the crossing line. "Remember to write."

"But," Arnold said, a panicked expression on his face. "But—"

"Enough!" Freya said. "Be gone! Or else."

Arnold sagged, and stepped across the divide between the stations. Soon the city left the spaceport station behind.

"Well," Freya said. "That's done."

I stared at her. "You just helped a murderer to escape!"

She lifted an eyebrow. "Exile is a very severe punishment; in fact in my cultural tradition it was the usual punishment for murder committed in anger or self-defense."

I waved a hand dismissively. "This isn't the Iceland of Eric the Red. And it wasn't self-defense—Sandor Musgrave was outright murdered."

"Well," she said, "*I* never liked him."

I told you before: she has no sense of right and wrong. It is a serious defect in a detective. I could only wave my arms in incoherent outrage; and my protests have never carried much weight with Freya, who claims not even to believe them.

We left the station. "What's that you were saying to Arnold about chalk?" I said, curiosity getting the better of me.

"That's the clue you provided, Nathaniel—somewhat transformed. As you reminded me, Musgrave was pointing at the patio, and Heidi's patio is made of a block of the Dover cliffs. Dover cliffs, as you know, are composed of *chalk*. So I returned to the painting, and cut through the back to retrieve samples of the chalk used in the underdrawing, which had been revealed to me by infrared photography." She turned a corner and led me uptown. "Chalk, you see, has its own history of change. In Monet's time chalk was made from natural sources, not from synthetics. Sure enough, the chalk I took from the canvas was a natural chalk. But natural chalk, being composed of marine ooze, is littered with the fossil remains of unicellular algae called coccoliths. These coccoliths are different depending upon the source of the chalk. Monet used Rouen chalk, appropriately enough, which was filled with the coccoliths *Maslovella barnesae* and *Cricolithus pemmatoidens.* The coccoliths in our painting, however, are *Neococcolithes dubius.* Very dubious indeed—for this is a North American chalk, first mined in Utah in 1924."

"So Monet couldn't have used this chalk! And there you had your proof that the painting is a fake."

"Exactly."

I said doubtfully, "It seems a subtle clue for the dying Musgrave to conceive of."

"Perhaps," Freya said cheerfully. "Perhaps he was only pointing in the direction of the patio by the accident of his final movements. But it was sufficient that the coincidence gave me the idea. The solution of a crime often depends upon imaginary clues."

"But how did you know Arnold was the forger?" I asked. "And why, after taking the trouble to concoct all those paints, did he use the wrong chalk?"

"The two matters are related. It could be that Arnold only knew he needed a natural chalk, and used the first convenient supply without knowing there are differences between them. In that case it was a mistake —his only mistake. But it seems unlike Arnold to me, and I think rather that it was the forger's signature. In effect, the forger said, if you take a slide of the chalk trapped underneath the paint, and magnify it five thousand times with an electron microscope, you will find me. This chalk never used by Monet is my sign. —For on some level every forger hopes to be discovered, if only in the distant future—to receive credit for the work.

"So I knew we had a forger on Mercury, and I was already suspicious of Arnold, since he was the dealer who brought the painting to Mercury, and since he was the only guest at Heidi's party with the opportunity to kill Musgrave; he was missing during the crucial moments—"

"You *are* a liar."

"And it seems Arnold was getting desperate; I searched among his recent bills, and found one for three suction plates. So when we found him on the track I was quite sure."

"He stuck himself to the track?"

"Yes. The one on his right wrist was electronically controlled, so after setting the other two he tripped the third between his teeth. He hoped that we would discover him there after missing him at the museum, and think that there was someone else who wished him harm. And if not, the cowcatchers would pull him free. It was a silly plan, but he was desperate after I set up that appointment with him. When I confronted him with all this, after we rescued him from the tracks, he broke down and confessed. Sandor Musgrave had discovered that the Monet was a fake while blackmailing the Evans family in England, and after forcing Heidi to give him a job, he worked on the painting in secret until he found proof. Then he blackmailed Arnold into bankruptcy, and when on Solday he pressed Arnold for more money, Arnold lost his composure and took advantage of the confusion caused by the opening of the Great Gates to smack Musgrave on the head with one of Heidi's mirrors."

I wagged a finger under her nose. "And you set him free. You've gone too far this time, Freya Grindavik."

She shook her head. "If you consider Arnold's case a bit longer, you might change your mind. Arnold Ohman has been the most important art dealer on Mercury for over sixty years. He sold the Vermeer collection to George Butler, and the Goyas to Terminator West Gallery, and the Pissarros to the museum in Homer Crater, and those Chinese landscapes you love so much to the city park, and the Kandinskys to the Lion of the Grays. Most of the finest paintings on Mercury were brought here by Arnold Ohman."

"So?"

"So how many of those, do you think, were painted by Arnold himself?"

I stopped dead in the street, stunned at the very idea. "But—but that only makes it worse! Inestimably worse! It means there are fakes all over the planet!"

"Probably so. And no one wants to hear that. But it also means Arnold Ohman is a very great artist. And in our age that is no easy feat. Can you imagine the withering reception his painting would have received if he had done original work? He would have ended up like Harvey Washburn and all the rest of them who wander around the galleries like dogs. The great art of the past crashes down on our artists like meteors, so that their minds resemble the blasted landscape we roll over. Now Arnold has escaped that fate, and his work is universally admired, even loved. That Monet, for instance—it isn't just that it passes for one of the cathedral series; it could be argued that it is the *best* of them. Now is this a level of greatness that Arnold could have achieved—would have been *allowed* to achieve—if he had done original work on this museum planet? Impossible. He was forced to forge old masters to be able to fully express his genius."

"All this is no excuse for forgery or murder."

But Freya wasn't listening. "Now that I've exiled him, he may go on forging old paintings, but he may begin painting something new. That possibility surely justifies ameliorating his punishment for killing such a parasite as Musgrave. And there is Mercury's reputation as art museum of the system to consider. . . ."

I refused to honor her opinions with a reply, and looking around, I saw that during our conversation she had led me far up the terraces. "Where are we going?"

"To Heidi's," she said. And she had the grace to look a little shame-faced—for a moment, anyway. "I need your help moving something."

"Oh, no."

"Well," Freya explained, "when I told Heidi some of the facts of the case, she insisted on giving me a token of her gratitude, and she overrode all my refusals, so . . . I was forced to accept." She rang the wall bell.

"You're joking," I said.

"Not at all. Actually, I think Heidi preferred not to own a painting she knew to be a fake, you see. So I did her a favor by taking it off her hands."

When Delaurence let us in, we found he had almost finished securing *Rouen Cathedral—Sun Effect* in a big plastic box. "We'll finish this," Freya told him.

While we completed the boxing I told Freya what I thought of her conduct. "You've taken liberties with the *law*—you lied right and left—"

"Well boxed," she said. "Let's go before Heidi changes her mind."

"And I suppose you're proud of yourself."

"Of course. A lot of lab work went into this."

We maneuvered the big box through the gate and into the street, and carried it upright between us, like a short flat coffin. We reached Freya's villa, and immediately she set to work unboxing the painting. When she had freed it she set it on top of a couch, resting against the wall.

Shaking with righteous indignation, I cried, "That *thing* isn't a product of the past! It isn't *authentic*. It is only a *fake*. Claude Monet *didn't paint it.*"

Freya looked at me with a mild frown, as if confronting a slightly dense and very stubborn child. "So what?"

After I had lectured her on her immorality a good deal more, and heard all of her patient agreement, I ran out of steam. "Well," I muttered, "you may have destroyed all my faith in you, and damaged Mercury's art heritage forever, but at least I'll get a good story out of it." This was some small comfort. "I believe I'll call it *The Case of the Thirty-third Cathedral of Rouen.*"

"What's this?" she exclaimed. "No, of course not!" And then she insisted that I keep everything she had told me that day a secret.

I couldn't believe it. Bitterly I said, "You're like those forgers. You want *somebody* to witness your cleverness, and I'm the one who is stuck with it."

She immediately agreed, but went on to list all the reasons no one else could ever learn of the affair—how so many people would be hurt—including her, I added acerbically—how so many valuable collections would be ruined, how her plan to transform Arnold into a respectable honest Plutonian artist would collapse, and so on and so forth, for nearly an hour. Finally I gave up and conceded to her wishes, so that the upshot of it was, I promised not to write down a single word concerning this particular adventure of ours, and I promised furthermore to say nothing of the entire affair, and to keep it a complete secret, forever and ever.

But I don't suppose it will do any harm to tell you.

Time fascinates us. Is it the true Fourth Dimension, or is that just a glib definition made in an effort to hide the fact that we don't understand it at all? Science fiction writers since H. G. Wells have enjoyed speculating about Time, and in the following story Harlan Ellison shows there are still new ways of looking at it.

"Paladin of the Lost Hour" did not begin as a story; Ellison began writing it as a television script for The Twilight Zone *series on CBS, which will be revived this fall. Halfway through the script, he took time out to write the story—and in the process, he says, new ideas came to him that greatly improved the script when he finished it.*

It will be interesting to compare the story to the TV version in a few months.

PALADIN OF THE LOST HOUR

HARLAN ELLISON

This was an old man. Not an incredibly old man; obsolete, spavined; not as worn as the sway-backed stone steps ascending the Pyramid of the Sun to an ancient temple; not yet a relic. But even so, a *very* old man, this old man perched on antique shooting stick, its handles open to form a seat, its spike thrust at an angle into the soft ground and trimmed grass of the cemetery. Gray, thin rain misted down at almost the same angle as that at which the spike pierced the ground. The winter-barren trees lay flat and black against an aluminum sky, unmoving in the chill wind. An old man sitting at the foot of a grave mound whose headstone had tilted slightly when the earth had settled; sitting in the rain and speaking to someone below.

"They tore it down, Minna.

"I tell you, they must have bought off a councilman.

"Came in with bulldozers at six o'clock in the morning, and you *know* that's not legal. There's a Municipal Code. Supposed to hold off till at least seven on weekdays, eight on the weekend; but there they were at six, even *before* six, barely light for godsakes. Thought they'd sneak in and do it before the neighborhood got wind of it and called the landmarks committee. Sneaks: they come on *holidays*, can you imagine!

"But I was out there waiting for them, and I told them, 'You can't do it, that's Code number 91.3002, sub-section E,' and they lied and said they had special permission, so I said to the big muckymuck in charge, 'Let's see your waiver permit,' and he said the Code didn't apply in this case because it was supposed to be only for grading, and since they were demolishing and not grading, they could start whenever they felt like it. So I told him I'd call the police, then, because it came under the heading of Disturbing the Peace, and he said . . . well, I know you hate that kind of language, old girl, so I won't tell you what he said, but you can imagine.

"So I called the police, and gave them my name, and of course they didn't get there till almost quarter after seven (which is what makes me think they bought off a councilman), and by then those 'dozers had leveled most of it. Doesn't take long, you know that.

"And I don't suppose it's as great a loss as, maybe, say, the Great Library of Alexandria, but it was the last of the authentic Deco design drive-ins, and the carhops still served you on roller skates, and it was a landmark, and just about the only place left in the city where you could still get a decent grilled cheese sandwich pressed very flat on the grill by one of those weights they used to use, made with real cheese and not that rancid plastic they cut into squares and call it 'cheese food.'

"Gone, old dear, gone and mourned. And I understand they plan to put up another one of those mini-malls on the site, just ten blocks away from one that's already there, and you know what's going to happen: this new one will drain off the traffic from the older one, and then that one will fail the way they all do when the next one gets built, you'd think they'd see some history in it; but no, they never learn. And you should have seen the crowd by seven-thirty. All ages, even some of those kids painted like aborigines, with torn leather clothing. Even they came to protest. Terrible language, but at least they were concerned. And nothing could stop it. They just whammed it, and down it went.

"I do so miss you today, Minna. No more good grilled cheese." Said the *very* old man to the ground. And now he was crying softly, and now the wind rose, and the mist rain stippled his overcoat.

Nearby, yet at a distance, Billy Kinetta stared down at another grave. He could see the old man over there off to his left, but he took no further notice. The wind whipped the vent of his trenchcoat. His collar was up but rain trickled down his neck. This was a younger man, not yet thirty-five. Unlike the old man, Billy Kinetta neither cried nor spoke to memories of someone who had once listened. He might have been a geomancer, so silently did he stand, eyes toward the ground.

One of these men was black; the other was white.

Beyond the high, spiked-iron fence surrounding the cemetery two boys crouched, staring through the bars, through the rain; at the men absorbed by grave matters, by matters of graves. These were not really boys. They were legally young men. One was nineteen, the other two months beyond twenty. Both were legally old enough to vote, to drink alcoholic beverages, to drive a car. Neither would reach the age of Billy Kinetta.

One of them said, "Let's take the old man."

The other responded, "You think the guy in the trenchcoat'll get in the way?"

The first one smiled; and a mean little laugh. "I sure as shit hope so." He wore, on his right hand, a leather carnaby glove with the fingers cut off, small round metal studs in a pattern along the line of his knuckles. He made a fist, flexed, did it again.

They went under the spiked fence at a point where erosion had created a shallow gully. "Sonofabitch!" one of them said, as he slid through on his stomach. It was muddy. The front of his sateen roadie jacket was filthy. "Sonofabitch!" He was speaking in general of the fence, the sliding under, the muddy ground, the universe in total. And the old man, who would now *really* get the crap kicked out of him for making this fine sateen roadie jacket filthy.

They sneaked up on him from the left, as far from the young guy in the trenchcoat as they could. The first one kicked out the shooting stick with a short, sharp, downward movement he had learned in his Tae-Kwon Do class. It was called the *yup-chagi*. The old man went over backward.

Then they were on him, the one with the filthy sonofabitch sateen roadie jacket punching at the old man's neck and the side of his face as he dragged him around by the collar of the overcoat. The other one began ransacking the coat pockets, ripping the fabric to get his hand inside.

The old man commenced to scream. "Protect me! You've got to protect me . . . it's necessary to protect me!"

The one pillaging pockets froze momentarily. What the hell kind of thing is that for this old fucker to be saying? Who the hell does he think'll

protect him? Is he asking *us* to protect him? I'll protect you, scumbag! I'll
kick in your fuckin' lung! "Shut 'im up!" he whispered urgently to his
friend. "Stick a fist in his mouth!" Then his hand, wedged in an inside
jacket pocket, closed over something. He tried to get his hand loose, but
the jacket and coat and the old man's body had wound around his wrist.
"C'mon loose, motherfuckah!" he said to the very old man, who was still
screaming for protection. The other young man was making huffing
sounds, as dark as mud, as he slapped at the rain-soaked hair of his victim.
"I can't . . . he's all twisted 'round . . . getcher hand outta there so's I
can . . ." Screaming, the old man had doubled under, locking their
hands on his person.

And then the pillager's fist came loose, and he was clutching—for an
instant—a gorgeous pocket watch.

What used to be called a turnip watch.

The dial face was *cloisonné*, exquisite beyond the telling.

The case was of silver, so bright it seemed blue.

The hands, cast as arrows of time, were gold. They formed a shallow V
at precisely eleven o'clock. This was happening at 3:45 in the afternoon,
with rain and wind.

The timepiece made no sound, no sound at all.

Then: there was space all around the watch, and in that space in the
palm of the hand, there was heat. Intense heat for just a moment, just
long enough for the hand to open.

The watch glided out of the boy's palm and levitated.

"Help me! You *must* protect me!"

Billy Kinetta heard the shrieking, but did not see the pocket watch
floating in the air above the astonished young man. It was silver, and it
was end-on toward him, and the rain was silver and slanting; and he did
not see the watch hanging free in the air, even when the furious young
man disentangled himself and leaped for it. Billy did not see the watch
rise just so much, out of reach of the mugger.

Billy Kinetta saw two boys, two young men of ratpack age, beating
someone much older; and he went for them. Pow, like that!

Thrashing his legs, the old man twisted around—over, under—as the
boy holding him by the collar tried to land a punch to put him away. Who
would have thought the old man to have had so much battle in him?

A flapping shape, screaming something unintelligible, hit the center of
the group at full speed. The carnaby-gloved hand reaching for the watch

grasped at empty air one moment, and the next was buried under its owner as the boy was struck a crackback block that threw him face-first into the soggy ground. He tried to rise, but something stomped him at the base of his spine; something kicked him twice in the kidneys; something rolled over him like a flash flood.

Twisting, twisting, the very old man put his thumb in the right eye of the boy clutching his collar.

The great trenchcoated maelstrom that was Billy Kinetta whirled into the boy as he let loose of the old man on the ground and, howling, slapped a palm against his stinging eye. Billy locked his fingers and delivered a roundhouse wallop that sent the boy reeling backward to fall over Minna's tilted headstone.

Billy's back was to the old man. He did not see the miraculous pocket watch smoothly descend through rain that did not touch it, to hover in front of the old man. He did not see the old man reach up, did not see the timepiece snuggle into an arthritic hand, did not see the old man return the turnip to an inside jacket pocket.

Wind, rain and Billy Kinetta pummeled two young men of a legal age that made them accountable for their actions. There was no thought of the knife stuck down in one boot, no chance to reach it, no moment when the wild thing let them rise. So they crawled. They scrabbled across the muddy ground, the slippery grass, over graves and out of his reach. They ran; falling, rising, falling again; away, without looking back.

Billy Kinetta, breathing heavily, knees trembling, turned to help the old man to his feet; and found him standing, brushing dirt from his overcoat, snorting in anger and mumbling to himself.

"Are you all right?"

For a moment the old man's recitation of annoyance continued, then he snapped his chin down sharply as if marking end to the situation, and looked at his cavalry to the rescue. "That was very good, young fella. Considerable style you've got there."

Billy Kinetta stared at him wide-eyed. "Are you sure you're okay?" He reached over and flicked several blades of wet grass from the shoulder of the old man's overcoat.

"I'm fine. I'm fine but I'm wet and I'm cranky. Let's go somewhere and have a nice cup of Earl Grey."

There had been a look on Billy Kinetta's face as he stood with lowered

eyes, staring at the grave he had come to visit. The emergency had removed that look. Now it returned.

"No, thanks. If you're okay, I've got to do some things."

The old man felt himself all over, meticulously, as he replied, "I'm only
superficially bruised. Now if I were an old woman, instead of a spunky old
man, same age though, I'd have lost considerable of the calcium in my
bones, and those two would have done me some mischief. Did you know
that women lose a considerable part of their calcium when they reach my
age? I read a report." Then he paused, and said shyly, "Come on, why
don't you and I sit and chew the fat over a nice cup of tea?"

Billy shook his head with bemusement, smiling despite himself. "You're
something else, Dad. I don't even know you."

"I like that."

"What: that I don't know you?"

"No, that you called me 'Dad' and not 'Pop.' I *hate* 'Pop.' Always
makes me think the wise-apple wants to snap off my cap with a bottle
opener. Now *Dad* has a ring of respect to it. I like that right down to the
ground. Yes, I believe we should find someplace warm and quiet to sit and
get to know each other. After all, you saved my life. And you know what
that means in the Orient."

Billy was smiling continuously now. "In the first place, I doubt very
much I saved your life. Your wallet, maybe. And in the second place, I
don't even know your name; what would we have to talk about?"

"Gaspar," he said, extending his hand. "That's a first name. Gaspar.
Know what it means?"

Billy shook his head.

"See, already we have something to talk about."

So Billy, still smiling, began walking Gaspar out of the cemetery.
"Where do you live? I'll take you home."

They were on the street, approaching Billy Kinetta's 1979 Cutlass.
"Where I live is too far for now. I'm beginning to feel a bit peaky. I'd like
to lie down for a minute. We can just go on over to your place, if that
doesn't bother you. For a few minutes. A cup of tea. Is that all right?"

He was standing beside the Cutlass, looking at Billy with an old man's
expectant smile, waiting for him to unlock the door and hold it for him till
he'd placed his still-calcium-rich but nonetheless old bones in the passenger seat. Billy stared at him, trying to figure out what was at risk if he
unlocked that door. Then he snorted a tiny laugh, unlocked the door, held

it for Gaspar as he seated himself, slammed it and went around to unlock the other side and get in. Gaspar reached across and thumbed up the door lock knob. And they drove off together in the rain.

Through all of this the timepiece made no sound, no sound at all.

Like Gaspar, Billy Kinetta was alone in the world.

His three-room apartment was the vacuum in which he existed. It was furnished, but if one stepped out into the hallway and, for all the money in all the unnumbered accounts in all the banks in Switzerland, one were asked to describe those furnishings, one would come away no richer than before. The apartment was charisma poor. It was a place to come when all other possibilities had been expended. Nothing green, nothing alive, existed in those boxes. No eyes looked back from the walls. Neither warmth nor chill marked those spaces. It was a place to wait.

Gaspar leaned his closed shooting stick, now a walking stick with handles, against the bookcase. He studied the titles of the paperbacks stacked haphazardly on the shelves.

From the kitchenette came the sound of water running into a metal pan. Then tin on cast iron. Then the hiss of gas and the flaring of a match as it was struck; and the pop of the gas being lit.

"Many years ago," Gaspar said, taking out a copy of Moravia's *The Adolescents* and thumbing it as he spoke, "I had a library of books, oh, thousands of books—never could bear to toss one out, not even the bad ones—and when folks would come to the house to visit they'd look around at all the nooks and crannys stuffed with books; and if they were the sort of folks who don't snuggle with books, they'd always ask the same dumb question." He waited a moment for a response and when none was forthcoming (the sound of china cups on sink tile), he said, "Guess what the question was."

From the kitchen, without much interest: "No idea."

"They'd always ask it with the kind of voice people use in the presence of large sculptures in museums. They'd ask me, 'Have you read all these books?' " He waited again, but Billy Kinetta was not playing the game. "Well, young fella, after a while the same dumb question gets asked a million times, you get sorta snappish about it. And it came to annoy me more than a little bit. Till I finally figured out the right answer.

"And you know what that answer was? Go ahead, take a guess."

Billy appeared in the kitchenette doorway. "I suppose you told them you'd read a lot of them but not all of them."

Gaspar waved the guess away with a flapping hand. "Now what good would that have done? They wouldn't know they'd asked a dumb question, but I didn't want to insult them, either. So when they'd ask if I'd read all those books, I'd say, 'Hell no. Who wants a library full of books you've already read?' "

Billy laughed despite himself. He scratched at his hair with idle pleasure, and shook his head at the old man's verve. "Gaspar, you are a wild old man. You retired?"

The old man walked carefully to the most comfortable chair in the room, an overstuffed Thirties-style lounge that had been reupholstered many times before Billy Kinetta had purchased it at the American Cancer Society Thrift Shop. He sank into it with a sigh. "No sir, I am not by any means retired. Still very active."

"Doing what, if I'm not prying?"

"Doing ombudsman."

"You mean, like a consumer advocate? Like Ralph Nader?"

"Exactly. I watch out for things. I listen, I pay some attention; and if I do it right, sometimes I can even make a little difference. Yes, like Mr. Nader. A very fine man."

"And you were at the cemetery to see a relative?"

Gaspar's face settled into an expression of loss. "My dear old girl. My wife, Minna. She's been gone, well, it was twenty years in January." He sat silently staring inward for a while, then: "She was everything to me. The nice part was that I knew how important we were to each other; we discussed, well, just *everything*. I miss that the most, telling her what's going on.

"I go to see her every other day.

"I used to go every day. But. It. Hurt. Too much."

They had tea. Gaspar sipped and said it was very nice, but had Billy ever tried Earl Grey? Billy said he didn't know what that was, and Gaspar said he would bring him a tin, that it was splendid. And they chatted. Finally, Gaspar asked, "And who were you visiting?"

Billy pressed his lips together. "Just a friend." And would say no more. Then he sighed and said, "Well, listen, I have to go to work."

"Oh? What do you do?"

The answer came slowly. As if Billy Kinetta wanted to be able to say that he was in computers, or owned his own business, or held a position of import. "I'm night manager at a 7-Eleven."

"I'll bet you meet some fascinating people coming in late for milk or one of those slushies," Gaspar said gently. He seemed to understand.

Billy smiled. He took the kindness as it was intended. "Yeah, the cream of high society. That is, when they're not threatening to shoot me through the head if I don't open the safe."

"Let me ask you a favor," Gaspar said. "I'd like a little sanctuary, if you think it's all right. Just a little rest. I could lie down on the sofa for a bit. Would that be all right? You trust me to stay here while you're gone, young fella?"

Billy hesitated only a moment. The very old man seemed okay, not a crazy, certainly not a thief. And what was there to steal? Some tea that wasn't even Earl Grey?

"Sure. That'll be okay. But I won't be coming back till two A.M. So just close the door behind you when you go; it'll lock automatically."

They shook hands, Billy shrugged into his still-wet trenchcoat, and he went to the door. He paused to look back at Gaspar sitting in the lengthening shadows as evening came on. "It was nice getting to know you, Gaspar."

"You can make that a mutual pleasure, Billy. You're a nice young fella."

And Billy went to work, alone as always.

When he came home at two, prepared to open a can of Hormel chili, he found the table set for dinner, with the scent of an elegant beef stew enriching the apartment. There were new potatoes and stir-fried carrots and zucchini that had been lightly battered to delicate crispness. And cupcakes. White cake with chocolate frosting. From a bakery.

And in that way, as gently as that, Gaspar insinuated himself into Billy Kinetta's apartment and his life.

As they sat with tea and cupcakes, Billy said, "You don't have anyplace to go, do you?"

The old man smiled and made one of those deprecating movements of the head. "Well, I'm not the sort of fella who can bear to be homeless, but at the moment I'm what vaudevillians used to call 'at liberty.' "

"If you want to stay on a time, that would be okay," Billy said. "It's not very roomy here, but we seem to get on all right."

"That's strongly kind of you, Billy. Yes, I'd like to be your roommate for a while. Won't be too long, though. My doctor tells me I'm not long for this world." He paused, looked into the teacup and said softly, "I have to confess . . . I'm a little frightened. To go. Having someone to talk to would be a great comfort."

And Billy said, without preparation, "I was visiting the grave of a man who was in my rifle company in Viet Nam. I go there sometimes." But there was such pain in his words that Gaspar did not press him for details.

So the hours passed, as they will with or without permission, and when Gaspar asked Billy if they could watch the television, to catch an early newscast, and Billy tuned in the old set just in time to pick up dire reports of another aborted disarmament talk, and Billy shook his head and observed that it wasn't only Gaspar who was frightened of something like death, Gaspar chuckled, patted Billy on the knee and said, with unassailable assurance, "Take my word for it, Billy . . . it isn't going to happen. No nuclear holocaust. Trust me, when I tell you this: it'll never happen. Never, never, not ever."

Billy smiled wanly. "And why not? What makes *you* so sure . . . got some special inside information?"

And Gaspar pulled out the magnificent timepiece, which Billy was seeing for the first time, and he said, "It's not going to happen because it's only eleven o'clock."

Billy stared at the watch, which read 11:00 precisely. He consulted his wristwatch. "Hate to tell you this, but your watch has stopped. It's almost five-thirty."

Gaspar smiled his own certain smile. "No, it's eleven."

And they made up the sofa for the very old man, who placed his pocket change and his fountain pen and the sumptuous turnip watch on the now-silent television set, and they went to sleep.

One day Billy went off while Gaspar was washing the lunch dishes, and when he came back, he had a large paper bag from Toys "R" Us.

Gaspar came out of the kitchenette rubbing a plate with a souvenir dish towel from Niagara Falls, New York. He stared at Billy and the bag. "What's in the bag?" Billy inclined his head, and indicated the very old man should join him in the middle of the room. Then he sat down crosslegged on the floor, and dumped the contents of the bag. Gaspar stared with startlement, and sat down beside him.

So for two hours they played with tiny cars that turned into robots when the sections were unfolded.

Gaspar was excellent at figuring out all the permutations of the Transformers, Starriors and GoBots. He played well.

Then they went for a walk. "I'll treat you to a matinee," Gaspar said. "But no films with Karen Black, Sandy Dennis or Meryl Streep. They're always crying. Their noses are always red. I can't stand that."

They started to cross the avenue. Stopped at the light was this year's Cadillac Brougham, vanity license plates, ten coats of acrylic lacquer and two coats of clear (with a little retarder in the final "color coat" for a slow dry) of a magenta hue so rich that it approximated the shade of light shining through a decanter filled with Chateau Lafite-Rothschild 1945.

The man driving the Cadillac had no neck. His head sat thumped down hard on the shoulders. He stared straight ahead, took one last deep pull on the cigar, and threw it out the window. The still-smoking butt landed directly in front of Gaspar as he passed the car. The old man stopped, stared down at this coprolitic metaphor, and then stared at the driver. The eyes behind the wheel, the eyes of a macaque, did not waver from the stoplight's red circle. Just outside the window, someone was looking in, but the eyes of the rhesus were on the red circle.

A line of cars stopped behind the Brougham.

Gaspar continued to stare at the man in the Cadillac for a moment, and then, with creaking difficulty, he bent and picked up the smoldering butt of stogie.

The old man walked the two steps to the car—as Billy watched in confusion—thrust his face forward till it was mere inches from the driver's profile, and said with extreme sweetness, "I think you dropped this in our living room."

And as the glazed simian eyes turned to stare directly into the pedestrian's face, nearly nose-to-nose, Gaspar casually flipped the butt with its red glowing tip, into the back seat of the Cadillac, where it began to burn a hole in the fine Corinthian leather.

Three things happened simultaneously:

The driver let out a howl, tried to see the butt in his rear-view mirror, could not get the angle, tried to look over his shoulder into the back seat but without a neck could not perform that feat of agility, put the car into neutral, opened his door and stormed into the street trying to grab Gaspar. "You fuckin' bastid, whaddaya think you're doin' tuh my car you asshole bastid, I'll kill ya . . ."

Billy's hair stood on end as he saw what Gaspar was doing; he rushed back the short distance in the crosswalk to grab the old man; Gaspar would not be dragged away, stood smiling with unconcealed pleasure at the mad bull rampaging and screaming of the hysterical driver. Billy yanked as hard as he could and Gaspar began to move away, around the front of the Cadillac, toward the far curb. Still grinning with octogeneric charm.

The light changed.

These three things happened in the space of five seconds, abetted by the impatient honking of the cars behind the Brougham; as the light turned green.

Screaming, dragging, honking, as the driver found he could not do three things at once: he could not go after Gaspar while the traffic was clanging at him; could not let go of the car door to crawl into the back seat from which now came the stench of charring leather that could not be rectified by an inexpensive Tijuana tuck-'n-roll; could not save his back seat and at the same time stave off the hostility of a dozen drivers cursing and honking. He trembled there, torn three ways, doing nothing.

Billy dragged Gaspar.

Out of the crosswalk. Out of the street. Onto the curb. Up the side street. Into the alley. Through a backyard. To the next street from the avenue.

Puffing with the exertion, Billy stopped at last, five houses up the street. Gaspar was still grinning, chuckling softly with unconcealed pleasure at his puckish ways. Billy turned on him with wild gesticulations and babble.

"You're *nuts!*"

"How about that?" the old man said, giving Billy an affectionate poke in the bicep.

"Nuts! Looney! That guy would've torn off your head! What the hell's wrong with you, old man? Are you out of your boots?"

"I'm not crazy. I'm responsible."

"Responsible!?! Res*pon*sible, fer chrissakes? For what? For all the butts every yotz throws into the street?"

The old man nodded. "For butts, and trash, and pollution, and toxic waste dumping in the dead of night; for bushes, and cactus, and the baobab tree; for pippin apples and even lima beans, which I despise. You show me someone who'll eat lima beans without being at gunpoint, I'll show you a pervert!"

Billy was screaming. "What the hell are you talking about?"

"I'm also responsible for dogs and cats and guppies and cockroaches and the President of the United States and Jonas Salk and your mother and the entire chorus line at the Sands Hotel in Las Vegas. Also their choreographer."

"Who do you think you are? God?"

"Don't be sacrilegious. I'm too old to wash your mouth out with laundry soap. Of course I'm not God. I'm just an old man. *But I'm responsible.*"

Gaspar started to walk away, toward the corner and the avenue, and a resumption of their route. Billy stood where the old man's words had pinned him.

"Come on, young fella," Gaspar said, walking backward to speak to him, "we'll miss the beginning of the movie. I hate that."

Billy had finished eating, and they were sitting in the dimness of the apartment, only the lamp in the corner lit. The old man had gone to the County Art Museum and had bought inexpensive prints—Max Ernst, Gêrome, Richard Dadd, a subtle Feininger—which he had mounted in Insta-Frames. They sat in silence for a time, relaxing; then murmuring trivialities in a pleasant undertone.

Finally, Gaspar said, "I've been thinking a lot about my dying. I like what Woody Allen said."

Billy slid to a more comfortable position in the lounger. "What was that?"

"He said: I don't mind dying, I just don't want to be there when it happens."

Billy snickered.

"I feel something like that, Billy. I'm not afraid to go, but I don't want to leave Minna entirely. The times I spend with her, talking to her, well, it gives me the feeling we're still in touch. When I go, that's the end of Minna. She'll be well and truly dead. We never had any children, almost everyone who knew us is gone, no relatives. And we never did anything important that anyone would put in a record book, so that's the end of us.

For me, I don't mind; but I wish there was someone who knew about Minna . . . she was a remarkable person."

So Billy said, "Tell me. I'll remember for you."

Memories in no particular order. Some as strong as ropes that could pull the ocean ashore. Some that shimmered and swayed in the faintest breeze like spiderwebs. The entire person, all the little movements, that dimple that appeared when she was amused at something foolish he had said. Their youth together, their love, the procession of their days toward middle age. The small cheers and the pain of dreams never realized. So much about him, as he spoke of her. His voice soft and warm and filled with a longing so deep and true that he had to stop frequently because the words broke and would not come out till he had thought away some of the passion. He thought of her and was glad. He had gathered her together, all her dowry of love and taking care of him, her clothes and the way she wore them, her favorite knickknacks, a few clever remarks: and he packed it all up and delivered it to a new repository.

The very old man gave Minna to Billy Kinetta for safekeeping.

Dawn had come. The light filtering in through the blinds was saffron. "Thank you, Dad," Billy said. He could not name the feeling that had taken him hours earlier. But he said this: "I've never had to be responsible for anything, or anyone, in my whole life. I never belonged to anybody . . . I don't know why. It didn't bother me, because I didn't know any other way to be."

Then his position changed, there in the lounger. He sat up in a way that Gaspar thought was important. As if Billy were about to open the secret box buried at his center. And Billy spoke so softly the old man had to strain to hear him.

"I didn't even know him.

"We were defending the airfield at Danang. Did I tell you we were 1st Battalion, 9th Marines? Charlie was massing for a big push out of Quang Ngai province, south of us. Looked as if they were going to try to take the provincial capital. My rifle company was assigned to protect the perimeter. They kept sending in patrols to bite us. Every day we'd lose some poor bastard who scratched his head when he shouldn't of. It was June, late in June, cold and a lot of rain. The foxholes were hip-deep in water.

"Flares first. Our howitzers started firing. Then the sky was full of tracers, and I started to turn toward the bushes when I heard something coming, and these two main-force regulars in dark blue uniforms came toward me. I could see them so clearly. Long black hair. All crouched over. And they started firing. And that goddam carbine seized up, wouldn't fire; and I pulled out the banana clip, tried to slap in another, but they saw me and just turned a couple of AK-47's on me . . . God, I remember everything slowed down . . . I looked at those things, seven-point-six-two millimeter assault rifles they were . . . I got crazy for a second, tried to figure out in my own mind if they were Russian-made, or Chinese, or Czech, or North Korean. And it was so bright from the flares I could see them starting to squeeze off the rounds, and then from out of nowhere this lance corporal jumped out at them and yelled somedamn-thing like, 'Hey, you VC fucks, looka here!' except it wasn't that . . . I never could recall what he said actually . . . and they turned to brace him . . . and they opened him up like a baggie full of blood . . . and he was all over me, and the bushes, and oh god there was pieces of him floating on the water I was standing in . . ."

Billy was heaving breath with impossible weight. His hands moved in the air before his face without pattern or goal. He kept looking into far corners of the dawn-lit room as if special facts might present themselves to fill out the reasons behind what he was saying.

"Aw, geezus, he was *floating* on the water . . . aw, christ, *he got in my boots!*" Then a wail of pain so loud it blotted out the sound of traffic beyond the apartment; and he began to moan, but not cry; and the moaning kept on; and Gaspar came from the sofa and held him and said such words as *it's all right*, but they might not have been those words, or *any* words.

And pressed against the old man's shoulder, Billy Kinetta ran on only half sane: "He wasn't my friend, I never knew him, I'd never talked to him, but I'd seen him, he was just this guy, and there wasn't any reason to do that, he didn't know whether I was a good guy or a shit or anything, so why did he do that? He didn't need to do that. They wouldn't of seen him. He was dead before I killed them. He was gone already. I never got to say thank you or thank you or . . . *anything!*

"Now he's in that grave, so I came here to live, so I can go there, but I try and try to say thank you, and he's dead, and he can't hear me, he can't hear anything, he's just down there, down in the ground, and I can't say thank you . . . oh, geezus, geezus, why don't he hear me, I just want to say thanks . . ."

Billy Kinetta wanted to assume the responsibility for saying thanks, but that was possible only on a night that would never come again; and this was the day.

Gaspar took him to the bedroom and put him down to sleep in exactly the same way one would soothe an old, sick dog.

Then he went to his sofa, and because it was the only thing he could imagine saying, he murmured, "He'll be all right, Minna. Really he will."

When Billy left for the 7-Eleven the next evening, Gaspar was gone. It was an alternate day, and that meant he was out at the cemetery. Billy fretted that he shouldn't be there alone, but the old man had a way of taking care of himself. Billy was not smiling as he thought of his friend, and the word *friend* echoed as he realized that, yes, this was his friend, truly and really his friend. He wondered how old Gaspar was, and how soon Billy Kinetta would be once again what he had always been: alone.

When he returned to the apartment at two-thirty, Gaspar was asleep, cocooned in his blanket on the sofa. Billy went in and tried to sleep, but hours later, when sleep would not come, when thoughts of murky water and calcium night light on dark foliage kept him staring at the bedroom ceiling, he came out of the room for a drink of water. He wandered around the living room, not wanting to be by himself even if the only companionship in this sleepless night was breathing heavily, himself in sleep.

He stared out the window. Clouds lay in chiffon strips across the sky. The squealing of tires from the street.

Sighing, idle in his movement around the room, he saw the old man's pocket watch lying on the coffee table beside the sofa. He walked to the table. If the watch was still stopped at eleven o'clock, perhaps he would borrow it and have it repaired. It would be a nice thing to do for Gaspar. He loved that beautiful timepiece.

Billy bent to pick it up.

The watch, stopped at the V of eleven precisely, levitated at an angle, floating away from him.

Billy Kinetta felt a shiver travel down his back to burrow in at the base of his spine. He reached for the watch hanging in air before him. It floated away just enough that his fingers massaged empty space. He tried to catch it. The watch eluded him, lazily turning away like an opponent who knows he is in no danger of being struck from behind.

Then Billy realized Gaspar was awake. Turned away from the sofa, nonetheless he knew the old man was observing him. And the blissful floating watch.

He looked at Gaspar.

They did not speak for a long time.

Then: "I'm going back to sleep," Billy said. Quietly.

"I think you have some questions," Gaspar replied.

"Questions? No, of course not, Dad. Why in the world would I have questions? I'm still asleep." But that was not the truth, because he had not been asleep that night.

"Do you know what 'Gaspar' means? Do you remember the three wise men of the Bible, the Magi?"

"I don't want any frankincense and myrrh. I'm going back to bed. I'm going now. You see, I'm going right now."

" 'Gaspar' means master of the treasure, keeper of the secrets, paladin of the palace." Billy was staring at him, not walking into the bedroom; just staring at him. As the elegant timepiece floated to the old man, who extended his hand palm-up to receive it. The watch nestled in his hand, unmoving, and it made no sound, no sound at all.

"You go back to bed. But will you go out to the cemetery with me tomorrow? It's important."

"Why?"

"Because I believe I'll be dying tomorrow."

It was a nice day, cool and clear. Not at all a day for dying, but neither had been many such days in Southeast Asia, and death had not been deterred.

They stood at Minna's gravesite, and Gaspar opened his shooting stick to form a seat, and he thrust the spike into the ground, and he settled onto it, and sighed, and said to Billy Kinetta, "I'm growing cold as that stone."

"Do you want my jacket?"

"No. I'm cold inside." He looked around at the sky, at the grass, at the rows of markers. "I've been responsible, for all of this, and more."

"You've said that before."

"Young fella, are you by any chance familiar, in your reading, with an old novel by James Hilton called *Lost Horizon?* Perhaps you saw the movie. It was a wonderful movie, actually much better than the book. Mr. Capra's greatest achievement. A human testament. Ronald Colman was superb. Do you know the story?"

"Yes."

"Do you remember the High Lama, played by Sam Jaffe? His name was Father Perrault?"

"Yes."

"Do you remember how he passed on the caretakership of that magical hidden world, Shangri-La, to Ronald Colman?"

"Yes, I remember that." Billy paused. "Then he died. He was very old, and he died."

Gaspar smiled up at Billy. "Very good, Billy. I knew you were a good boy. So now, if you remember all that, may I tell you a story? It's not a very long story."

Billy nodded, smiling at his friend.

"In 1582 Pope Gregory XIII decreed that the civilized world would no longer observe the Julian calendar. October 4th, 1582 was followed, the next day, by October 15th. Eleven days vanished from the world. One hundred and seventy years later, the British Parliament followed suit, and September 2nd, 1752 was followed, the next day, by September 14th. Why did he do that, the Pope?"

Billy was bewildered by the conversation. "Because he was bringing it into synch with the real world. The solstices and equinoxes. When to plant, when to harvest."

Gaspar waggled a finger at him with pleasure. "Excellent, young fella. And you're correct when you say Gregory abolished the Julian calendar because its error of one day in every one hundred and twenty-eight years had moved the vernal equinox to March 11th. That's what the history books say. It's what *every* history book says. But what if?"

"What if *what?* I don't know what you're talking about."

"What if: Pope Gregory had the knowledge revealed to him that he *must* readjust time in the minds of men? What if: the excess time in 1582 was eleven days and one hour? What if: he accounted for those eleven days, vanished those eleven days, but that one hour slipped free, was left loose to bounce through eternity? A very special hour . . . an hour that must *never* be used . . . an hour that must never toll. What if?"

Billy spread his hands. "What if, what if, what if! It's all just philosophy. It doesn't mean anything. Hours aren't real, time isn't something that you can bottle up. So what if there *is* an hour out there somewhere that . . ."

And he stopped.

He grew tense, and leaned down to the old man. "The watch. Your watch. It doesn't work. It's stopped."

Gaspar nodded. "At eleven o'clock. My watch works; it keeps very special time, for one very special hour."

Billy touched Gaspar's shoulder. Carefully he asked, "Who are you, Dad?"

The old man did not smile as he said, "Gaspar. Keeper. Paladin. Guardian."

"Father Perrault was hundreds of years old."

Gaspar shook his head with a wistful expression on his old face. "I'm eighty-six years old, Billy. You asked me if I thought I was God. Not God, not Father Perrault, not an immortal, just an old man who will die too soon. Are you Ronald Colman?"

Billy nervously touched his lower lip with a finger. He looked at Gaspar as long as he could, then turned away. He walked off a few paces, stared at the barren trees. It seemed suddenly much chillier here in this place of entombed remembrances. From a distance he said, "But it's only . . . what? A chronological convenience. Like daylight saving time; Spring forward, Fall back. We don't actually *lose* an hour; we get it back."

Gaspar stared at Minna's grave. "At the end of April I lost an hour. If I die now, I'll die an hour short in my life. I'll have been cheated out of one hour I want, Billy." He swayed toward all he had left of Minna. "One last hour I could have with my old girl. That's what I'm afraid of, Billy. I have that hour in my possession. I'm afraid I'll use it, god help me, I want so much to use it."

Billy came to him. Tense, and chilled, he said, "Why must that hour never toll?"

Gaspar drew a deep breath and tore his eyes away from the grave. His gaze locked with Billy's. And he told him.

The years, all the days and hours, exist. As solid and as real as mountains and oceans and men and women and the baobab tree. Look, he said, at the lines in my face and deny that time is real. Consider these dead weeds that were once alive and try to believe it's all just vapor or the mutual agreement of Popes and Caesars and young men like you.

"The lost hour must never come, Billy, for in that hour it all ends. The light, the wind, the stars, this magnificent open place we call the universe. It all ends, and in its place—waiting, always waiting—is eternal darkness. No new beginnings, no world without end, just the infinite emptiness."

And he opened his hand, which had been lying in his lap, and there, in his palm, rested the watch, making no sound at all, and stopped dead at eleven o'clock. "Should it strike twelve, Billy, eternal night falls; from which there is no recall."

There he sat, this very old man, just a perfectly normal old man. The most recent in the endless chain of keepers of the lost hour, descended in possession from Caesar and Pope Gregory XIII, down through the centuries of men and women who had served as caretakers of the excellent timepiece. And now he was dying, and now he wanted to cling to life as every man and woman clings to life no matter how awful or painful or empty, even if it is for one more hour. The suicide, falling from the bridge, at the final instant, tries to fly, tries to climb back up the sky. This weary old man, who only wanted to stay one brief hour more with Minna. Who was afraid that his love would cost the universe.

He looked at Billy, and he extended his hand with the watch waiting for its next paladin. So softly Billy could barely hear him, knowing that he was denying himself what he most wanted at this last place in his life, he whispered, "If I die without passing it on . . . it will begin to tick."

"Not me," Billy said. "Why did you pick me? I'm no one special. I'm not someone like you. I run an all-night service mart. There's nothing special about me the way there is about you! I'm *not* Ronald Colman! I don't want to be responsible, I've *never* been responsible!"

Gaspar smiled gently. "You've been responsible for me."

Billy's rage vanished. He looked wounded.

"Look at us, Billy. Look at what color you are; and look at what color I am. You took me in as a friend. I think of you as worthy, Billy. Worthy."

They remained there that way, in silence, as the wind rose. And finally, in a timeless time, Billy nodded.

Then the young man said, "You won't be losing Minna, Dad. Now you'll go to the place where she's been waiting for you, just as she was when you first met her. There's a place where we find everything we've ever lost through the years."

"That's good, Billy, that you tell me that. I'd like to believe it, too. But I'm a pragmatist. I believe what exists . . . like rain and Minna's grave and the hours that pass that we can't see, but they *are*. I'm afraid, Billy. I'm afraid this will be the last time I can speak to her. So I ask a favor. As payment for my life spent protecting the watch.

"I ask for one minute of the hour, Billy. One minute to call her back, so we can stand face-to-face and I can touch her and say goodbye. You'll be the new protector of this watch, Billy, so I ask you please, just let me steal one minute."

Billy smiled and nodded. "We can spare the time."

Gaspar reached out with his free hand and took Billy's. It was an affectionate touch. "That was the last test, young fella. Oh, you know I've been testing you, don't you? This important item couldn't go to just anyone. And you passed the test, my friend, my last friend. When I said I could bring her back from where she's gone, here in this place we've both come to so often to talk to someone lost to us, I knew you would understand that *anyone* could be brought back in that stolen minute. And you let me take it instead of using it for yourself.

"I'm content, Billy. Minna and I don't need that minute. But if you're to carry on for me, I think you *do* need it. So I give you a going-away present . . ."

And he started the watch, whose ticking was as loud and as clear as a baby's first sound; and the sweep-second hand began to move away from eleven o'clock.

Then the wind rose, and the sky seemed to cloud over, and it grew colder, with a remarkable silver-blue mist that rolled across the cemetery; and though he did not see it emerge from that grave at a distance far to the right, Billy Kinetta saw a shape move toward him. A soldier in the uniform of a day past, and his rank was Lance Corporal. He came toward Billy Kinetta, and Billy went to meet him as Gaspar watched.

They stood together and Billy spoke to him. And the man whose name Billy had never known when he was alive, answered. And then he faded, as the seconds ticked away. Faded, and faded, and was gone. And the silver-blue mist rolled through them, and past them, and was gone; and the soldier was gone.

Billy stood alone.

When he turned back to look across the grounds to his friend, he saw that Gaspar had fallen from the shooting-stick. He lay on the ground. Billy rushed to him, and fell to his knees and lifted him onto his lap. Gaspar was still.

"Oh, god, Dad, you should have heard what he said. Oh, geez, he let me go. He let me go so I didn't even have to say I was sorry. He told me he didn't even *see* me in that foxhole. He never knew he'd saved my life. I said thank you and he said no, thank *you*, that he hadn't died for nothing. Oh, please, Dad, please don't be dead yet. I want to tell you . . ."

And the old man, the very old man, opened his eyes.*

"May I remember you to my old girl, Billy?" And his eyes closed and his caretakership was at an end, as his hand opened on the most excellent timepiece, now stopped again, at one minute past eleven, floated from his palm and waited till Billy Kinetta extended his hand, and then it floated down and lay there silently. Safe. Protected.

There in the place where all lost things returned, the young man sat on the cold ground, rocking the body of his friend. And he was in no hurry to leave. There was time.

* *The author gratefully acknowledges the importance of a discussion with Ms. Ellie Grossman in the creation of this work of fiction.*

Sometimes the ordinary world becomes very strange. It doesn't even require a change in the laws of nature or a visitation by creatures from the stars. Consider, for instance, waking up to find a giraffe in your bedroom who begins to eat the blankets from your bed . . .

Juleen Brantingham's first science fiction story appeared in Universe 9, *and she's gone on to appear in many other sf and fantasy publications with stories as original and delightful as this one. Currently she is working on her first novel.*

GIRAFFE TUESDAY

JULEEN BRANTINGHAM

When Violynne woke that morning there was one standing over her bed. It seemed ordinary enough as giraffes go: cream-colored with black spots; that ridiculous neck, of course; tall at the shoulders and sloping down to the rear; whisk-like tail adding a final note of whimsy. Its stubby horns grazed the ceiling of her bedroom and its soft brown eyes regarded her with a kindly air. It bowed to her with enormous dignity and more than a little awkwardness.

"Good day," it said. Violynne was bemused because she had heretofore believed giraffes to be voiceless. "Do you mind?" it continued when she did not respond to its greeting. "We seem to be out of giraffe biscuits and my stomach is beginning to think my throat's been cut." Chortling with what she thought excessive appreciation of its own humor, it proceeded to eat the coverlet from her bed.

She should have stopped it, she supposed. The coverlet had been a gift from her mother. But she had never before—to her knowledge—had a giraffe in her bedroom and she was disinclined to deny it anything. Added to that was her astonishment at the spectacle of the coverlet progressing down the inside of that long neck in lumps and slithers. It was only her ensuing queasiness that at last enabled her to avert her gaze.

Violynne accomplished her morning ablutions, clothed herself in her ordinary buttoned-down fashion, and edged around the giraffe, which was then licking up shreds of chenille with appreciative slurps and slobberings.

Making her way to her apartment kitchenette, she opened the cupboard where she kept breakfast cereals and found a single half-empty box labeled *Giraffe Whumpies*. The printing on the box did not enlighten her as to whether Whumpies were merely named for the animal, a part of its diet, or (St. Francis forbid!) processed giraffe meat. She poured some into a bowl and discovered that the flakes looked no different from the crispy crunchies she usually consumed for her morning meal. Taking a carton of milk from the refrigerator ("Milk from Genial Giraffes"), she sat down to eat and to consider the situation.

If you have never had a day like Violynne's Giraffe Tuesday you may wonder that she took it all so calmly. But she had always been somewhat unobservant and it was her personal though unexpressed opinion that such is the richness of life, hers was not an unusual case.

Previously she had had the experience of hearing a cheery little tune, seemingly for the first time, and when she whistled it for her lover, John, had been informed that it was the national anthem of Upper Magnolia and thus a part of the standard repertoire of every musical organization from the Calcutta Philharmonic to the Peachtree Street Kazoo Band.

On another occasion she had been enthusing to her acquaintances about an unusually shaped skyscraper she had noticed when taking a new route to her place of employment. She felt very odd indeed when it was revealed to her that not only was the said building one hundred and seventy-seven years old but also her parents had been married there in the chapel on the eighteenth floor, her kindergarten class had been located in its second sub-basement, and her dentist had his offices in an identical structure just across the street.

Violynne tried not to brood about it excessively but her failing had cost her, at various times, a scholarship, a husband, and a realtor's license, not to mention the respect of her family and friends.

She had been seven years old before she discovered that there are two sexes among humankind. One day she was living in what she believed to be a perfectly normal world and the next there were boys and men all over it. She had no doubt they had been there before she observed them but to her wondering eyes it was a sudden great infestation, as if beings from another planet had landed and overnight usurped the places of half the people she knew. Jokes whispered to her in the schoolyard acquired new meaning; the fads for miniskirts and codpieces were no longer an expression, entirely, of personal quirkiness; and her one parent's affinity for beer, hearty laughter, and sardines in garlic oil was more easily understood.

Considering the problems she had subsequently had with the masculine sex, she thought giraffes might be an easier blessing to which she must accustom herself.

As she sat there, thoughtfully chewing her Giraffe Whumpies, she cast back in her mind for memories of the long-necked beasts. She'd had an ordinary city-grown childhood with no pets other than an occasional dime-store goldfish. She had gone to university and fulfilled her military service with never a thought of giraffes crossing her mind in any significant manner. She had a commonplace job at a button factory.

The one oddity in her life was her Dali-mustachioed lover, John, who was employed by the government in some ultra-secret capacity. He spent his leisure hours collecting thesauri and annoying his building superintendent by blowing soap bubbles in the elevators. No giraffes there. Or so she thought.

But could her memory be trusted? After all, on that significant day in her eighth year, previously mentioned, when she saw a penis for the first time, she had inquired in horror-stricken tones as to what ghastly accident had befallen her poor friend. Into her mind had leaped visions of vacuum cleaner hoses running amuck or deforming chemicals polluting the bath water.

The gales of laughter her inquiry had evoked made her loath to risk such an event a second time. She determined to go about her day as if giraffes were no more out of the ordinary than asbestos pot holders.

After washing her breakfast dishes she took her coat from the closet and prepared to depart for the button factory. However, this was not to be. Somehow, while she had been occupied in the kitchenette, the giraffe had sneaked past her, on tip-toe, most likely, or tip-hoof. She found it waiting by the front door with a leash and a spangled red collar in its mouth.

Violynne frowned with displeasure, never before having considered the disadvantages of owning a pet with legs rather than fins. "Just once around the block," she told it with no hint of fondness in her voice, for she held a responsible position at the button factory and if she were late, at some time in the future there would be people who would have to go around with trousers and shirtwaists gaping open for lack of buttons. Who knew what disasters could result from such a misfortune?

The giraffe simpered in a manner that warned Violynne it was accustomed to having its own way.

She had a brief moment of concern when she depressed the elevator button but she need not have worried. The elevator car was much more capacious than she remembered, easily tall enough to accommodate the giraffe.

It snuggled up to her as the car descended, licked her on her forehead, and twisting its neck around and about so it could gaze deeply into her eyes, demonstrated such a warm affection for her that she felt her resentment melt entirely away. Feeling somewhat awkward with embarrassment, she patted its nose once or twice.

"Tell me, giraffe, have you a name?"

"Why, of course," said the animal. "You yourself gave me the name Fido when I was but a wee puppy."

"Puppy?" Violynne inquired.

Fido lowered its—his?—head as they passed through the doorway and came into the lobby. (NOW RENTING! said a sign upon a silver stand there. GIRAFFES WELCOME!) She could see a worried frown on its brow.

"Do I mean kitten?" Fido wondered.

"*Calf* must be the proper word," she said with a confident air. Since she was bearing one end of the leash and Fido had the other fastened to the collar around his neck, she felt it only just that she should be the one to make these decisions and if later she were to be proved wrong—why, what of it? There was an order to the world and each being must be made aware of its proper place.

As they strolled down the street together, Violynne and her gentle giraffe, she was pleased to note that others were also exercising their pets. The shapes, colors, and varieties of giraffe were quite astonishing. She saw some no taller than her waist, others as large as delivery vans. Some had pelts of snowy white, spotted with yellow, red, or blue. Some had hairless skins as black as moonless night. Most had coats as short and straight as Fido's but some sported curls and ringlets while others were longhairs. Among the latter there was even more variety, the length allowing for braids and waves. The fancier ones had gems and gewgaws bound up in their tresses, of which they seemed very vain.

Giraffe owners were a friendly lot, nodding and smiling at each other, stopping to pass the time of day in brief conversation while attracting envious glances from giraffeless pedestrians. The pets, too, were sociable and would pause to twine necks or to press cheeks together. It was an endearing sight.

Upon hearing rapid foot- and hoof-steps behind her Violynne turned and discovered she was being overtaken by a man and a panting purple giraffe racing to catch a bus. Naturally, politeness demanded that she step aside and as she did so she heard ill-humored grumbling from a man standing by a shopfront.

"Ruining the breed, that's what they're doing. Simply *ruining* the breed."

The sign above the shop stated PEDIGREED GIRAFFES and from the man's bearing Violynne surmised this could be none other than the owner of that establishment. Fido began to graze from a box of giraffe-nip mounted at a convenient height over the window. Violynne's heart quickened its beat, for here she saw an opportunity to cure her ignorance about the animal everyone else had seemingly known and loved since childhood but she had noticed for only the first time on this strange Giraffe Tuesday.

"Good morning," she said. Gesturing with her head toward the purple giraffe now climbing the steps of the bus, she added, "Odd color for a giraffe, don't you think?"

The man's face brightened at this expression of agreement with his position, for such was the impression she had intended her words to give.

"Quite right!" he expostulated. "It makes a true animal lover heartsick to see what unscrupulous breeders have done. Such overbred specimens are always frail and sickly. I've even heard it said they become so stupid they cannot talk."

Violynne took this to mean he had no purple giraffes among his stock and, what is more, had had more than one request for them.

"There should be a law against it!" she said, feigning shock and disapproval.

She chatted with the man for several minutes and dropped a few innocent questions, attempting to learn a few basic facts regarding giraffe ownership. The man was most helpful, mentioning vitamins and curry combs, voice and posture lessons.

Casting about wildly for some explanation that would fit giraffes into her previously faulty worldview, she said, "Perhaps you can settle an argument I have been having with a friend. The question arose as to how long the giraffe has been domesticated. My friend says it first occurred two or three hundred years ago but it seems to me the event was much more recent than that."

At once the man's scorn returned full force and he turned on her the burning eyes of a true fanatic. "I can see," he said, "that neither you nor your friend know anything at all about this noble animal. The giraffe was the first domesticated animal, its origins lost in the myths of prehistory. Indeed, there are those who avow it was not man who tamed the giraffe, but giraffe who tamed the man, requiring a workbeast to brush its coat, to cultivate and prepare the delicacies it prefers, and to provide conversation by the fireside at night."

"Is that right?" Violynne asked, bemused. How could she have missed something that must have been mentioned in every social studies and biology lesson in elementary school? Hoping to get back into the man's good graces, for he might be a source of further information, she said, "You know, I have been thinking it would be pleasant to hear the patter of little hooves around my apartment. Might you have for sale a female of this size and type?"

The man's scorn doubled and redoubled as he looked upon gentle Fido, waiting patiently, still grazing at the box of giraffe-nip. "I do not deal in mongrels," he said shortly, and turned on his heel to enter his shop.

Violynne, who only moments before had been feeling a slight sense of discomfort because her pet was so plain and ordinary, was now roused to anger.

"Fido is not a mongrel," she said with as much hauteur as she could muster. "He is a domestic shorthair."

The owner of the giraffe shop (whom she could now see was not worthy of her time, for who but a man without a soul would dare to earn a living from the sale of giraffes?) did not deign to answer except to slam the door of his establishment, setting the bell a-jangle. But then dear Fido put his great head upon her shoulder and whispered such words of comfort and affection into her ear that her heart was filled near to bursting.

Almost immediately upon turning away from the giraffe shop, that den of iniquity, Violynne's gaze fell upon one giraffe before whom all, pets and owners and unaccompanied pedestrians alike, stood aside and stared in awe. Its fur was of an unspotted pearl gray and looked to be as soft as the fur of a chinchilla. Its eyes were as blue as the purest of mountain pools. Most astounding of all was its neck, which was twisted as a corkscrew, ending in a half-turn so the giraffe was perpetually looking back to see where it had been. As it ambled down the street with its owner it was gazing back at Fido and Violynne, not rudely staring but with rather a queenly expression on its face.

Violynne was about to turn away, fearing yet another slur upon her pet's lineage, another blow to Fido's tender feelings, even though it might be unspoken, when something about the appearance of the corkscrew-necked giraffe's owner caught her attention. It was the sight of the tips of mustachios projecting beyond each side of the man's head. Could it be? Dare she hope?

"John?" she called out in a hesitant manner.

Indeed, it was he. Her lover turned and his expression brightened the moment his gaze fell upon her, the tips of his Dali mustachios rising a full three inches as he smiled.

"Violynne, my darling, I did not see you standing there. Or rather, should I say I did not expect to see you at this time of the morning, so, of course, I could not. Shall you not be late arriving at the button factory?"

Violynne thought with regret of gaping trousers and shirtwaists. "Yes, I'm afraid that I shall but some things cannot be helped. Oh, John, I have had an eventful morning!"

An expression of concern crossed his face and his mustachios could almost be said to have drooped. "Sweetheart! Not so eventful, I sincerely hope, that you have had no time to consider the question I put to you last evening?"

Violynne pondered as Fido licked the back of the gray giraffe's head. What question could her lover have expressed the previous evening? She searched her memory in vain. Had there been such a question, the experience of waking this Tuesday morning to find a giraffe in her bedroom had driven it quite out of her mind.

Seeing her apparent distress, John hastened to remind her. "My dearest one, I begged you most humbly to grant me the honor of becoming my spouse. I hope you can understand how eagerly I have been awaiting your reply."

"Ahh," Violynne breathed with sadness and regret. Had she been reminded of the question earlier that morning there would have been no hesitation in answering, for she loved John dearly. However, the encounter with the owner of the giraffe shop and her developing affection for Fido and the sight of John's spectacular companion had all combined to make her doubt that there could be wedded bliss in the future for her and John.

John's mustachios reached a five and seven o'clock position on his face. "Oh, I fear I see the answer upon your face and I cannot bear it! Say it is not so, my darling. Say that you shall not reject me."

There was the sound of soft sobbing in the morning air. With a start Violynne realized it issued, not from her lover, but from the spiral-necked giraffe, whose face she could not see due to its peculiarly twisted anatomy. Apparently these animals were so sensitive that they were a perfect reflection of their owners' emotions. Even Fido, when he turned to gaze at her, was moist-eyed, though he spoke not a word.

"The giraffes—" she explained, somewhat overcome herself.

"The giraffes?" John repeated. "Please tell me it is not the giraffes that have changed your feelings for me. My darling, I did it only to give you pleasure. An amusing little pre-engagement gift, I thought. Could I have erred?"

"You, John? You had something to do with—with giraffes?" She felt so confused. She was almost certain it was the government John worked for —surely not as a giraffe breeder. Curses upon this faulty memory of hers! Unconsciously she began to stroke the soft fur of Fido's neck. So dear to her he was. Could he have been a gift from her lover?

John looked down modestly and began to scuff the toe of one polished shoe against the sidewalk. "Yes, it was I," he confessed. Then, looking slyly from one side to another as if to assure himself there were no eaves-droppers in the vicinity, he added, "I tried to think of some delightful little thing to mark the beginning of what I hope will be a joyful marriage. Giraffes are so—so *fantastical*, don't you think? Like unicorns. It was an abuse of my position, I know, but—"

"Your position?" she inquired, more puzzled than before.

One mustachio tickled her chin as he leaned forward to whisper. "My position as Reality Adjuster for the government, of course. I arrange to eliminate all the things threatening our national security. But, darling, when I arranged for the giraffes I was also all but certain I had arranged that you and I, alone out of all the world, would remember that they have not always been a part of our lives. Did I make a mathematical miscalculation somewhere?"

Understanding dawned upon Violynne like a glorious sunburst. It had not been her own failing that was responsible for her ignorance of giraffes in everyday life! In spite of the assertion of the snobbish owner of the giraffe shop, the noble beast had not been the first to be domesticated. Indeed, they had not acquired their current place in the world until John had exercised his ultra-secret skills—an abuse of his position, certainly, but accomplished in all innocence on her behalf.

"Oh, my darling, what a wonderful gift! How could I say anything but *yes* to the man who tries so hard to please me?" But as he leaned forward to kiss her upon the cheek and to press her hand with unspoken passion, Violynne was assailed by a brief moment of uncertainty.

"But, my dear one," she whispered, nodding toward Fido and the pearl-gray giraffe, who seemed to have captured or been captured by the affectionate fervor of the moment. "Perhaps you *did* make one slight miscalculation. What of our sweet companions and their possible—progeny? The laws of genetics—"

"*Bah* upon the laws of genetics!" he cried grandly, taking her arm and escorting her down the street past guard giraffes at the bank, past singing giraffes begging for pennies, past rat-catching giraffes at the greengrocer's. "I will arrange for the laws of genetics to be subtracted from reality the instant you become my bride!"

She reached up to tweak the tip of one of his mustachios. "Not all of them, I hope."

The disciplines of medicine and genetics have been making rapid strides toward giving us greatly lengthened lives, perhaps even immortality. But scientific research requires large amounts of funding, so probably when breakthroughs are made in this area the benefits will go first to the very rich. Here's a story about New Year's Eve in the year 2100, about the wealthy few who will be attending their second turn-of-the-century party, and the reactions of the less fortunate who may still be limited to "normal" life spans.

Arthur Jean Cox has been publishing thought-provoking science fiction stories for thirty-five years . . . which means he's now of an age when speculations about longevity naturally concern him. So shall they concern all of us, and sooner than we probably think.

EVERGREEN

ARTHUR JEAN COX

Gay, lilting music spilled into the hallway from the ballroom—"The Ballroom in the Sky," as it billed itself, for it was on an upper floor of a lofty Manhattan hotel—and no passerby failed to turn a momentarily quickened eye toward its large door. That door was flanked by two small evergreen trees in ceramic jars and each tree was flanked, on the side nearest the door, by a man. These were both serious men, with watchful eyes and positively grim haircuts: men who meant business, although everyone in the room behind them meant play. For more than music spilled into the hallway. There was also laughter and the happy chatter of some three hundred men and women who seemed to be celebrating a triumph of some sort or to be congratulating themselves on their own sense of life. In these respects they were, of course, very much like any New Year's Eve crowd . . . and, as a matter of fact, it *was* New Year's Eve. In another two hours and twenty-eight minutes there would begin, at the stroke of midnight, the year 2100.

There were not many passersby, but there were a few; and one turned more than his quickened eye toward the large door. He turned also his feet, until he was stopped by the two guards, who had moved forward to block his way.

"May we help you, sir?"

"I would like to see Mr. Grandcourt."

"And what," asked the guard to his right—a soft-looking man, but so very large that he dwarfed both the passerby and the other guard—"what is the nature of your business with him?"

"I'm afraid it's personal."

Their eyes searched his face. It was an ordinary enough face, although its eyes were still a little too quickened; the face of a man of, say, forty.

"Personal?" It was again the large guard who spoke; the other was clearly a subordinate personage. "You are acquainted with Mr. Grandcourt, then?"

"Oh, yes! I've known Dave for years. We went to school together."

And the faces of the two guards froze.

But the passerby didn't notice. He was craning his neck to look past the guards into the Ballroom. It was a glittering crowd that he saw there: obviously affluent, distinctly youngish, and very well groomed—if you made allowance (as he did) for an eccentric uniformity of dress. For the men all wore green tuxedoes and the women flaring gowns of muted greens and yellows. But he didn't care: he'd found what he was looking for. "There's Dave now—standing at that table over there under the windows and looking out over the crowd with that imperial gaze of his."

And in his eagerness he started forward, raising his arm as if to hail the man he had come to see. But neither movement was completed. Both guards fell upon him and bore him to the floor. He was pinned to the carpet and the object he held in his uplifted hand was wrenched from his grip. And, suddenly, other men with grim haircuts had come running down the hallway and they too laid hands upon the passerby. He was hoisted to his feet and hustled out of sight so quickly and so very quietly that one might almost have fancied he would never be seen again. And they took with them the small but deadly explosive device with which he had meant to greet his old friend.

All this was done so efficiently that the three hundred men and women in the Ballroom never knew that it had taken place or that they had ever been, for a passing moment, in any danger. And the music swept some scores of them across the mirrored dance floor in a lilting, gliding movement.

It was now 10 P.M. And at this moment there could be detected a change in the tempo of the humming swarm in the Ballroom, but only on one side, at the edge of the crowd nearest the door. For someone had entered there, someone who was trailed after a little uncertainly, even a little sheepishly, by the two guards. People passing by stopped and stared at this newcomer. Men and women dining at nearby tables suspended that interesting activity, forks and spoons poised near their mouths. The nearest dancing couples faltered and slowed, the face of each partner turned in her direction.

There was something shocking in the appearance of this woman. Everyone felt that; it was reflected in every face. Someone watching those faces might have seen here and there very much the same words trembling silently but visibly upon more than one pair of lips: *"Old . . . terribly old."* And then the next moment one would have seen something very strange: those lips became still and then smiled a curious inward ironic smile. And yet it was undeniable that she was old—old and horribly decayed. Her face was spotted and bruised and wrinkled beyond repair. Her hair was gray and very scanty. The arms projecting from her ridiculously fluffy dress were painfully thin, almost as thin as the two canes with which she tested the floor before her as she advanced. Her gown spared the viewers any glimpse of her legs and for that they might well have been grateful. The dark eyes that glittered from her ruined face were the only things about her that seemed truly alive—the objection that could have been made to them, that was made to them, was that they were *too* alive. And, as she advanced, ripples of pity, disgust, horror, and—could it be?—guilt spread outward from her through the crowd . . . spread outward and slowly faded away.

A man came forward and confronted her. He was a tall man with a forehead so high and hair so light in texture and color that one's first glancing impression was that he was bald. But he wasn't bald; and once one noticed that, one revised one's estimate of his age downward from, say, fifty to within a year or two of thirty.

He looked the woman over with a cold, suspicious eye. He examined her dress carefully, as if there might be something concealed under it other than her horrible legs. He seemed to be almost afraid of her canes. So much so that he was hardly able to turn his eyes away from them to the large guard hovering to her right. "Gibraltar?"

Gibraltar replied with something suspiciously like a humorous intonation: "She's okay, Dave. And, Dave, she meets the requirement."

"That's right, Mr. Grandcourt," said the other guard. "The people with her showed us her birth certificate. She was born"—and he chuckled—"on the third of July 1997."

Dave was not amused. His suspicious eye took in the small knot of grinning people standing in the hallway and a sign, standing just inside the door, with large black letters forbidding entry to all who failed to meet a very rigorous requirement, before he turned it back to the woman. "What do you want, ma'am?"

"Sir"—a thin sibilance, like a single strand of cobweb, issued from the lipless mouth. "Sir, I want nothing. I am a *memento mori*, the skeleton at the feast. I am here to remind you that you too are mortal."

Dave hooded his eyes. "Thank you. And now that you have delivered your message, Madame Mayfly, you may totter back to those who sent you. I would be very much obliged to you if you would do me the great favor of not dying in the next few minutes. Wait until you're well away from the building before you fall over."

"Just a minute, Dave," said a woman, stepping out of the half-circle of people that was forming about them. "Let's not be cruel. And besides . . ."

He rounded on her, almost fiercely. She was a tall woman, with auburn hair and pleasant, if not exactly pretty, features. "And what, may I ask, is the date of your birth?"

She appeared to be about thirty; but her reply was: "25 February 1972."

He winced, mockingly touched his forehead, as if he were touching a forelock, though he had none.

"And besides," she went on, "it makes a very picturesque contrast, don't you see?"

"I rather think I do," said Dave dryly. "It's the contrast I object to."

"I'll pose with her," said 25 February. And to the younger woman: "Would you mind posing, dear?"

"Not at all, my dearie-dear. I'm quite accustomed to posing, you know." Her smile was touched with a pathetic pride. "I was Miss Flushing of 2016."

"If you don't mind," said Dave to 25 February, "I think I see the possibility of an even more striking contrast." He turned to Gibraltar.

"There's a girl in the kitchen named April-May. You'll know her when you see her. Fetch her here. And bring those two photographers here."

"Yes, Dave." The guard raised his hand, as if to touch *his* forelock, caught himself, and ran his hand through his close-cropped hair instead. He disappeared through the swinging doors of the kitchen some thirty yards farther on at the back of the room. They all waited (the decayed woman shaking with palsy, like an antique car with the motor idling) until he came back into sight, shepherding before him, as if she were a suspect being brought in for questioning, a slim blond girl. As she was brought closer, those in the half-circle about Dave saw that he indeed had an eye for contrast where the "old" lady was concerned. For April-May was extremely pretty, with blond ringlets, blue eyes, and the flawless complexion of a child. Her face was thin but sweet; though at the moment, as she hurried forward, wiping her hands on her apron, it was rather worried.

And she had a tremulous voice. "Yes, sir?"

"Don't be afraid, my dear," said Dave. And it was obvious that she had nothing to fear from *him*, for his frozen face had thawed by quite a few degrees. "There's nothing wrong. We simply want you to pose with this lady here."

The girl and the decayed woman looked at each other. Dave noticed that there was no shock, no antipathy, no disgust in the face of either. The fresh and budding girl looked at the one hundred-and-two-year-old woman with an expression no different from that with which she regarded everyone else in the room; and the malicious glitter in the eye of the decayed woman was somewhat softened.

But 25 February had been nettled by something. "April-May, you look like you're not more than sixteen. Are you sure you're old enough to have a work permit?"

The girl stammered, "I'm older than I look. . . ."

And all the Evergreens standing about laughed, though not unkindly.

"Isn't everyone?" asked a man standing at Dave's elbow. He appeared to be within a year or two of thirty—and a stranger might have said that he would be fat at fifty.

"No, Sleek," said Dave, "not everyone." And to 25 February: "You needn't concern yourself with that. You may outrank me in age, but I'm still in charge of these matters. I've already satisfied myself about her permit. I assure you that no one gets in here without being thoroughly screened. And April-May's a great acquisition for the Banquet. She makes the most delicious little desserts." And he looked upon her rather as if she were a dessert herself.

"Men!" said 25 February scornfully and turned away. "Why," she said delightedly, "why, here's her twin! See that boy there—he's not much older than she is."

Dave looked around, saw a slim, red-jacketed fellow with light brown, almost blond hair, bearing a tray to a table.

"One of my Mayfly waiters. In fact, he's waiting on my table, so he's my waiter in the other sense too. Strange. I hadn't noticed . . ."

"Well," murmured 25 February, "perhaps you never notice waiters— only dessert girls." And to the junior security man: "Bring that boy here, will you?" The guard glanced at Dave, who absently nodded permission, his lofty brow still furrowed in puzzlement.

The boyish-looking waiter was torn from his duties, came forward.

"What a fledgling he is!" exclaimed 25 February. "Fragments of the eggshell are still clinging to him!"

The subject of her remarks glanced down and about at his red tunic, as if he had taken her remarks literally, which caused his arrival at the half-circle to be greeted with laughter. He looked about at the laughers with an inquiring smile and wide-open eyes.

"What is your name?" asked 25 February.

"Ogg," said the waiter. "Jimmy Ogg. O-g-g."

"A euphonious name," said Sleek.

"Well, Jimmy, we'd like to take some pictures. Would you mind posing with these two ladies here?"

"Yes," said Sleek. "Be a good egg, Ogg."

Jimmy shrugged and obligingly moved forward; and as the people parted from in front of him, he saw the two "ladies" for the first time. He stopped, as the dancers had done when they had first seen the doddering woman; and then he went on bravely and took up a position at her side. But it was April-May whom he looked at over her bent and nodding head. He was almost as fresh-looking as April-May, though undoubtedly a year or two older. He continued to stare, and she lowered her eyes, smiling shyly. A blush spread over her face . . . and was answered by a blush in his.

Again there was laughter from the group standing about.

"Now, *that,*" said someone, "is something you don't often see these days."

"The old, old story," intoned Sleek.

"Like takes to like," said 25 February, with a glance at Dave, the meaning of which was: "She's for him, not for the likes of you, sir."

And it was Dave's turn to be nettled.

The photographers were already present and the cameras made their unnecessary but satisfying little sounds. They took pictures of the three; and then, for sharper contrast, of the two "ladies" with so much disparity between their ages.

"Don't worry," said Dave into Sleek's ear. "I have no intention of allowing those photographs to be published."

"Enough!" whispered the decayed woman. "It's past my bedtime." She began working herself about to face the doorway, with quick jerky little movements like those of a spider. "Remember: be not proud. Your days too are numbered. Good night."

"Good night," agreed Dave, with more feeling than was required by courtesy. He watched her picking her way with her two canes toward the door, then revolved his disgusted eye toward the senior guard.

"I wouldn't do that again if I were you, Gibraltar. What if she had died here? Think what a focusing point for hatred that would be! Think what the media would make of it. And think what that mob down there would make of it, if they heard of it. And, believe me, they would—within half an hour."

Gibraltar was abashed. "Gosh, Dave, I didn't think of that."

For down on the wet street was a restless crowd, smoldering with a bitterness that threatened to flame into violence at any moment; but it was kept at bay (across Broadway and across Fifty-second Street) by raincoated policemen clip-clopping down the glistening asphalt on anachronistic horses. Some of those who turned their faces up to the rain and shouted and sang were so old that they could no longer hope that the genetic reprogramming would take hold. Others had chosen to have children and now resented the condition the government had attached to its permission to add to the world's population. Many, perhaps most, knew that their credit ratings would never be good enough to purchase the "Tune-Up," as it was called, even if those mysterious quotas (about which there were so many doubts) remained unchanged. But, regardless of which class they fell into, they all chanted slogans or carried placards that implied that their grief and rage were not of a mere personal nature but rested on the very highest of grounds. Some of those grounds were political, but most were religious: for it had come to be widely believed that anyone who had chosen to have more than the biblical threescore-and-ten in this world had forfeited all hope of Eternal Life in the next.

But why should that happier crowd in "The Ballroom in the Sky" care? It was safe enough. No Mayfly was admitted to the hotel without some sort of legitimate business there. And no one less than one hundred years old was admitted to the Ballroom itself, except under one condition: that he or she come in as part of the servants' staff, as Jimmy had. No, the Evergreens needn't concern themselves. The police, the hotel guards, and their own numbers gave them safety. All their energies could be expended in one glorious blaze of welcome to the coming century. All had seen the present one come in; and all hoped, not too unreasonably, to welcome in the century *after* the one that began tonight at midnight.

The half-circle dispersed. The dancers picked up the tempo again and the eaters gave their undivided attention to their plates. Sleek moved back to his table. But Jimmy Ogg and April-May stood where they were, neither speaking, neither moving.

"All right, Ogg," said Dave, preparing to follow Sleek's example. "It's over. You can go back to work."

"In a minute," said Jimmy.

Dave stopped and turned, his face grim. He stabbed a finger at the red jacket. "You will do it *now!* Do you know who I am?"

"Yes," said Jimmy, not looking away from April-May. "You're President Emeritus of the Waiters' Union, President of the Caterers' Guild, National Secretary of the Evergreen Society . . ."

"That's enough!" snapped Dave, who heard impertinence in this recitation of his titles. "You obviously know enough to realize that if I say you don't work again as a waiter in this town, you'll never work again. The only reason I don't send you out that door right now is because we're so shorthanded tonight. Otherwise," went on Dave, his anger growing as he spoke, "otherwise, I would. So back to work, and back to work now!"

The girl whispered, "You'd better do it."

"You won't run away?"

She laughed, as if at the absurdity of the notion . . . and Jimmy brushed by Dave on his way back to his station. Dave looked after him, then turned to the girl and made an ironical, exasperated gesture with both hands.

"He's a *waiter*, for God's sake!"

April-May inclined her head to one side, then flashed out brightly with "But, Mr. Grandcourt, didn't *you* begin life as a waiter?"

He had, of course. But somehow it didn't matter and it had never mattered. He hadn't really, so to speak, been a waiter: no more than a secret agent who assumes the guise of a waiter is really a waiter. And he had never for a moment lost his contempt for his fellow waiters.

But this would be a little difficult to explain to April-May . . . and before he had quite found the words to do so, she was on her way back to the kitchen.

He watched her disappear through the swinging doors, then turned his face again to where Jimmy was hovering about his table in the middle distance; watched him intently, his brow wrinkled. It cleared. *"Ogilby!"* he muttered. And he walked rapidly to the back of the Ballroom, though not to the kitchen.

A short while later Jimmy was tapped on the shoulder by a passing waiter. "You're wanted in the office."

The office was a small room with the usual furnishings: a desk, some chairs, an ornamental letter tray, and a PIN terminal. A single overhead lamp sent a cone of light down upon the desk; the rest of the room was in shadow. Dave Grandcourt stood before the desk, his face turned toward Jimmy standing in the doorway; and behind the desk stood a tall man wearing a black, not a green, tuxedo. He was a man who at one time would have been called "distinguished," but now the silver hair at his temples carried a less flattering implication.

"Come in," said Dave. And when Jimmy had done so Dave said, "May I see your union card?"

Jimmy, with a wry, resigned smile, removed the plastic card from a breast pocket and handed it to him. Dave studied it while Jimmy glanced idly about at the dark corners of the room. There were stacks of folding chairs in one corner and what appeared to be pieces of theatrical backdrop scenery propped against the far wall. "Let's see," murmured Dave, without looking up, "you must be about sixty years old?"

Jimmy was at first blank, then looked at the silver-templed man behind the desk, who said in a slow and puzzled voice, "Why . . . yes, as a matter of fact, I am."

Dave's laugh was of the snorting I-can't-believe-I-heard-that kind. "I didn't mean you, Griesé. I meant our young friend here, who has a union card issued forty years ago." He examined Jimmy as if he were some previously unclassified specimen of insect. "One thing is obvious—you're *not* an Evergreen. So only one solution is possible: You stole this card off your father's desk."

Jimmy was a little startled by this deduction, but he replied with conviction and a touch of warmth, "I did *not* steal it!"

"Didn't you? It doesn't matter. Even if he handed it to you voluntarily, there's still a crime involved. The only difference is: he's an accessory. By the way, I seem to remember your father's name as Ogilby and I notice that that's the name on the card. And yet you say your name is Ogg?"

Jimmy shrugged. "Ogg suits me better."

Griesé nodded, easily accepting this. Choosing their own names after they had left home had become a widespread fashion among the young.

But Dave's face was still glazed over with suspicion. "Why did you do it?"

Jimmy grinned. "I wanted to attend the Banquet. I thought it would be a lot of fun. And this"—he touched his red jacket with a forefinger—"is the only way I could. Am I fired?"

Dave didn't reply immediately. Tapping the card against the knuckles of his left hand, he now studied Griesé in much the same way he had studied Jimmy.

"Mr. Griesé knows nothing about this," said Jimmy. "When the men you'd picked as waiters came through the lobby of the hotel on the way up here to report to him, I simply joined them and handed him my PIN card and that union card. Naturally, he assumed that you had hired me."

"Naturally," said Dave.

Jimmy repeated: "Am I fired?"

Dave's smile was very slow in forming . . . and so slight as to seem hardly worth the wait. "No . . . no, I don't think so. We're very short on waiters tonight. And, besides, I don't want anything to mar this historic occasion, not while it's in progress. So you're perfectly welcome to hang around for . . . what did you call it? . . . the fun. You may go back to your station. But I think I'll retain this superannuated card; as head of the Waiters' Union, I have the right to do that. Well? Is there something else?"

For Jimmy had hesitated. He turned his inquiring blue eyes on Dave. "You say you knew my father?"

Dave's green eye, turned sideways, was sardonic. "Our paths crossed briefly some years back. I found him . . . a little lacking in respect, let us say, and I was going to have him kicked out of the Union; but he saved me the trouble by disappearing before the showdown—on the very evening of the Hearing, as I recall. He must have remembered that he had pressing business elsewhere. It may be"—and he allowed his smile to reappear—"that your resemblance to him is more than physical. You may go."

Jimmy left. The door had hardly clicked shut behind him when a man came out from behind the theatrical scenery propped against the wall. He wore the red jacket of a waiter, but he had a face so remarkably hard-looking that it wouldn't have greatly recommended him as a waiter to a prospective employer—his uncompromising mouth alone would have cost him many a job. Dave stepped to this man and whispered into his gristled ear three, perhaps four words. They may have been words of dismissal, for the man touched his forelock very briskly and left the room.

Griesé's eyes followed him out the door, then came sliding back to his employer, as if fascinated. The two men stared at each other for some moments in silence.

And then Dave, softly: "Mr. Griesé, may I suggest that you don't worry about *his* skin? There's only one thing you need fret yourself about, and that is that you hired as a waiter a Mayfly not previously screened by me. That is an act of inexcusable negligence at best; and, for all I know, it may be something worse."

Griesé backed away from the desk a little, shaking his head. "You don't believe that, Mr. Grandcourt. And I know as well as you do that you're not turning that boy over to your secret police because you think he's some sort of anti-Evergreen spy or assassin. You don't think that for a moment. You're either acting out of sheer malignity or you have some other motive I don't know about."

"Griesé," said Dave, dropping his voice so low that it could barely be heard, "you're fired. And there's something else. You will never be an Evergreen. Oh, I know—your name is on the List and you're up for processing in January. But I'm removing your name. I can do that, and you, sir, may consider it done."

The blood drained from Griesé's face: his face and white hair stood out in startling contrast to his black tuxedo. It cost him an effort to speak, but he managed it.

"Mr. Grandcourt, I want that extra century or so of life. But, by God, there are some things I won't do for it, and nodding my head and smiling while you torture and maybe murder that boy is one of them. I won't go along with that, and if there's anything I can do to prevent it, I will."

"There's nothing you can do to prevent it. And may I make a suggestion? You have only a few years of life left now. If you want to keep those few years, I suggest you disappear very quickly. I won't come looking for you; but if you're still here after midnight, things will go badly for you."

He regarded the silver-haired (and younger) man with an expression in which respect and contempt were for the moment uneasily mingled. And then, as the stricken Griesé turned to retrieve his overcoat from the back of a chair, there was only contempt. "Mayfly!" he said with infinite scorn, and walked out of the room.

He was suddenly very hungry. But he had eyes for things other than his table, where his friends were already dining. He glanced aside twice. Once at the hard-featured man in the red jacket who stood unobtrusively to one side of the room. The idiot!—he had *saluted* him! If Jimmy Ogg had seen that, he might have guessed that Dave Grandcourt's titles included one not generally known. And he looked too, once, in the direction of the kitchen, as if with some thought to future appetites.

He resumed his seat beside his friend Sleek and found that 25 February was at the same table. She must have asked someone to trade places with her, so that she could be at this table—and why should she do that, he asked himself, except to be near *him?* Actually, he decided, discreetly surveying her as she ate, she wasn't at all bad . . . except when brought into unhappy contrast with April-May.

He was served by a quietly efficient Jimmy Ogg, all unconscious of what was waiting for him at the end of the evening. Dave smiled to himself. He ordered the beef and when it came ate it with real enjoyment, although what passed for beef these days usually bored him. The others had mostly finished eating and Sleek was holding forth in his usual whimsical way on the difficulties of living life incognito among the Mayflies. He had become very adept, he said, at acquiring forged PIN cards and at establishing covers; but no matter how ingenious he was, he still had to move on every dozen or so years when it became apparent that he wasn't aging at the usual rate. Dave listened with only one ear. He didn't have that problem himself, because he lived apart from people in a high-security building. It was because of Sleek, and others like him, who insisted on living what they called "normal lives," that no television cameras or outside photographers were allowed within a thousand feet, in any direction, of the Ballroom: they didn't want to run the risk of being recognized by their "friends."

A helicopter chose that moment to come shuddering by, startlingly close, and the lofty windows quaked and chattered in sympathy. The assembled diners all looked in that one direction, instantly apprehensive, and in the lull that followed everyone thought they heard (although it was clearly impossible) a faint shout from the angry streets below. But the apprehension dropped away almost as soon as it became conscious and the Evergreens denied that it had ever existed with a brave burst of laughter and talk. It had probably been a news-wasp, thought Dave, trying to sneak a peek. But he knew it hadn't succeeded: for *he* had chosen the drapes.

Two Mayfly waiters approached. One was Jimmy Ogg, who presented a rather startling appearance. He bore in each hand a flaming brand, like some apocalyptic Angel of Destruction; but his amiable purpose was simply to light the Blackbeard Rum Pudding that the other waiter—a remarkably hard-looking man, with an uncompromising mouth—was placing before each diner.

"Ogg, Son of Fire," murmured Sleek, with a sly look around.

"What a lovely boy that is!" said 25 February, after Jimmy had gone and she and the others were putting April-May's pudding to the proof. "He has a kind of glow to him, the glow of youth, innocence, and boundless hope. Who was it who said, 'No young man believes he will ever die'?"

"Hazlitt," said Dave. "You know, Miss February, to a boy of seventeen you're probably an old hag—and that would be true even if you really were only twenty-eight and not a hundred twenty-eight." He instantly regretted having tossed this little barb, which was certainly below his dignity; to soften the sting a little, he added, "Of course, *I* have a different perspective. . . ."

"Yes," said 25 February, with so much bitterness in her voice that he was taken by surprise; "we have seen some evidence of your 'perspective.'"

And he again smiled to himself. *It will take about two weeks with this one.* Two weeks during which, with a series of shoves and sharp little taps, he would walk her backwards until she tripped and sprawled across his bed. But did he really want that? Well, maybe. . . . She wasn't at all bad. But still, he would much prefer to see the lovely, the tender, the delicious

April-May sprawling on his bed, perhaps tearfully pleading as he stripped the clothes from her body. . . .

His flashing fantasy was blotted out by the voice of a bugle. The crowd came to attention. The dancers drifted back to their tables and all eyes were turned to the dais, where there stood a green-tuxedoed and wasp-like figure on fragile legs. But the figure had a mighty voice that boomed out over the audience:

"I am Stentor."

And, as if this were some sort of signal, all the waiters began filing out of the room into the kitchen—as if Mayfly ears were not to be allowed to hear what Stentor had to say . . . although his next words were innocuous enough.

"I am happy to announce that of the one hundred and one Founding Members of the Evergreen Society, sixty-two are with us tonight."

Wild applause from the several hundred present members of the society. 25 February, with a painful contraction still about her eyes, applauded almost desperately.

"Of the thirty-nine who are missing," went on the clarion voice, "it is believed that five are still alive in various parts of this planet. Three of those, and the sixty-two here tonight, have promised to be with us on our next Centennial celebration, on the eve of the year 2200."

Again, wild applause: although everyone there knew that at least half of those would be lost to what was called "attrition."

"In a moment we shall have the Contest of the Elders, to see who shall be our Man or Woman of the Century. But first . . ."

Stentor waved a hand. The trumpet sound again, bravely at first and then with a dying fall into something like a catcall. A ripple of laughter moved through the room, a stir of excitement. And at that moment all the waiters who had so mysteriously vanished when Stentor had begun to speak made a sudden reappearance. They burst out of the swinging doors of the kitchen, two abreast, each balancing on the fingers of one hand a heaping platter. They moved quickly and with a kind of comic emphasis, and a platter was placed on each and every table. The platters were piled with buns, and the diners instantly fell upon the buns like starved savages and disemboweled them with knives and buttered their insides and slavered them with jams and jellies. It was all done in a minute or two, though with a great bustle of chatter and laughter; and as it was being done the waiters filed to one side of the room and lined up just under the windows.

The faces of the celebrants all turned toward the dais . . . and a large screen some fifteen feet square slowly unrolled from the ceiling in front of the dais until its bottom reached within a foot or so of the floor. The screen displayed the familiar countenance of Isaac Asimov, a popular science writer of the last half of the twentieth century. It was a haughty expression that had been caught in this photo: head tilted backward a little, lips forming a slight moue, nose in the air. Even as it was descending there had burst from the audience whistles, raucous cheers and jeers, loud catcalls, and foot stompings. And now the purpose of those heaping platters, of those hundreds of buttered and jellied buns, became evident—for a barrage, a hailstorm, a blizzard of buns rained through the air, pelted and spattered the screen, which dimpled and winced under their impact. There was much laughing and shouting, some persons standing in the aisles and pitching the buns like baseballs, some standing up at the tables and lobbing them like hand grenades. And, through the miracle of modern animation, Isaac Asimov's expression changed from one of disdain to dismay and fright, eyes and mouth wide.

The picture began slowly rewinding, withdrawing from sight into the scroll near the ceiling, like a snail retreating into its shell; and as it did so the whistles and foot stompings gradually ceased. It was gone, and the audience burst into unanimous applause, enthusiastically congratulating itself on its own triumphant sense of community. Such a warmth of feeling moved through the room that even the Mayfly waiters felt the tug of it. All smiled or grinned; all, that is, except the waiter who stood beside Jimmy Ogg. 25 February's brow lost that contraction of pain; she threw back her head and laughed. And it may be that even the high forehead of Dave Grandcourt was touched by a mellower gleam.

The uproar subsided and the diners sank into their seats. A signal was given by a captain; and the waiters, moving in a single file (like a train of ants, in their red jackets), each claimed a wicker basket from a stack of baskets behind the orchestra and moved to collect the piles of scattered buns from the dance floor. The waiter who had stood beside Jimmy at the wall had kept up a string of sarcastic remarks during the Ritual Bunning of Asimov; and he apparently had more to say along the same lines, for he stuck close to Jimmy. He wasn't a very personable man, but there was something ingratiating in his assumption that Jimmy would naturally share his resentment of the Evergreens. His face, as he stooped to pick up the buns, was reflected by the mirrored floor, showing his uncompromising mouth twisted a little by bitterness.

"Do they think Asimov *invented* the Flaw?" he asked, disgustedly chucking buttered and jellied buns into his basket. Jimmy, bending near him, voiced no opinion; and he went on, "Of course, you know all about Asimov's Flaw?"

Jimmy was doubtful. "I don't believe I've ever met the man. But, you know," he added tolerantly, "most of us have some sort of flaw."

The other gave the reflection of Jimmy's face in the floor a hard, searching look—and then snorted. "Does your mother let you cross the street alone, kid?" And he fell silent, as if momentarily defeated.

They finished the harvesting of the buns and were soon standing again, like the others, with their backs against the wall. Jimmy was not inclined to talk, but his newfound friend's need to confide in him was still unsatisfied.

"Okay, kid," he said out of the corner of his mouth nearest Jimmy, "I'll take pity on your ignorance and tell you what this bunning business is all about. I'll tell you why these people hate Isaac Asimov so.

"You see"—looking straight ahead and hardly moving his lips, like a conspirator divulging guilty secrets—"what we call a 'natural death' is really a form of suicide. From Nature's viewpoint there's no reason for us to hang around once our kids are old enough to take care of themselves, so a self-destruct mechanism is triggered which prevents the cells of our bodies from repairing themselves and so we get old and sick and die. What the younger Dr. Ives did was, he discovered a way to defuse the self-destruct mechanism and this made it possible for people to remain in the prime of life and no longer die of 'old age,' as it was called. It was even thought for a while they might live forever. But Isaac Asimov had already discovered that there's a limit to which human life can be extended. He called it his clinker theory, but it's now called Asimov's Fatal Flaw.

"You see, even if the self-destruct mechanism *is* defused and the cells keep on repairing and renewing themselves, a small number of mistakes will still occur. The genetic mechanism of a cell is extremely complicated and delicate, so it sometimes happens that a defect will occur when a cell reproduces itself; the result is that this new cell becomes a kind of dead end. This happens about twice in a hundred thousand duplications. That doesn't sound like much, I know, and in a normal lifetime of sixty or seventy years it wouldn't matter—but it matters very much over a period of two hundred years, because there's one of those rising-curve effects. You see what this means? It means that even our friends, the Evergreens, are not immortal. They're around longer than we are, but already some who looked perfectly okay have dropped dead because groups of dead cells have accumulated in vital parts of their brains or in the places that manufacture the enzymes we can't get along without. And there's no cure for that." He chuckled, as if this afforded him some gratification. "No, and there never will be. It's been estimated that the average life of an Evergreen can be only—*only!*—two hundred years. And the greedy rascals, they're not satisfied. They want more! But they're not going to get more and they know it, because of Asimov's Fatal Flaw. That's why they hate the very name of Asimov."

He was silent a moment. He stood looking out across the large room crowded with the laughing and playful Evergreens; and then, speaking very softly, as if to himself: "I think that if everyone can't have long life, then no one should have it."

"I don't agree," said Jimmy. "I'd like to see everyone live longer and healthier and happier lives. But if they can't, that's no reason why *some* shouldn't, even if it's only a few."

The hard-faced waiter turned toward him a little and regarded him a long while. He shook his head sadly. "Your mother should have kept you at home tonight, kid."

11 P.M. The orchestra, and not just the bragging trumpet, sounded again. Stentor came forward.

"It is now the moment for the Contest of the Elders. We trust that those seated about each table have already identified the eldest at that table. As I call upon each table, that person must stand and proclaim himself or herself. If challenged, he or she must be able to prove his or her date of birth."

As luck had it, the oldest at the first table was very young, having been born in 1997. He was almost as young as that horribly decayed woman, but he was nevertheless the oldest at his table. The man at the second table somewhat restored the balance. He had been born August 19, 1948 —he followed the old system of stating the month first, then the day. He had not taken his reprogramming until 2008; but, despite his then sixty years, the process had "taken" and . . . "Well, here I am." Applause. The man at Table Three had been born 27 April 1985. By an odd coincidence, another man at the same table had been born the same day, but, it had been discovered, two hours later . . . "and so I take precedence." Laughter.

Tables Four and Five. And then: "Dave?" said Stentor.

But Dave Grandcourt astonished everyone present by not rising. He replied from where he sat.

"Not this time, Bob. It's true that I'm one of the Founding Members of this Society. It's also true that I'm one of the very first persons to receive the reprogramming, which I had from the hands of the younger Dr. Ives himself. But I am by no means the oldest member here, nor, as it happens, the oldest at this table, although I had meant to be. I am junior by three years to the lady who sits across from me. As you know, an Evergreen woman, unlike Mayfly women, is never"—he turned a sly glance across the table—"ashamed of her age. And so I think she might be persuaded to rise and introduce herself."

She did. "I was born 25 February 1972." And she confessed to having been christened with a name, like any other human being: Margaret Pressburger.

And so it went, as rapidly as possible, for the midnight hour was approaching, through forty tables. Most of those present had been born in the 1980s and '90s, but they, with some exceptions, kept their seats. Those who rose to their feet had been born, mostly, in the 1960s and '70s. There were a few from the 1950s and one man who had been born in 1949 on Christmas Day. 1949? Could it be, then, that the man at Table Two whose long life had begun on 19 August 1948 was the oldest person present?

Stentor thought so. "It would seem," he mused, "that the Convention has found its Elder."

There was scattered applause and a tooting of paper horns.

"Not so fast!" cried a voice. It had come from Table Three. "There's someone here"—and the speaker rose and lurched forward clumsily, scraping a chair. There was laughter from the nearby tables, for they saw that he was tipsy. "There's someone here," he tried again, pointing to a man seated at his table and wearing a tam-o'-shanter, "who has declined to tell us his birthday. I think we should know his age before we . . . we . . . what? . . . commit ourselves."

Stentor decided to fall in line behind this. His brassy voice carried a note of facetiousness. "Will you please rise, sir?"

The man who had been pointed out rose to his feet, but with a somewhat rueful expression. Most of those in the room now saw for the first time that he was wearing below his green tuxedo jacket not tuxedo trousers but a kilt. Again there was laughter, again a few remarks (someone observing that the tartan was that of the MacDonald clan). Others stared not so much at his kilt as at his face. The man himself was in no way abashed by the laughter, the remarks, or the stares. He stood there with one arm akimbo, his handsome and dignified face gravely amused: posing a bit, perhaps, but carrying it off.

Stentor asked, "Sir, why the kilt?"

"That," said its wearer, "would be a long story."

"Never mind, then. Life is too short," quipped Stentor. "But would you confide in us, briefly, the date of your birth?"

The kilted man seemed a bit reluctant to part with it, but did so:

"12 August 1907."

The audience gasped as one . . . and then there was applause—hesitant at first, but growing in confidence and volume, and punctuated by shouts of recognition. For they knew him at last. Only the tam and the kilt had prevented them from recognizing him from old pictures (and that may have been the purpose of those articles of dress). The shouts became concerted, became a chant that grew and swelled and rocked the room.

"Who is the Man Who Led the Way?"

And it answered itself:

"GEORGE CLAY!"

And two or three voices, raggedly overlapping, cried from diverse parts of the room:

"Who is the man who's here today?"

And the congregation responded:

"GEORGE CLAY!"

And one man at the very back of the room rose and shouted:

"And who's the man who's here to stay?"

And any doubts anyone might have had about this proposition were swept away by the unanimous, enthusiastic reply:

"GEORGE CLAY!"

Yes, George Clay! The applause and enthusiasm were unbounded. Various persons rushed forward to greet Clay, to shake his hand. One of these was Dave Grandcourt, who almost ran from his remote (as it seemed at the moment) Table Seven to grab both of Clay's hands and agitate them. There were not many men he admired, but this was one of them.

George Clay—the first Evergreen and still flourishing, that man who in old age had been, by the strangest set of chances, struck at once young and long-lived. But of course that was a story too well known to everyone present to need retelling.

It took a while for this tumult to die. It hadn't yet done so completely when Stentor overrode it and brought the room to order. Most of the congratulators of George Clay gravitated back to their tables, but Dave Grandcourt, still glowing with elation, held his ground.

"I believe," pronounced Stentor with a genial humor, "that we may safely assume that *you* are the oldest person here, Mr. Clay."

Cheers and laughter.

But once again there came that same startling interruption:

"Not so fast!"

And a man stood up, a man at Table Eleven in the second row, not ten feet from where George Clay and Dave Grandcourt stood. The other people at the table where this man had been sitting looked up at him, first with slack mouths (he evidently had not prepared them for his announcement) and then with some continuing uncertainty. Truth to tell, there was something a little odd about him, although it was difficult to say just what it was. It wasn't, of course, age that set him apart, because, like everyone else, he appeared to be within a year or two of thirty. He certainly wasn't distinguished by gray hair: his, in fact, was almost oppressively black. He wasn't distinguished by an impressive bearing, because his middle-sized frame seemed to have gone a little soft. And it wasn't by nobility of countenance; for his face showed a peculiarly intense, almost aggressive, blandness: as if a meek man had decided to be arrogant, or an arrogant man to be meek.

"I believe," said this man, speaking very deliberately and somewhat coarsely, "that I can lay claim to a longer life than can George Clay."

The ripple of astonishment that spread through the room was followed by a quieter one of skepticism . . . with, here and there, little eddies and whorls of outright disbelief and scorn.

"Well, sir," said Stentor cautiously, "can you prove that? Do you have with you proof of age?"

"That man," said the challenger, leveling an arm at George Clay, who stood looking on with a good deal of interest and yet without concern, "offered no proof of age."

"He doesn't need to," replied Stentor. "There are those here who know him from very long ago and those who recognize him by sight. But we do not know you, sir. I am afraid that you will have to show us some proof of your rather astonishing claim."

The challenger shrugged. "Oh, well, if you insist . . ."

And he reached inside his jacket. He extracted something and held it out, not toward Stentor or his nearest neighbor, but toward George Clay, as if offering him such proof as was needed.

A deafening explosion clapped the walls of the large room and George Clay flung up his arms and toppled backward like a falling tree.

There were shouts, screams, shattering glass, chairs being scraped back and clattering to the floor—and the assailant, screaming an incoherent curse, dashed toward the fallen patriarch, with gun extended. People everywhere stood frozen where they were, or ducked or huddled, or fell to the floor.

And Dave Grandcourt, diving gracefully in a single movement, hid his forehead and his body under the table in front of which his hero had stood.

The screaming man halted at George Clay's feet and pointed the gun at his head, as if to finish him off execution style.

But Jimmy Ogg had reacted with astonishing swiftness. His red jacket blurred as he moved away from the wall and past an intervening table. He flung himself upon the gunman. They grappled and swayed. There was another shot, not so loud, it seemed, as the first; in fact, curiously muffled —and a woman at the nearest table screamed and clutched her leg.

The other man outweighed him by forty pounds, but Jimmy showed unexpected strength. He seized the man's gun hand at the wrist and forced it upward and out. The hand jerked convulsively and the gun discharged itself again and again, deafeningly but harmlessly, into the soft roll at the ceiling bearing Asimov's scrolled features.

But all this time the security guards had been converging upon them from all parts of the room, moving (as it seemed to some) in slow motion. Gibraltar was foremost; and he and two, three, four others now fell upon the struggling couple and wrestled them to the ground, handling Jimmy rather roughly in the process.

Jimmy at last managed to get to his feet. He moved back out of harm's way . . . and bumped into Dave Grandcourt, who at that moment looked out from under Table Three, one flap of the cloth draped over his forehead. Jimmy stepped aside and Dave crawled out and raised himself to his feet, looking about with a dismayed face.

There were people clustered about and bending over George Clay and there rose from one of them the glad cry:

"He's alive!"

And Clay's voice was heard, protesting feebly, "I'm all right . . . all right."

The guards, having wrestled the would-be assassin to the floor, now wrestled him to his feet; and he was borne backward, arms outflung, heels dragging, toward the large door—shouting as he went and with a laugh wildly and bitterly triumphant:

"Fools! Your life is but a day and is gone. You are like the grass that is cut down. But I, *I* shall have Life Everlasting!"

"Maybe," said the grim-faced waiter, who now stood near Jimmy again. He was holding in his hand the plastic gun the fanatic had used and was examining it with a professional eye. "Maybe. But it won't be continuous with the one you have now."

Dave was at first rather sheepish; but with a little effort, and very little loss of time, he recovered his arrogance. He had already taken in the entire situation and, straightening himself, he resumed his role as one of the Elders of the Convention.

He saw first to George Clay. But after he had seen that Clay's wound was not critical, and that the woman's wound was only superficial, and that the hotel medics were forcing their way through the throng toward the injured parties, he came back to Jimmy Ogg. His manner was lofty yet, but not so severe as it had been.

"You may congratulate yourself. I had been planning a little surprise for you at the end of the evening."

"Had been?" said Jimmy. His hair was disheveled and his face was very pale. He was fidgeting with his red jacket, pulling it more tightly about his midriff, as if he wanted to button it; but the buttons had been torn off in the struggle.

"Yes, had been." And he glanced at the grim-faced waiter, who nodded and moved away. "But because of this little service you have done us, I'm going to forget that you obtained entrance here under false colors. Your heroic action," he said, turning upon Jimmy what looked very much like a disparaging eye, "proves that your presence here was innocent. I suppose you really did mean just to see the fun. And you saw it, didn't you? You're very pale, Jimmy Ogg. But now you have something to brag to your father about . . . if he's still around."

He was silent a moment, looking out over the dining room like the survivor of a battle over a battlefield. Everywhere he looked, he saw shock and grief and the aftermath of hysteria. There were men and women huddled in their chairs, slumped over their tables, or fearfully clinging to each other. Nearby, a woman who had fainted was lying on the floor, anxiously tended by her friends. His face was sickened by disgust and self-disgust. His eyes were hooded. His lips moved. "Our long lives, our precious long lives and our desire to protect them, have made cowards of us all. It has made a coward of me. We are not fit to rule. I am not fit to rule."

His half-hooded eyes revolved back to Jimmy. "You saved George Clay's life and for that I'm going to let you live. I'm going to let you live out the rest of your natural life span."

"Thanks," said Jimmy.

"But that's it. You'll never be an Evergreen. There are *two* lists. And I'm putting your name on the second."

Jimmy smiled and shrugged.

"Yes, I know, Mayfly. That doesn't bother you. You think you're going to live forever, just as everyone your age does. That's why you dashed forward to grab the gunman, while I took cover. The possibility that you can actually die hasn't sunk in yet. But it will. Your courage is grounded in ignorance and in lack of imagination—and I'm going to cut those grounds out from under you. You think you're a hero and I'm a coward . . . but we'll see how much of a hero you are forty years from now when you're banging on my door and pleading to be made an Evergreen. You may go, Mayfly."

"Thank you. I'll just stop in the kitchen and collect April-May on the way."

An expletive burst from Dave. "You believe in pressing your luck, don't you, Mayfly?" He broke off, because 25 February 1972, *née* Margaret Pressburger, was approaching. She was crying and wringing her hands. She flung herself upon Dave.

"You were so *brave!*" She buried her face in his green jacket. "I forgive you. I forgive you everything."

Grandcourt was only momentarily baffled. It seemed that in the confusion and uproar she had not quite followed the sequence of events. He gave Jimmy a rueful, sideways, threatening look.

"Okay," he said. Margaret was sobbing and couldn't hear. "Okay"—with resignation and, again, a touch of disgust—"I suppose that girl is more in your age group than in mine."

"I should think so," said Jimmy, and moved off.

The hard-faced waiter touched his forelock, or perhaps saluted him, as he passed. He made his way between the tables (ignoring persons who plucked at him, trying to order drinks) to the kitchen. But he didn't enter the kitchen immediately. He stopped a few yards to one side of the swinging doors and leaned against the wall there, steadying himself with one hand. His face was still very pale, his forehead damp. Some minutes passed before he had quite recomposed himself and had adjusted his tunic and hair and wiped his brow.

He went into the kitchen.

April-May, her dessert duties done, was sitting beside a small table, facing the doors as if she were waiting for someone. On the other side of the table was a kitchen chair, also facing the doors. Jimmy sat down in it, as if claiming it.

Silence for a long moment; and then their eyes met and they laughed.

"I had an idea you might be here," said Jimmy. "I had an idea that someone, anyway, might be here and I hoped it would be you. And so I came."

"I knew you would be here," said April-May. "It was the one place where your curiosity and humor would be sure to bring you. And I thought you might come looking for me. So I came."

There was another pause and then Jimmy asked slowly, "Where is He Who Tamed the Horses?"

Her eyes, turned sideways, reproved him for his irony. "My beloved Harry was destroyed in the crash of the Topeka Space Shuttle." She added, quoting Borges, " 'The Gods who live past all imploring, abandoned him to that tiger, Fire.' "

"I'm sorry," said Jimmy. And then: "The Topeka Space Shuttle crash? That was some time ago. You've been alone all this while?"

"Yes."

"I'm sorry about that too."

She sat watching him with a sly, sweet smile. "You've loved me for a long time, haven't you?"

His smile was so tender it was almost painful to see—only the boyishness of his face kept it from suggesting unfathomable heartbreak and loneliness. "For *ages.*"

"And how long will you go on loving me?"

His reply was a whisper. "Forever."

She laughed again. *"That* long?"

His right arm was resting on the table. She moved her hand sideways across the table until her fingers barely touched his. He lifted his hand to cover hers, leaned forward a little to do so . . . and winced.

She looked at him with concern; and, by way of explanation, he opened his red jacket. On the white cambric shirt underneath, on his right side, was a red spot about the size of a dime.

She whispered, "Does it still hurt?"

"Only a little. The healing process is almost completed. The bullet went right through me and struck the leg of a woman seated behind me. But I will need food soon."

"I'll get you some."

But for the moment she didn't move, not wanting to break the contact with his hand.

Behind them someone was scraping pans, clattering and splashing them in the soapy water. And, occasionally, through the swinging doors would come a waiter or one of the security personnel, who in passing would give them a glance of incurious appraisal or, seeing their touching hands, an amused and ready understanding.

They didn't care who came or went. They spoke in very low voices; and besides, they spoke in a language that had been forgotten, except by a few, when the pyramids were as yet undreamed of. It was a language that had broken the stillness of the dawn in the glad, bright morning of the race, when the men with hair streaming behind them like manes had chased the horses and had hallooed to each other across the great rolling steppes of Central Asia. It was the language with which they had greeted the Man Without Flaw when he had stepped from the glistening sphere that had dropped from the sky, who, before departing, had almost negligently granted them the Boon.

"There can't be many of us left now," said Jimmy. "Perhaps there's only the two of us."

"Perhaps," agreed April-May.

There was a sudden, thunderous hullabaloo from the larger room: cheers, applause, and the tooting of paper horns drowned by the blaring orchestra. It was now midnight—midnight of New Year's Eve of the year 2100, the first few seconds of the twenty-second century. And there swept over them, the two who sat there in the kitchen, a wave of music and melodious laughter. It seemed that the Evergreens had quite recovered themselves: for the song was exuberant, the laughter triumphant and self-congratulatory. The boy and the girl, with the freshness of the dawn still and forever upon them, looked at each other . . . and smiled sadly. For the swinging doors had swung inward and had hung open for a moment, as if forced open by a gust of gaiety, and they had been granted a glimpse of the Evergreens at play. They were gliding to the music across the mirrored dance floor like mayflies above the surface of a pond.

This is not a pleasant story, as anyone who recognizes the name in the title will know instantly. "Mengele" is a powerful story about a war criminal who is apparently still alive somewhere: a man of science who may still be conducting his atrocious experiments. But it's more than that; it's a story about the essential nature of evil that suggests very disturbing things about how easy and natural those experiments may be.

Lucius Shepard, who made his debut in Universe 13, *is an alumnus of the Clarion SF Writers' Workshop whose thoughtful stories have graced the pages of most of the science fiction magazines recently. His first novel,* Green Eyes, *was published as one of the New Ace Science Fiction Specials last year and elicited rave reviews; he's currently working on his second novel.*

MENGELE

LUCIUS SHEPARD

During the Vietnam War I served as an aerial scout, piloting a single-engine Cessna low above the jungles, spotting targets for the F-16s. It was not nearly so dangerous as it sounds; the VC preferred to risk the slim chance of being spotted rather than giving away their positions by shooting me down, and most of my flights were made in an atmosphere of relative peace and quiet. I had always been a loner, perhaps even a bit of a misanthrope, and after my tour was up, after returning to the States, I found these attitudes had hardened. War had either colored my perceptions or dropped the scales from my eyes, for everywhere I went I noticed a great dissolution. In the combat zones and shooting galleries, in the bombed-looking districts of urban decay, in the violent music and the cities teeming with derelicts and burned-out children, I saw reflected the energies that had created Vietnam; and it occurred to me that in our culture war and peace had virtually the same effects. The West, it seemed, was truly in decline. I was less in sympathy with those who preached social reform than with the wild-eyed street evangelists who proclaimed the last days and the triumph of evil. Yet evil struck me then as too emotional and unsophisticated a term, redolent of swarming demons and medieval plagues, and I preferred to think of it as a spiritual malaise. No matter what label was given to the affliction, though, I wanted no part of it. I came to think of my wartime experiences, the clean minimalism of my solo flights, as an idyll, and thus I entered into the business of ferrying small planes (Phelan's Air Pherry I called it, until I smartened up).

My disposition to the business was similar to that of someone who is faced with the prospect of crossing a puddle too large to leap; he must plot a course between the shallow spots and then skip on tiptoe from point to point, landing as lightly as possible in order to avoid a contaminating splash. It was my intent to soar above decay, to touch down only in those places as yet unspoiled. Some of the planes I ferried carried cargos, which I did not rigorously inspect; others I delivered to their owners, however far away their homes. The farther away the better, to my mind. By my reckoning I have spent fifteen months in propeller-driven aircraft over water, a good portion of this over the North Atlantic; and so, when I was offered a substantial fee to pilot a twin-engine Beechcraft from Miami to Asunción, the capital of Paraguay, it hardly posed a challenge.

From the outset, though, the flight proved to be anything but unchallenging: The Beechcraft was a lemon. The right wing shimmied, the inside of the cabin rattled like an old jalopy, and the radio was constantly on the fritz, giving up the ghost once and for all as I crossed into Paraguayan airspace. I had to set down in Guayaquil for repairs to the electrical system, and then, as I was passing over the Gran Chaco—the great forest that sprawls across western Paraguay, a wilderness of rumpled, dark green hills—the engines died.

In those first seconds of pure silence before the weight of the world dragged me down and the wind began ripping past, I experienced an exhilaration, an irrational confidence that God had chosen to make an exception of me and had repealed the law of gravity, that I would float the rest of the way to Asunción. But as the nose of the plane tipped earthward and a chill fanned out from my groin, I shook off this notion and started fighting for my life. A river—the Pilcomayo—was glinting silver among the hills several miles to my left; I banked into a glide and headed toward it. Under ordinary conditions I would have had time to pick an optimal stretch of water, but the Beechcraft was an even worse glider than airplane, and I had to settle for the nearest likely spot: a fairly straight section enclosed by steep, piney slopes. As I flashed between the slopes, I caught sight of black-roofed cottages along the shore, a much larger house looming on the crest. Then I smacked down, skipping like a stone for at least a hundred yards. I felt the tail lift, and everything became a sickening whirl of dark green and glare, and the hard silver light of the river came up to shatter the windshield.

I must have regained consciousness shortly after the crash, for I recall a face peering in at me. There was something malformed about the face, some wrongness of hue and shape, but I was too dizzy to see clearly. I tried to speak, managed a croak, and just this slight effort caused me to lose consciousness again. The next thing I recall is waking in a high-ceilinged room whose size led me to believe that I was inside the large house I had noticed atop the slope. My head ached fiercely, and when I put a hand to my brow I found it to be bandaged. As soon as the aching had diminished, I sat up and looked around. The decor of the room had a rectitude that would have been appropriate to a mausoleum. The walls and floors were of gray marble inscribed by veins of deeper gray; the door —a featureless rectangle of ebony—was flanked by two black wooden chairs; the bed itself was spread with a black silk coverlet. I assumed the drapes overhanging the window to be black also, but on closer inspection I discovered that they were woven of a cloth that under various intensities of light displayed many colors of darkness. These were the only furnishings. Carefully, because I was still dizzy, I walked to the window and pulled back the drapes. Scattered among the pines below were a dozen or so black roofs—tile, they were—and a handful of people were visible on the paths between them. There was a terrible, slow awkwardness to their movements that brought to mind the malformed face I had seen earlier, and a nervous thrill ran across the muscles of my shoulders. Farther down the slope the pines grew more thickly, obscuring the wreckage of the plane, though patches of shining water showed through the boughs.

I heard a click behind me, and turning I saw an old man in the doorway. He was leaning on a cane, wearing a loose gray shirt that buttoned high about his throat, and dark trousers—apparently of the same material as the drapes; he was so hunched that it was only with great difficulty he was able to lift his eyes from the floor (an infirmity, he told me later, that had led to his acquiring an interest in entomology). He was bald, his scalp mottled like a bird's egg, and when he spoke the creakiness of his voice could not disguise a thick German accent.

"I'm pleased to see you up and about, Mr. Phelan," he said, indicating by a gesture that I should sit on the bed.

"I take it I have you to thank for this," I said, pointing to my bandage. "I'm very grateful, Mr. . . . ?"

"You may call me Dr. Mengele." He shuffled toward me at a snail's pace. "I have of course learned your name from your papers. They will be returned to you."

The name Mengele, which had the sound of a dull bell ringing, was familiar; but I was neither Jewish nor a student of history, and it was not until after he had examined me, pronouncing me fit, that I began to put together the name and the facts of his age, his accent, and his presence in this remote Paraguayan village. Then I remembered a photograph I had seen as a child: a fleshy, smiling man with dark hair cut high above his ears was standing beside a surgical table, where lay a young woman, her torso draped by a sheet; her legs were exposed, and from the calves down all the flesh had been removed, leaving the skeleton protruding from the bloody casings of her knees. *Josef Mengele in his surgery at Auschwitz* had read the caption. That photograph had had quite an effect on me, because of its horrific detail and also because I had not understood what scientific purpose could have been served by this sort of mutilation. I stared at the old man, trying to match his face with the smiling, fleshy one, trying to feel the emanation of evil; but he was withered and shrunken to the point of anonymity, and the only impression I received from him was of an enormous vitality, a forceful physical glow such as might have accrued to a healthy young man.

"Mengele," I said. "Not . . ."

"Yes, yes!" he said impatiently. *"That* Mengele. The mad doctor of the Third Reich. The monster, the sadist."

I was repelled, and yet I did not feel outrage as I might have had I been Jewish. I had been born in 1948, and the terrors of World War II, the concentration camps, Mengele's hideous pseudo-scientific experiments, they had the reality of vampire movies for me. I was curious, intensely so, in the way a child becomes fascinated with a crawling thing he has turned up from beneath a stone: he is inclined to crush it, but more likely to watch it ooze along.

"Come with me," said Mengele, shuffling toward the door. "I can offer you dinner, but afterward I'm afraid you must leave. We have but one law here, and that is that no stranger may pass the night within our borders." I had not observed any roads leading away from the village, and when I asked if I might have use of a radio, he laughed. "We have no communication with the outside world. We are self-sufficient here. None of the villagers ever leave, and rarely do we have visitors. You will have to make your way as best you can."

"Are you saying I'll have to walk?" I asked.

"You have no choice. If you head south along the river, some twenty or twenty-five kilometers, you will reach another village and there you will find a radio."

The prospect of being thrown out into the Gran Chaco made me even less eager for his company, but if I were going on a twenty-five-kilometer hike I needed food. His pace was so slow that our walk to the dining room effectively constituted a tour of the house. He talked as we went, telling me—surprisingly enough—of his conversion to Nazism (National Socialism, he termed it) and his work at the camps. Whenever I asked a question he would pause, his expression would go blank, and after a moment he would pose a complicated answer. I had the idea that his answers were pre-rehearsed, that he had long ago anticipated every possible question and during those pauses he was rummaging through a file. In truth I only half listened to him, being disconcerted by the house. It seemed less a house than a bleak mental landscape, and though I was accompanied by the man whose mind it no doubt reflected, I felt imperiled, out of my element. We passed room after room of gray marble and black furnishings identical to those I have already noted, but with an occasional variant: a pedestal supporting nothing but an obsidian surface; a bookshelf containing rows of black volumes; a carpet of so lusterless and deep a black that it looked to be an opening into some negative dimension. The silence added to my sense of endangerment, and as we entered the dining room, a huge marble cell distinguished from the other rooms by a long ebony table and an iron chandelier, I forced myself to pay attention to him, hoping the sound of his voice would steady my nerves. He had been telling me, I realized, about his flight from Germany.

"It hardly felt like an escape," he said. "It had more the air of a vacation. Packing, hurried goodbyes, and as soon as I reached Italy and met my Vatican contact, it all became quite relaxing. Good dinners, fine wines, and at last a leisurely sea voyage." He seated himself at one end of the table and rang a small black bell: it had been muffled in some way and barely produced a note. "It will be several minutes before you are served, I fear," he went on. "I did not know when you would be sufficiently recovered to eat."

I took a seat at the opposite end of the table. The strangeness of the environment, meeting Mengele, and now his reminiscences, all coming on the heels of my crash . . . it had left me fuddled. I felt as if I were phasing in and out of existence; at one moment I would be alert, intent upon his words, and the next I would be wrapped in vagueness and staring at the walls. The veins of the marble appeared to be writhing, spelling out messages in an archaic script.

"This house," I said suddenly, interrupting him. "Why is it like it is? It doesn't seem a place in which a man—even one with your history—would choose to live."

Again, that momentary blankness. "I believe you may well be a kindred spirit, Mr. Phelan," he said, and smiled. "Only one other has asked that particular question, and though he did not understand my answer at first, he came to understand it as you may someday." He cleared his throat. "You see, several years after I had settled in Paraguay I underwent a crisis of conscience. Not that I had regrets concerning my actions during the war. Oh, I had nightmares now and again, but no more than such as come to every man. No, I had faith in my work, despite the fact that it had been countenanced as evil, and as it turned out, that work proved to be the foundation of consequential discoveries. But perhaps, I thought, it *was* evil. If this were the case, well, I freely admitted to it . . . and yet I had never seen myself as an evil man. Only a committed one. And now the focus of my commitment—National Socialism—had failed. It was inconceivable to me, though, that the principles underlying it had failed, and I came to the conclusion that the failure could probably be laid to a misapprehension of those principles. Things had happened too fast for us. We had always been in a hurry, overborne by the needs of the country; we had been too pressured to act coherently, and the movement had become less a religion than a church. Empty, pompous ritual had taken the place of contemplated action. But now I had no pressure and all the time in the world, and I set out to understand the nature of evil."

He sighed and drummed his fingers on the table. "It was a slow process. Years of study, reading philosophy and natural history and cabalistic works, anything that might have a bearing on the subject. And when finally I did understand, I was amazed that I had not done so sooner. It was obvious! Evil was not—as it had been depicted for centuries—the tool of chaos. Creation was the chaotic force. Why, you can see this truth in every mechanism of the natural world, in the clouds of pollen, the swarms of flies, the migrations of birds. There is precision in those events, but they are nonetheless chaotic. Their precision is one born of overabundance, a million pellets shot and several dozen hitting the mark. No, evil was not chaotic. It was simplicity, it was system, it was the severing stroke of a knife. And most of all, it was inevitable. The entropic resolution of good, the utter simplification of the creative. Hitler had always known this, and National Socialism had always embodied it. What were the blitzkrieg and the concentration camps if not tactical expressions of that simplicity? What is this house if not its esthetic employment?" Mengele smiled, apparently amused by something he saw written on my face. "This understanding of mine may not strike you as revelatory, yet once I did understand everything I had been doing, all my researches began to succeed whereas previously they had failed. By understanding, of course, I do not mean that I merely acknowledged the principle. I absorbed it, I dissolved in it, I let it rule me like magic. I *understood!*"

I am not sure what I might have said—I was revolted by the depth of his madness, his iniquity—but at that moment he turned to the door and said, "Ah! Your dinner." A man dressed in the same manner as Mengele was shuffling across the room, carrying a tray. I barely glanced at him, intent upon my host. The man moved behind my chair and, leaning in over my shoulder, began to lay down plates and silverware. Then I noticed his hand. The skin was ashen gray, the fingers knobbly and unnaturally long—the fingers of a demon—and the nails were figured by half-moons of dead white. Startled, I looked up at him.

He had almost finished setting my place, and I doubt I stared at him for more than a few seconds, but those seconds passed as slowly as drops of water welling from a leaky tap. His face had a horrid simplicity that echoed the decor of the house. His mouth was a lipless slit, his eyes narrow black ovals, his nose a slight swelling perforated by two neat holes; he was bald, his skull elongated, and each time he inclined his head I could see a ridge of bone bisecting the scalp like the sagittal crest of a lizard. All his movements had that awful slowness I had observed in the people of the village. I wanted to fling myself away from the table, but I maintained control and waited until he had gone before I spoke.

"My God!" I said. "What's wrong with him?"

Mengele pursed his lips in disapproval. "The deformed are ever with us, Mr. Phelan. Surely you have seen worse in your time."

"Yes, but . . ."

"Tell me of an instance." He leaned forward, eager to hear.

I was nonplused, but I told him how one night in New York City—my home—I had been walking in the East Village when a man had come toward me from the opposite corner; his collar had been turned up, his chin tucked in, so that most of his face was obscured; yet as he had passed, the flare of the streetlight had revealed a grimacing mouth set vertically just beneath his cheekbone, complete with tiny teeth. I had not been able to tell if he had in addition a normal mouth, and over the years I had grown uncertain as to whether or not it had been a hallucination. Mengele was delighted and asked me to supply more descriptive details, as if he planned to add the event to his file.

"But your servant," I asked. "What of him?"

"Merely a decoration," he said. "A creature of my design. The village and the woods abound with them. No doubt you will encounter a fair sampling on your walk along the Pilcomayo."

"Your design!" I was enraged. "You made him that way?"

"You cannot have expected my work to have an angelic character." Mengele paused, thoughtful. "You must understand that what you see here, the villagers, the house, everything, is a memorial to my work. It has the reality of one of those glass baubles that contain wintry rural scenes and when shaken produce whirling snowstorms. The same actions are repeated over and over, the same effects produced. There is nothing for you to be upset about. The people here are content to serve me in this fashion. They understand." He pointed to the plates in front of me. "Eat, Mr. Phelan. Time is pressing."

I looked down at the plates. They were black ceramic. One held a green salad, and the other slices of roast beef swimming in blood. I have always enjoyed rare beef, but in that place it seemed an obscenity. Nonetheless, I was hungry, and I ate. And while I did, while Mengele told me of his work in genetics—work that had created monstrosities such as his servant—I determined to kill him. We were natural enemies, he and I. For though I had no personal score to settle, he exulted in the dissolution that I had spent most of my postwar life in avoiding. It was time, I thought, to do more than avoid it. I decided to take the knife with which I cut my beef and slash his throat. Perhaps he would appreciate the simplicity.

"Naturally," he said, "the creation of grotesques was not the pinnacle of my achievements. That pinnacle I reached nine years ago when I discovered a means of chemically affecting the mechanisms that underlie gene regulation, specifically those that control cell breakdown and rebuilding."

Being no scientist, I was not sure what he meant. "Cell breakdown?" I said. "Are you . . ."

"Simply stated," he said, "I learned to reverse the process of aging. It may be that I have discovered the secret of immortality, though it is not yet clear how many treatments the body will accept."

"If that's true, why haven't you treated yourself?"

"Indeed," he said with a chuckle. "Why not?"

There was no doubt in my mind that he was lying about his great triumph, and this lie—which put into an even darker perspective the malignancy of his work, showing it to be purposeless, serving no end other than to further the vileness of his ego—this lie firmed my resolve to kill him. I gripped the knife and started to push back my chair; but then a disturbing thought crossed my mind. "Why have you revealed yourself to me?" I asked. "Surely you know that I'm liable to mention this to someone."

"First, Mr. Phelan, you may never have a chance to mention it; a twenty-five-kilometer walk along the Pilcomayo is no Sunday stroll. Second, whom would you tell? The officialdom of this country are my associates."

"What about the Israelis? If they knew of this place, they'd be swarming all over you."

"The Israelis!" Mengele made a noise of disgust. "They would not find me here. Tell them if you wish. I will give you proof." He opened a drawer in the end of the table and from it removed an ink bottle and a sheet of paper; he poured a few drops of ink onto the paper, and after a moment pressed his thumb down to make a print; then he blew on the paper and slid it toward me. "Show that to the Israelis and tell them I am not afraid of their reprisals. My work will go on."

I picked up the paper. "I suppose you've altered your prints, and this will only prove to the Israelis that I'm a madman."

"These fingerprints have not been altered."

"Good." I folded the paper and stuck it into my shirt pocket. Knife in hand, I stood and walked along the table toward him. I am certain he knew my intention, yet his bemused expression did not falter; and when I reached his side he looked me in the eyes. I wanted to say something, pronounce a curse that would harrow him to hell; his calm stare, however, unnerved me. I put my left hand behind his neck to steady him and prepared to draw the blade across his jugular. But as I did, he seized my wrist in a powerful grip, holding me immobile. I clubbed him on the brow with my left hand, and his head scarcely wobbled. Terrified, I tried to wrench free and managed to stagger a few paces away, pulling him after me. He did not attack; he only laughed and maintained his grip. I battered him again and again, I clawed at his face, his neck, and in so doing I tore the buttons from his shirt. The two halves fell open, and I screamed at what I saw.

He flung me to the floor and shrugged off the torn shirt. I was transfixed. Though he was still hunched, his torso was smooth-skinned and powerfully muscled, the torso of a young man from which a withered neck had sprouted; his arms, too, bulged with muscle and evolved into gnarled, liver-spotted hands. There was no trace of surgical scarring; the skin flowed from youth to old age in the way a tributary changes color upon merging with the mainstream. "Why not?" he had answered when I asked why he did not avail himself of his treatments. Of course he had, and—in keeping with his warped sensibilities—he had transformed himself into a monster. The sight of that shrunken face perched atop a youthful body was enough to shred the last of my rationality. Ablaze with fear, I scrambled to my feet and ran from the room, bursting through the main doors and down the piney slope, with Mengele's laughter echoing behind.

Night had fallen, a three-quarter moon rode high, and as I plunged along the path toward the river, in the slants of silvery light piercing the boughs I saw the villagers standing by the doors of their cottages. Some moved after me, stretching out their arms . . . whether in supplication or aggression, I was unable to tell. I did not stop to take note of their particular deformities, but glimpsed oblate heads, strangely configured hands, great bruised-looking eyes that seemed patches of velvet woven into their skins rather than organs with humors and capillaries. Breath shrieked in my throat as I zigzagged among them, eluding their sluggish attempts to touch me. And then I was splashing through the shallows, past the wreckage of my plane, past those godforsaken slopes, panicked, falling, crawling, sending up silvery sprays of water that were like shouts, pure expressions of my fear.

Twenty-five kilometers along the Río Pilcomayo. Fifteen miles. Twelve hours. No measure could encompass the terrors of that walk. Mengele's creatures did, indeed, abound. Once, while pausing to catch my breath, I spotted an owl on a branch that overhung the water. A jet-black owl, its eyes glowing faintly orange. Once a vast bulk heaved up from midstream, just the back of the thing, an expanse of smooth dark skin: it must have been thirty feet long. Once, at a point where the Pilcomayo fell into a gorge and I was forced to go overland, something heavy pursued me through the brush, and at last, fearing it more than the rapids, I dove into the river; as the current bore me off, I saw its huge misshapen head leaning over the cliff, silhouetted against the stars. All around I heard cries that I did not believe could issue from an earthly throat. Bubbling screeches, grinding roars, eerie whistles that reminded me of the keening made by incoming artillery rounds. By the time I reached the village of which Mengele had spoken, I was incoherent and I remember little of the flight that carried me to Asunción.

The authorities questioned me about my accident. I told them my compass had malfunctioned, that I had no idea where I had crashed. I was afraid to mention Mengele. These men were his accomplices, and besides, if his creatures flourished along the Pilcomayo, could not some of them be here? What had he said? "The deformed are ever with us, Mr. Phelan." True enough, but since my experiences in his house it seemed I had become sensitized to their presence. I picked them out of crowds, I encountered them on street corners, I saw the potential for deformity in every normal face. Even after returning to New York, every subway ride, every walk, every meal out brought me into contact with men and women who hid their faces—all having the gray city pallor—yet who could not quite disguise some grotesque disfigurement. I suffered nightmares; I imagined I was being watched. Finally, in hopes of exorcizing these fears, I went to see an old Jewish man, a colleague of Simon Wiesenthal, the famous Nazi hunter.

His office in the East Seventies was a picture of clutter, with stacks of papers and folios teetering on his desk, overflowing file cabinets. He was as old a man as Mengele had appeared, his forehead tiered by wrinkles, cadaverous cheeks, weepy brown eyes. I took a seat at the desk and handed him the paper on which Mengele had made his thumbprint. "I'd like this identified," I said. "I believe it belongs to Josef Mengele."

He stared at it a moment, then hobbled over to a cabinet and began shuffling through papers. After several minutes he clicked his tongue against his teeth and came back to the desk. "Where did you get this?" he asked with a degree of urgency.

"Does it match?"

He hesitated. "Yes, it matches. Now where did you get it?"

As I told my story, he leaned back and closed his eyes and nodded thoughtfully, interrupting me to ask an occasional question. "Well," I said when I had finished. "What are you going to do?"

"I don't know. There may be nothing I can do."

"What do you mean?" I said, dumbfounded. "I can give you the exact position of the village. Hell, I can take you there myself!"

He let out a weary sigh. "This"—he tapped the paper—"this is not Mengele's thumbprint."

"He must have altered it," I said, desperate to prove my case. "He *is* there! I swear it! If you would just . . ." And then I realized something. "You said it matched?"

The old man's face seemed to have sagged further into decay. "Six years ago a man came to the office and told me almost verbatim the story you have told. I thought he was insane and threw him out, but before he left he thrust a paper at me, one that bore a thumbprint. That print matches yours. But it does not belong to Mengele."

"Then it is proof!" I said excitedly. "Don't you see? He may have altered it, but this proves that he exists, and the existence of the village where he lives."

"Does he live there?" he asked. "I'm afraid there is another possibility."

I was not sure what he meant at first; then I remembered Mengele's description of the village. ". . . what you see here, the villagers, the house, everything, is a memorial to my work. It has the reality of one of those glass baubles that contain wintry rural scenes and when shaken produce whirling snowstorms." The key word was "everything." I had likened the way he had paused before giving answers to rummaging through a file, but it was probably more accurate to say he had been recalling a memorized biography. It had been a stand-in I had met, a young man made old or the reverse. Mengele was many years gone from the village, gone God knows where and in God knows what disguise, doing his work. Perhaps he was once again the fleshy, smiling man whose photograph I had seen as a child.

The old man and I had little else to say to one another. He was anxious to be rid of me; I had, after all, shed a wan light on his forty years of vengeful labor. I asked if he had an address for the other man who had told him of the village; I thought he alone might be able to offer me solace. The old man gave it to me—an address in the West Twenties—and promised to initiate an investigation of the village; but I think we both knew that Mengele had won, that *his* principle, not ours, was in accord with the times. I was hopeless-feeling, stunned, and on stepping outside I became aware of Mengele's victory in an even more poignant way.

It was a gray, blustery afternoon, a few snowflakes whirling between the drab façades of the buildings; the windows were glinting blackly, reflecting opaque diagonals of the sky. Garbage was piled in the gutters, spilling onto the sidewalks, and wedges of grimy, crusted snow clung to the bumpers of the cars. Hunched against the wind, holding their coat collars closed over their faces, pedestrians struggled past. What I could see of their expressions was either hateful or angry or worried. It was a perfect Mengelian day, all underpinnings visible, everything pared down to ordinary bone; and as I walked along, I wondered for how much of it he was directly responsible. Oh, he was somewhere turning out grotesques, working scientific charms, but I doubted his efforts were essential to that gray principle underlying the factory air, the principle he worshipped, whose high priest he was. He had been right. Good *was* eroding into evil, bright into dark, abundance into uniformity. Everywhere I went I saw that truth reflected. In the simple shapes and primary colors of the cars, in the mad eyes of the bag ladies, in the featureless sky, in the single-minded stares of businessmen. We were all suffering a reduction to simpler forms, a draining of spirit and vitality.

I walked aimlessly, but I was not surprised to find myself some time later standing before an apartment building in the West Twenties; nor was I any more surprised when shortly thereafter a particularly gray-looking man came down the steps, his face muffled by a scarf and a wool hat pulled low over his brow. He shuffled across the street toward me, unwrapping the scarf. I knew I would be horrified by his deformity, yet I was willing to accept him, to listen, to hear what comforts deformity bestowed; because, though I did not understand Mengele's principle, though I had not dissolved in it or let it rule me, I had acknowledged it and sensed its inevitability. I could almost detect its slow vibrations ringing the changes of the world with—like the syllables of Mengele's name—the sullen, unmusical timbre of a deadened bell.

Most of us, according to the polls, believe that science will give us wondrous lives in the future. But the nature of the human beast is such that no matter how much our lives may improve, they'll never be totally satisfactory to us. Consider a future in which everyone can have everything he or she wants—well, nearly everything. What might be missing? What will we long for?

The individual's own achievements, in such a world, will become of paramount importance. But what will "individual achievement" mean then?

"Originals" is in its own way—which is quite different from that of "Mercurial"—a science fiction detective story. But the problem is not murder, and the solution has more to do with society of the future than with "clues." Nonetheless, this is a science fiction detective story.

Pamela Sargent contributed a fine story to Universe 2, *thirteen years ago, when she was just starting her career. Since then she has published nine novels and four anthologies, three of them in the* Women of Wonder *series.*

ORIGINALS

PAMELA SARGENT

Lora dipped her spoon into the soup, then lifted it to her lips. The broth was clear, with a faint lemony taste; the vegetables, as always, were slightly crispy. Bits of parsley floated on top of the soup. Lora swallowed.

"Superb," she said, trying to smile. Antoine, the chef, stood near the table, searching her face with his morose brown eyes. "Really, it's delicious. You are an artist, Antoine." Antoine tilted his head; his chef's hat slipped a little.

Geraldo, Lora's partner, was slurping softly. "Good soup," he said. The rest of Lora's family was gazing at her expectantly, perhaps wondering why she had not been more effusive in her praise. Her three sons put down their spoons almost at the same moment, while her two little girls fidgeted, tugging at their gown straps. At the other end of the table, Junia was staring directly at Lora.

"I think it's one of the finest soups I've ever tasted," Junia announced. Antoine bowed.

Lora could not control herself any longer. Releasing a sigh, she dropped her spoon next to her bowl. "Oh," she murmured, giving the word all the misery she could muster. She covered her eyes for a moment. "You'll all find out soon enough." She leaned back in her chair. "Another disk was stolen, it seems. It was the one for this cauliflower soup."

"That is too much," her son Roald muttered as his brothers, Rex and Richard, nodded their heads. "I don't understand it. It just goes on and on." The three brothers scowled in unison. Rina tugged at her strap again, then brushed back a lock of blond hair; her sister, Celia, planted her elbows on the table. One of Celia's loose, dark tresses narrowly missed her bowl of soup. Junia sat back, folding her hands. Geraldo continued to eat.

"A pity," Antoine said in tragic tones.

"It's unbearable," Lora said in an unusually harsh voice. "I imagine that, at this very moment, millions of people are enjoying this same soup. What is the point of having our own chef and our own exclusive recipe disks if we can't keep them to ourselves and our invited guests?"

"I am most sorry, madame," Antoine said, gazing heavenward. "I shall create another soup, never fear. And there are still all the disks that remain. They far outnumber the purloined ones."

Lora glanced at him, suddenly irritated with his unhappy face. Gretchen Karell's chef was a cheerful Chinese gentleman who could barely contain his joy at the sight of his sumptuous dishes, while Antoine's seemed to bring him to the verge of tears. It was Gretchen who had left the message that morning, telling Lora that various food fanciers had suddenly acquired disks labeled *Antoine Laval's Cauliflower Soup.* Lora had longed to reach toward the screen and slap Gretchen's smug image.

"Still tastes good," Geraldo said as he finished.

"Really!" Lora gazed balefully at her partner's handsome but chubby face. "I simply can't understand how you can so blithely enjoy a soup that anyone can have now. I've always prided myself on our unique cuisine, and now it seems that it's becoming as common as dirt."

"I don't know how the disk could have been stolen," Junia said in her clear, sharp voice. "No one's been in this house except us for at least a month, and the house would have warned us of any intrusion. You always had guests here when the others were taken."

Lora winced. She had done her best to get along with Junia, who was soon to be the partner of her son Roald, but the young woman was tact-less. Junia had just pointed out what no one else at the table had wanted to mention—namely, that one of those present had to be the thief. That was the worst of it; Lora would have to be suspicious of her own family. Already, she was peering at each face, searching for signs of guilt, wonder-ing who would be capable of such a deed. Her three sons stared back with the same bland look in their identical blue eyes. Her two daughters were once again plucking at their gowns and she nearly burst out with a repri-mand, wanting to tell them to be still.

Geraldo signaled to Antoine, who departed for the kitchen to prepare the next course. Geraldo could not have stolen the disk. He had a hearty appetite, but at the same time, he didn't seem to care what he ate; it was one of his more disagreeable qualities. Lora tensed. Maybe that indiffer-ence made him more likely to steal. The treasured recipes did not mean that much to him, and he would enjoy them just as much no matter how many people had access to them. He was, she thought sadly, only a man of leisure at heart.

Lora covered her eyes again, waiting for someone to take pity and blurt out a confession. She would forgive the lapse, she decided, but only after a truly abject apology. But when she looked up, the robots were already clearing away the soup bowls in preparation for the next course, and no one had spoken.

"I'd like to speak to you," Lora said to the screen in her room. "Alone, please."

"Certainly," the house replied. An image formed on the screen; a kindly, gray-bearded man was now staring out at her, a personification of the mind that ran the house. Lora had always been uneasy whenever she spoke to the disembodied voice of her house cybermind and preferred the friendly, human image.

"We are now on a closed channel," the house said as the man's lips moved. "Please do go on."

"Who stole that disk?"

"You know I can't answer that. If I had known, I would have informed you of the fact."

"I thought you might have some ideas."

"I am completely in the dark." The house chuckled at that; it was night outside. "I don't watch the kitchen, you know."

"Show me the kitchen."

The man disappeared. She was now gazing at the kitchen, knowing that Antoine, who hated to be observed at work, was asleep in his bedroom.

The room looked like any well-equipped kitchen. Inside one pantry shelf, thousands of disks were concealed behind the polished wood doors. Each disk, when inserted into the kitchen's duplicator, would produce meat, fish, poultry, fresh fruits, vegetables, or other raw materials for Antoine to use in preparing a dish. Another shelf held disks with the patterns for wine and other beverages, and a third held spice and herb disks. There were cheese disks, cooking oil disks, butter disks. But in one corner, inside one special shelf, were Antoine's own recipe disks, each containing the pattern for one of his creations.

The duplicator itself, a tall, transparent column with metallic shelves jutting out from its sides, stood near one wall next to a disposal chute. Inside the chute, carried to it from other passages throughout the house's walls, sat much of the household's cast-off clothing, worn-out artifacts, garbage, trash, and dust—all of the materials needed for transmutation. When a disk was inserted into one of the duplicator's slots, the chute would drop the necessary amount of debris into the column. The duplicator would glow as energy created by fusion poured into it and the debris, broken down into its constituent atoms, would be transformed, becoming a bottle of wine, a roasted chicken, or some other food, depending on the pattern stored on the disk. One could also imprint a pattern on a blank disk by slipping the small round platter into a slot above the shelf holding the object one intended to store.

Lora had only a rudimentary understanding of how the duplicator worked, but she had learned a smattering of history and knew that commonplace objects had once been rare. The duplicator, given enough material and the endless stream of fusion energy, could change that material into anything the user wanted, as long as a pattern for that object was on a disk. Sometimes, in her more reflective moments, Lora's heart would go out to those who in past times had had to endure scanty supplies or even do without the bare necessities. There were no shortages now. She drew her brows together. That wasn't quite true. She had occasionally run out of detritus and had been forced to send the robots out foraging for dead leaves and twigs. Once, during a particularly festive party, she had even resorted to having the robots feed dirt from her flower garden into the duplicator in order to feed all the guests. There was, of course, always human waste, but Lora would never dream of using that in the kitchen duplicator. Such material was collected in another chute, to be sterilized and then transmuted by the duplicator in her sitting room into other things. One had to have *some* standards. Recycling was a wonderful and necessary thing, but there were limits.

Occasionally, Antoine had allowed Lora to enter the kitchen while he was cooking, a rare privilege and one that she was careful not to abuse. The last time she had been there, her chef had been trying out a recipe for *poulet persillade*. He had assembled his ingredients and had finished cooking the chicken dish for the fourth time; the first three attempts had not met with his approval and had been relegated to the chute.

Lora's mouth watered as she recalled the taste of the chicken in its light crust of bread crumbs, parsley, and shallots. But Antoine had not been satisfied until his fifth attempt. The disk that could duplicate the *poulet persillade* was now stored safely on a shelf. The dish could be reproduced; the *poulet persillade* would be perfect every time.

She frowned as she stared at her screen, searching the kitchen as if this might yield a clue. The robots that assisted Antoine were standing in one corner; they were always shut off when not working and could not have seen a thing. She might have to keep the shelves locked, and rebelled at that thought. What was the world coming to when she could not trust those nearest to her?

"Show me who left the house this week, and when, and what time each person returned," she said. The kitchen vanished as lists of names and times appeared. Lora emitted a small sigh. Everyone had left the house at various times; each had clearly had the opportunity to take a disk to town, dupe it, and return it to the shelf with no one the wiser. The kitchen, except when Antoine was cooking or duplicating meals, was usually empty.

"Oh, dear," she said sadly.

"It would be quite simple to discover the malefactor," the house murmured as the image of the bearded man reappeared. "I do have eyes and ears inside all of the rooms, you know."

"Oh, no," Lora responded, shocked at the notion of trespassing on her family's privacy. "That wouldn't do at all."

"I need to watch only the kitchen."

"Absolutely not," Lora said firmly. "You know Antoine would never stand for that. He might leave if he found out you were watching."

"Question everyone, then. I'll quickly ferret out anyone who's lying. I can read their physiological reactions and note any vocal stresses."

Lora sat up. "No. I won't turn my home into a police state." She shuddered. She had never spied on anyone in her life and was not about to start doing so now. Her family would never forgive her. She would never forgive herself.

"Then I really don't know how you plan to solve this problem," the house said haughtily.

"I'll find a way. The thief will make a mistake eventually." She wanted to believe that.

Unable to sleep, Lora finally got out of bed and tiptoed to the door connecting her room with Geraldo's. As she opened it, she heard his gentle snoring; she could not disturb him with her worries. Closing the door again, she crossed her room and went out into the corridor, then crept down the winding staircase to the hall below.

Silver moonlight shone through the wide windows. Occasionally, she found herself envying the ones who lived on the moon. Those people had to live in tunnels below ground, enduring out-of-date duplicated clothing and the same food millions of others ate, but their astronomical and scientific pursuits assured their social status. Only original work could win honor, although people who collected original, unduplicated objects also had some respect. The thought of the moondwellers reminded her of her own lowly position. Being a hostess was humble work. A house could have done it, but many still shied away from being entertained by only a voice. Lora's gatherings drew the brightest lights of society, and she was normally content to bask in their reflected glory. At least she had escaped being only a woman of leisure, wasting her time in idleness while surrounded by wealth. She needed to feel useful.

She moved toward the door and stepped out on the porch. Junia was sitting near one marble column, holding a glass; her chestnut hair seemed black in the shadows.

The young woman turned. "Lora." She lifted her glass. "Can't you sleep?"

"No. I'm afraid that this business with the disks is too disturbing." Lora sat down in a chair next to Junia, glancing at the young woman suspiciously. The thefts had begun after Junia had started visiting Roald. She had to be the culprit. Junia knew perfectly well that Lora had not been terribly pleased when Roald had announced his plans to take the young woman as his partner.

"Would you like a brandy?" Junia waved her glass. "I'll be glad to fetch one for you."

"No, thank you." Lora leaned back. "I don't know what to do. Even the house doesn't have a clue. It's just shameful. I'm afraid to have people over to dine. Imagine how embarrassing it would be to serve them an exclusive dish only to have it turn up in other houses later on. I'd lose what little position I have." She paused. "Poor Antoine. He has to spend so much time creating new dishes as it is."

"Oh, he doesn't seem to mind. He loves to cook. After all, it's what he was bred for."

"Indeed. But even Antoine deserves a rest." Lora gripped the arms of her chair, reflecting on how callous Junia often seemed to be. But then almost everyone lacked her own finer feelings. Lora's parents had wanted a sensitive child and that was what the geneticists had given them. "High-strung," Lora's mother had called her, taking pride in her daughter's fine tuning. She had in fact become so sensitive that visiting her parents as an adult had become an ordeal as she struggled not to disappoint them with any inadvertent crudity. Lora had been relieved when both her parents had decided to have a mind-wipe and assume new identities; now they didn't know who she was and she no longer had to visit.

"I've been thinking," Junia said as she brushed back a dark strand of hair. "You don't suppose Rina or Celia could have taken the disks, do you? They love to play little jokes. They put a frog in my bed the other night."

"Oh, dear."

"It doesn't matter. It really didn't frighten me."

Lora thought of the two girls. She had decided against having terribly sensitive offspring, but she had not believed the two children were capable of handling anything as slimy as a frog. Rina and Celia were supposed to be cute for the benefit of guests who enjoyed the presence of a family; they would hardly seem adorable if they played such pranks.

"Stealing disks," Lora murmured, "is hardly a joke."

"Oh, I know. But they might not think of it that way. They might not understand how serious it is."

Lora grimaced. If one of the girls was the thief, the other would surely know about it; they did almost everything together. She could go to one of her daughters and say that the other had owned up to the deed, and force an admission of guilt.

Thinking of such a confrontation repelled her. She had always left discipline, what little there was of it, to Geraldo and the robotic nanny. Anyway, she was beginning to wonder if Rina and Celia had the intelligence to plan such a thievery and carry it off without giving themselves away. She had not wanted intelligent children, either. Intelligent children asked too many hard questions and showed off their knowledge and ended with making their parents feel like fools; she had seen it happen in other households. What good did it do to have an accomplished child to brag about if the child considered one's own mind beneath contempt?

"Well, I'm sure Roald wouldn't steal anything," Junia went on. "Of course, I can't speak for his brothers."

Lora gazed out at the lawn. Beyond the cleared land around her house, the forest's pine trees sang as the wind stirred their branches. Junia would give herself away if she continued to chatter; only a guilty person would be trying to cast suspicion on others. She was now almost certain that the young woman was the thief, and wondered if she would have the strength to order her from the house. Roald might decide to leave with her.

Lora nearly wept as she thought of that. She might lose her son. Surely he was more important than having exclusive recipes. Could he be stealing them to get back at her for her original disapproval of Junia? What other motive might he have for such uncharacteristic behavior? Could he be trading the disks for unduplicated objects?

She shook her head. If Roald or anyone else in the house had been trading the disks for exclusive objets d'art, jewelry, unique historical artifacts, or anything else, some evidence would have turned up by now, and the person accepting the disks would have no motive for duplicating them for the world. Clearly, someone wanted only to make her own life as miserable as possible. Her own limited status was now in jeopardy. Her dinner parties drew people of great prestige with the promise of Antoine's cooking. How many would accept her invitations if they thought they could acquire the dishes elsewhere?

Junia cleared her throat. "I suppose you suspect me, Lora."

"Dear me," Lora said. "I suspect no one." She was again suspecting everyone. Perhaps it was a conspiracy, and they were all in on it; maybe they were tired of trying to be of some use to others and longed to lapse into leisure and laziness altogether. A tear trickled down her cheek as she wallowed in misery, feeling that the world had turned against her. She would become only a peasant, reduced to consuming an endless stream of goods and services.

"Oh, I can understand why you think I might have done it. I wish I could convince you that I didn't. I can't think of anything I'd like more than your approval. I know you didn't want me as a partner for Roald at first."

"Oh, dear." Junia, she thought darkly, had no delicacy at all.

"But we'll still be here, in the house. It's what we both want. You'll still have Roald nearby, and I know he couldn't bear to leave Rex and Richard —they're all so close."

"Junia, I do respect you. Really." Lora tried to give the words some conviction. The young woman might be a bit on the blunt side, but she was also kind and even-tempered; Roald could have done far worse. "It's only that I had hoped all three of my sons would find three partners together. They are a set, after all. If there were two more like you, I really wouldn't have any objection at all." She paused. "I don't suppose you would consider being a partner to all three."

"Oh, no," Junia said cheerfully. "It's Roald I love."

"Oh, well." Lora thought of her three sons. She had been so taken with Richard after removing him from his artificial womb that she had insisted on having two brothers cloned right away. Roald had been brought home ten years later, after a period in cryonic storage, and Rex ten years after that. She had received many compliments on her handsome sons, the same genotype at different ages; their physical similarity as individuals made them seem unique as a group.

Richard was now thirty-eight, Roald twenty-eight, and Rex eighteen; except for their blue eyes, they were all slimmer versions of Geraldo, which was fitting since he had contributed most of the genes. She had once dreamed of finding them three identical young women, or, failing that, one who would fall in love with all three, but it was not to be. Her sons, unhappily, had shown more individuality than she had expected; Rex parceled out his affections to various girls while Richard was not likely to partner at all. At least Junia had not insisted on her own house.

Her doubts, held at bay, suddenly bit at her mind again, nibbling at her small share of happiness. Rex might be giving the disks to his many loves. Richard was close to the Karells; could Gretchen, Lora's social rival, have encouraged his thievery? If only she could put her doubts aside. They all knew how easily she could be wounded; how could those she loved be so cruel? Her sons would never stoop to theft; had one of them truly wanted to hurt her, all he had to do was leave.

It had to be Junia. Even as Lora clung to that hypothesis, she questioned it. Junia, in addition to being a trifle rough around the edges, was intelligent. The young woman was only too aware that she would be the prime suspect; she had said so. She could not want Lora's ill will, not when she would have to live under the same roof.

Junia rose. "I'm going to bed." She yawned, not even troubling to cover her pretty mouth. "You should, too. No sense worrying about it. Whoever's stealing your disks will get tired of doing it eventually."

Lora and Geraldo breakfasted alone at the small table near the rose garden. She nibbled at a sectioned orange and a brioche as Geraldo feasted on an omelet, then helped himself to buckwheat cakes. Glancing at her partner's rounded belly, Lora made a mental note to tell Antoine that he should serve non-caloric foods for the next day or two. Antoine would not be happy about that; she could never convince him that such foods really did taste the same as others.

"Don't worry," Geraldo muttered as he reached for the syrup. "Junia'll make Roald a good partner." He looked past the garden toward the lawn, where Rex, Roald, and Richard were passing a football to one another; their brown, bare chests gleamed with sweat. Near them, a few robots were clipping the grass, collecting the blades in sacks to be used in the duplicator.

"I wasn't thinking of Junia." The morning light had revealed a gray hair on Geraldo's head; he would need another rejuvenation treatment before the rigors of the social season began.

"Are you still worried about the disks? Forget it, honey. We all know how you feel. I'm sorry you feel so rotten. I guess I didn't realize how upset you'd get about it."

She peered at him. "Exactly what do you mean, dear?" She waited to see if he was about to confess. Geraldo was generous by nature; he might not have been able to resist a friend's plea for a disk.

"Oh, you know. I mean, if the food's good, I'll eat it. I never really cared how many people had the recipe. I guess I forgot that it means more to you," he added hastily.

"It should mean something to you, too. Don't you care what people think? Aren't you concerned with our obligations?"

"Oh, of course. Well, I know I didn't do it. Antoine doesn't like me anywhere near the kitchen even when he's not there. I don't praise his efforts enough."

"I can't say I blame him," Lora said gently. "He wants people to savor his food, not gulp it."

"Rina and Celia couldn't have planned it, either. Mind you, I love our little girls, but if a thought ever entered their heads, they'd probably say, 'What's that?' " Geraldo narrowed his eyes. "Aha! *You* did it!" He put down his fork. "That's it. You did it so we'd all feel sorry for you and be nicer. You always did like a lot of sympathy—playing the victim and all."

Shocked, Lora began to weep.

"Hey!" Geraldo took her hand. "I was only kidding."

"That's cruel, Geraldo. I never thought you, of all people, could be so heartless."

"I didn't mean it."

"I don't enjoy being so touchy. It's not something I would have chosen. I know it's sometimes hard for all of you to keep from upsetting me." She dabbed at her tears with her napkin, knowing how ugly red, watery eyes and a puffy face were. "You don't know how many times I've considered reconditioning, but that would be like losing part of myself. I've even thought of mind-wiping."

Geraldo started.

"But then I wouldn't remember you. I'd lose everything."

Geraldo stroked her hand. "Lora, I like you just the way you are. You might be sensitive, but so what? It gives the rest of us something to aspire to, in a way. It just shows how civilized and delicate you are." He waved one arm expansively. "Why, if everyone were like you, it would be a much nicer world. We'd all be a lot more thoughtful of others' feelings."

She smiled, forgiving him. Geraldo had his faults, but he always knew how to heal her wounds, and he was invaluable at parties. His unpretentious manner could put the most nervous guest at ease; he was, in part, responsible for her own small success.

"Well," she whispered, and then her doubts returned; she still had no solution to her problem. "I don't know what to do," she continued. "I simply can't resort to spying on my own family, even if that's what the house wanted me to do. Antoine might leave, you know."

"Has he said so?" Geraldo mumbled, his mouth full of food.

"No. I'm afraid to speak to him about it. But you can imagine how he feels. If someone keeps stealing his disks, he may want to go to a house where there aren't any thieves." She was well aware that the chef's position on the social ladder was higher than her own; all she could really offer him was an appreciative and discerning audience for his efforts. "All of this larceny just means more work for him. Other chefs take time off, laze about most of the time, create new recipes only when inspiration strikes, while he has to labor constantly. Why, if he didn't, we'd scarcely have any exclusive recipes left. We'd have to duplicate disks from the public library!"

"Aren't you exaggerating a little?"

"Not at all. Ten stolen disks in less than a year, *ten.*" She bowed her head, thinking of the couscous, Antoine's crabmeat salad with green grapes and his special dressing, the cauliflower soup, the poached salmon with dill and a secret ingredient Antoine had refused to reveal—all duplicated now, all being consumed by others. "We'll have to have a backlog of disks, seeing that I don't know what might be stolen next. Maybe it's my own fault. I should never have bragged so far and wide about Antoine's cooking, and maybe this wouldn't have happened."

"You shouldn't think that. You wanted to do something with yourself, and that's good. You had to tell people about Antoine to draw them here. Why, without you, honey, I might still be back in that slum."

Lora shuddered, recalling the hill of mansions surrounded by trenches. The people in such a neighborhood craved so many things that they needed to ruin their grounds in an effort to provide enough mass for their duplicators. Luckily, she had not met Geraldo's family until after they became partners; she quailed at the memory of the Tudor house cluttered with velvet furniture, gold statues, Oriental carpets, closets packed with clothes, and paintings in gilt frames selected with no eye for style or period. One visit had been quite enough.

"Now Antoine will want to leave," she said bitterly. "He may put it off for a while, to spare my feelings, but he'll get around to it in time. And we'll never get another chef, not when others find out about our situation."

She sipped some coffee. Good chefs were so hard to come by. So few people wanted a child bred for that profession; whatever the eventual rewards might be, raising a child who was a picky eater was a torment.

Perhaps she could talk Antoine into having himself cloned. It didn't matter. It would take at least twenty years for the child to grow up and be trained as a chef, and in the meantime she would be reduced to eating food available to all.

"Listen," Geraldo said. "We know that the thief isn't one of our acquaintances, so we've narrowed the list of suspects. And you're sure to find out who the thief is for one reason."

She raised her head, gazing into his dark eyes. "And what is that?"

"You're so damned sensitive. You'll sense it. You'll see something in someone's manner that will give the thief away—something subtle, not obvious. Trust your instincts, Lora, and you'll solve this problem."

"And then what should I do? I simply don't have the stamina for a confrontation."

"Leave it to me. I'll take care of that."

After breakfast, Lora decided to take a stroll through the woods. Her sons ran into the house, returning with a brown cloak to protect her against the air, which had grown cooler. Richard had made the cloak himself; her sons were already gaining some small renown as designers of clothing. Rex draped the garment over her shoulders as Richard and Roald each planted a kiss on her cheek.

She peered intently into their blue eyes, trying to discern guilt in one open, honest face. Her sons had never lied to her, though there had been times, especially when Rex was talking about his latest amorous adventure, when she had wished that they were somewhat less open.

"Is anything wrong?" Richard asked, apparently noting her frown.

"Oh, no."

"If you see Junia," Roald said, "tell her I'm going over to the Karells' house later. She wanted to come along."

"Isn't she still upstairs?"

Roald shook his head. "She went for a walk a little while after Antoine went out."

Lora savored that morsel of information as she crossed the lawn. Was Junia following the chef? Antoine often went on solitary forays looking for wild plants to dupe for his recipes, and she suspected that he had a secret herb garden somewhere, carefully concealed. She thought of Roald. He had never been able to abide deceit; would he have fallen in love with a woman who would steal? Somehow she doubted it.

Antoine would leave; he would not tolerate the larceny indefinitely. If only—and even thinking such a thought was profoundly disturbing—the chef could be duplicated. How evil her musings had become. The penalty for duping a human being was severe; the offender would be deprived of access to any duplicator, reduced to eating only in restaurants and acquiring goods others had thrown away. With watchful cyberminds everywhere, discovery of such a crime was certain, which was why such offenses were rare. At any rate, such action would do no good even if she could overcome her conditioning long enough to push Antoine into the duplicator in order to get his pattern. The duplicated Antoine would only repeat his predecessor's actions and leave her, too.

Rina and Celia were sitting on the lawn, playing with various rubies, diamonds, and sapphires; the gems were scattered among the neatly trimmed blades.

"Hello, my darlings," Lora said as she approached her daughters. The girls looked up, gaping. Though Rina was fair, and Celia dark, they both had Lora's fine features. "What are you doing?"

The inquiry seemed to be causing the children some perplexity. Celia glanced at her sister, as if looking for enlightenment.

"Playing," Rina answered at last.

"A game," Celia added.

"Hadn't you better go inside?" Lora asked.

"Why?" Rina said.

"Because it's getting cold."

"Oh," Celia said, looking surprised.

"And you shouldn't gape, dears. You're both much too pretty to leave your mouths hanging open like that." The girls scrambled to pick up their gems, dropping several in the process and having to stoop for them again. Had one of them been the thief, Lora thought, broken disks would have been scattered over the kitchen floor.

She came to the woods, treading daintily over the pine needles on the ground. Here, at least, she could put her troubles behind her for a while. She listened to the birds; their musical chirping, accompanied by the whistling pines, lifted her spirits. The spell was broken as a grackle cawed, causing Lora to wince.

The dark thought she had been suppressing now floated to the surface. The house had ample opportunity to steal. It could easily set one of the robots to the task in the middle of the night, and erase any record of its movements. The air around her seemed to grow even colder.

What motive could the house have? She had heard of other cyberminds becoming bitchy or recalcitrant, growing disdainful of the human beings around them. Most, indeed, had a habit of behaving as if they were the superior intelligence.

She pressed her lips together. Perhaps the house wanted to displace her and take over her functions; maybe it had grown to resent being only an onlooker at her soirées. She imagined a conspiracy of houses communicating through secret channels, plotting against those whom they served. The thought was intolerable; how could she confront her own house with such an accusation? If she angered it, the house might decide to close down, and then she would have to move.

She leaned against a tree for a moment, then steadied herself. Surely those more brilliant than she had considered such a possibility. They would not allow cyberminds to become too rebellious, for there was no telling where such rebelliousness might lead.

She had walked farther than she had intended. The trees had thinned out; just beyond this edge of the forest, the Karells' stone house stood in a glade. Lora turned back, remembering how Gretchen Karell had gloated when leaving her message about the stolen soup. She would have to tell Roald not to invite the Karells to dinner.

As she retraced her steps, a voice rang out through the woods. "Hello!" It was Junia; Lora knew that piercing, clear tone well. She looked around, then glimpsed the young woman. Junia was standing with her back to Lora; she had spoken to Antoine. Neither had spotted Lora.

"Bonjour," the chef replied. He was carrying a basket filled with weedy-looking plants.

"Going back to the house?" Junia bent over to brush a bit of dirt from her pants.

"Yes. I have gathered enough for today."

"Can't you use disks for that stuff?"

Antoine drew himself up. "Occasionally truly fresh ingredients are required, mademoiselle. I have recorded many for later duplication, but I am always on the lookout, so to speak, for something new, something not yet recorded."

"Goodness." Junia leaned forward. "Just plants? Or do you hunt?"

"Certainly not, mademoiselle." Antoine was clearly appalled. "I am not so barbaric as to seek the death of an animal. The disks have spared me the necessity for such a crime."

"Well, that's a relief. I thought your rabbit stew was delicious. I'm glad it wasn't made with any residents of the forest."

Antoine's fingers fluttered; he was obviously moved by the compliment. "Alas, I sometimes mourn those creatures who had to die long ago so that their patterns could be preserved on disks. But those dark days are past. And we have this beautiful forest instead of a wheat field or lettuce patch. We should be grateful we no longer need to waste ourselves in such toil. Only those who enjoy gardening for its own sake need to till the earth and breed new strains for our eventual delectation."

"But you toil, Antoine." The two were walking now. Lora kept her distance from the pair as she followed. She was eavesdropping, but could not bring herself to reveal her presence. Chastising herself for her lack of character, she kept the pair in sight. The unknown thief had reduced her to being a sneak.

"Yes, I toil, mademoiselle," Antoine replied, "but it is what I was born to do. I cannot conceive of a greater pleasure than concocting a new tasty tidbit."

"But you're at it all the time. Surely you like to relax."

"My work is my relaxation."

"Then why don't you open your own restaurant? Or better yet, a private dining club? You'd get lots of members, I'm sure. People would trade you all sorts of things for your meals—why, you could have an unduplicated art collection if you wanted."

Antoine shook his head. "My cooking is my art, and I would not want the distractions of running a club. At any rate, there is more cachet to being a private chef."

"That's true. But why here? There are lots of families that would have you. You could go anywhere you like."

"I am happy here," Antoine answered. "And there is Madame Lora. She is so appreciative of my work. Such taste and discernment are not common nowadays when so many grab at everything without discrimination. We live in a world of coarsened palates, mademoiselle. In my previous station, the family I served would often sneak into the kitchen in the dead of night to dupe chili dogs." He shuddered. "I do not wish to feed pigs at the trough. Madame Lora's pleasure in my work is most gratifying, and she is careful to invite only those who will appreciate it."

Lora swelled with pride and nearly tripped over a root. Steadying herself, she held her breath, but Junia and Antoine continued on their way, unaware of her.

"I see your point," Junia said. "Praise from someone like Lora means a lot. She's so easily upset by a lot of things." Lora smiled to herself. There were some rewards in eavesdropping.

"Next to cooking, appreciation is what I live for," Antoine said. "I sleep soundly when I know that my food has been savored by others. I say to myself, only Antoine Laval could do this, only Antoine Laval is capable of producing such deliciousness. I am so pleased that you will be living with the young monsieur, that there will be another person of taste to enjoy my delicacies on a daily basis. With time, you may even approach Madame Lora in your discernment."

"That's very kind."

"It is no more than you deserve, mademoiselle."

"You're easy to appreciate. You're an artist, Antoine." Junia took his free arm. "It's such a pity about those stolen disks."

Antoine was silent. "Yes, a pity," he said at last. "I must work even more to create new dishes."

The two moved on. Lora waited until they were out of sight, then began to hurry toward the house along a different route; she was running by the time she reached the lawn.

Lora took a deep breath before entering the kitchen. Her hands were shaking; she had drunk a bottle of wine to steady her nerves.

Antoine, dressed in his hat and apron, stood before a shelf of disks making his selections for the evening. His robots stood by, still unactivated; the rest of the family was upstairs dressing for dinner.

She cleared her throat. The chef turned, raising an eyebrow. "Madame," Antoine said in wounded tones, "I have not requested your presence in my kitchen."

"I know who's been stealing the disks." She leaned against the counter as she summoned her courage.

Antoine's eyes widened.

"You've been stealing them, Antoine. Every once in a while, you take one to town and dupe it. It's true, isn't it?"

The chef clasped his hands together, then lowered his eyes. "I cannot deny it," he said after a long pause. "I have indeed been distributing my disks. I give them to a friend in town who makes other duplicates. He is most trustworthy, so I do not think you found out from him."

Lora nodded.

"How did I give myself away?" He glanced at the screen. "Has the house betrayed me by spying? I cannot believe you would allow it."

"No. You betrayed yourself in the woods today. I didn't mean to over-hear you and Junia, but I did." She looked away for a moment, embarrassed at having to admit her own minor lapse. "You said appreciation meant so much to you, more than almost anything. That's why you made sure every disk had your name on it. Hundreds of discerning diners must appreciate your handiwork every day. That's what you wanted. You still have the status of a private chef while pleasing so many others. You didn't even trade them for anything because you don't want anything else except to cook and have your efforts honored. There was nothing to give you away."

Antoine hung his head. "I am most chagrined, madame."

Lora sagged against the counter, too weak and hurt to cry. The chef quickly took her arm and led her to a stool, seating her. "How could you do it, Antoine? Haven't we been good to you? Haven't you always liked it here?"

"Of course." He wrung his hands. "I have dishonored myself. I promised you exclusive recipes and did not keep my word. I should have sought help when my desire for fame and appreciation became so great." He flung out his arms. "I shall never forgive myself!"

"Oh, dear." Lora pressed her fingertips to her temples.

"I am an artist!" Antoine beat his chest with one fist, then began to pace the room. "I long for honor and prestige, for there is nothing else to have in this world. I hunger for that as much as anyone. An artist must share his gift, or it will curdle inside him like spoiled milk. It will grow as sour as a wine bottled badly. It will become as flat as an ill-made soufflé. Oh, madame!"

Lora let her hand drop. "But all of the people who have come here honor you."

"That is true. But think of all the others who might."

She sighed.

"We are at an impasse," Antoine said more calmly. "I will have to go, yet no one will have me as a family chef when my misdeeds are known. I should have realized I could not keep a secret from one as sensitive as you." Taking off his hat, he threw it to the floor. "I shall work as a common chef, and make new disks for the public at large. It will be punishment enough. My friend gave my disks only to those who would fully appreciate them, I assure you, but now—" He waved a hand. "I shall be forced to cast my pearls before swine, or will have to serve them the slops they so desire. But worst of all, I shall lose your pleasure in my work."

"Oh, my."

He pointed at the shelf. "I shall leave you the exclusive disks still remaining," he said dramatically. "Alas, I may never have such a well-equipped kitchen again. It will take years to assemble one."

"Oh, dear," Lora said. "I can't bear to lose you, Antoine. I'd go mad."

"It is a compulsion, madame. I would have to be reconditioned to overcome it."

"No," she cried. "Your talent is much too precious. You mustn't risk damaging it with reconditioning. Only we know about this, Antoine. No one else has to know at all."

"But I know I shall dupe another disk eventually. Others will find out. Mademoiselle Junia is clever enough to do so. I cannot make you my accomplice in this crime. You would be disgraced."

"But you must stay." Lora rubbed her forehead, trying to think.

"How I longed to be widely honored!" Antoine raised his eyes to the ceiling. "Savoring one's talent is not enough—one must allow others to feast on one's accomplishments. I even dreamed of elevating the public taste through this stealthy distribution. I was wrong. I wanted to be both universal and exclusive, and that is not possible. I shall go." He began to untie his apron.

"Wait. There must be a solution." An idea was forming in her mind. She prodded at it mentally, hoping it was not half-baked. Perhaps the bits of historical knowledge she had acquired might be useful for more than simply entertaining her guests with anecdotes about the dark past. "Let me explain."

"Certainly, madame." Antoine, halfway to the door, was hesitating.

"In the old days, before duplicators, people who offered goods and services found that they had to create a demand for those things. So they advertised. That means they informed the public at large that such goods and services were available."

"That is what you do when you speak of your parties and my cooking to others."

"Yes, but these people had many other ways of spreading the information." Lora drew her brows together, unused to such sustained mental effort. "They put up posters and made little films and so forth. I saw a few in a public museum as a child. Of course, the claims were often exaggerated. But sometimes, for something new, simply providing information wasn't enough. So they came up with another idea—the free sample."

"The free sample?" The chef looked puzzled. "They gave them away? But in those troubled times, people gave nothing away except on special occasions—so I have always believed."

"But a free sample would create demand." Lora beamed, proud of her cogency. "One would use the sample and then want more of the product."

"I understand. But what has this to do with me?"

"Don't you see? What you've actually been doing is giving away samples and creating demand. When you look at it that way, it really doesn't seem so bad, does it?"

Antoine's face brightened a bit.

"So what we'll do is continue to give away free samples. You can dupe a disk once in a while, when your compulsion grows too strong, but we'll be open about it. Of course, you must also point out that even finer dishes are available in this house. People will be green with envy at the thought of what we eat here—why, you'll have more appreciation than you'll know what to do with!" And she, Lora thought, would increase her own reputation as a hostess even more. Everyone would clamor for invitations to dinner. Antoine would have his fame without sacrificing his position or principles. Her sensitive soul warmed at the notion of making him happy. "Will you stay?"

"Why, madame!" The chef was actually smiling. "Of course I will stay. You are brilliant."

"I am, if I do say so myself." Lora patted her hair. "You know, Antoine, those of us with some cultivation have been neglecting our responsibilities. We think that because people can have almost anything, we needn't create demand. That's a mistake. We should seek to lead people to finer things, encourage such folk to want them." That idea, like free samples, was an old one called *noblesse oblige*, but an old enough idea could seem quite new. "Most of us have been satisfied only to accept the admiration of those like us. True appreciation is our rarity—we should try to increase this wealth, if I may put it that way. I suspect that a lot of others will start offering free samples soon."

Antoine kissed his fingers. "You are an originator!"

"Oh, my," Lora murmured, accepting that highest of compliments. "It was really your idea," she added modestly. "I mean, you've provided the ingredients—I've only simmered the broth, so to speak. But you'll have even more work to do now."

"But I love my work." He hurried to her side; bowing, he kissed her hand. "I shall be content."

Lora hopped off the stool. "Enough. It's almost time for supper. Something substantial, I hope. With all this thinking, I've worked up quite an appetite."

"It will be delicious, I assure you. And exclusive."

Let's face it: If we ever achieve time travel, it's going to present us with a lot of problems. Even if we ignore time paradoxes and the like, there will be countless subtle and unexpected problems that may hit us in the face.

But even granting that, some of those problems might get even more strange than we could have predicted: humans are odd creatures even to themselves. Therefore, here's a very peculiar story about time travel and some people of whom you've heard, more or less.

Barry Malzberg has been writing science fiction for more than twenty years; if I tried to list all of his novels and short stories, the list might be longer than this story. Malzberg has also published a book of sf criticism, The Engines of the Night, *which you should read: not only does he say many sage and cogent things about the literature of the imagination but he also says them in a very entertaining way.*

JOHANN SEBASTIAN BRAHMS

BARRY N. MALZBERG

The purpose of this test is not to measure your knowledge but your potential. A specific demonstration of knowledge is irrelevant and may even be counted against you. Answer the questions honestly. Allow your emotions to predominate. The Examiners will take into account factors beyond your apprehension. You have forty-five minutes. When the instructions are given to stop, *stop immediately.* Do not finish the sentence you are working upon; do not complete the question. This test is in only partial fulfillment of other requirements which at their pleasure the Examiners will take into account. Good luck.

1. Who is the most significant figure of the Western Creative Period? Explain and justify.

2. What can you bring to this figure beyond the accumulated researches?

3. Psychotronics leads to well-defined damages. Define some of them.

4. What is the primary factor (if any) lacking in the figure described in (1)?

1. The most significant figure of the Western Period was Johann Sebastian Brahms. In his symphonies, his concertos, and his German Mass for chorus and soloists he brought a kind of tenderness to the concept of death which had not been previously glimpsed. Johann Sebastian Brahms lived a difficult life. He was the target of scorn and envy. In his lifetime very few of his works were performed. One was the Symphony Number 1, about which someone said, "That sounds like the Beethoven Symphony theme," and the witty Brahms replied, "Any donkey can tell that." Brahms was also in love with Clara Schubert, the wife of another composer, and this so disturbed him that he sought counseling from the famous doctor Sigmund Freud, who helped him with his problems. After his death in 1897 the work of Johann Sebastian Brahms reached its true place in the audience and was performed for over three hundred years! He was very significant because of the originality of his themes (despite that nasty remark I have quoted) and the deepness of his passion.

2. I think I have a true and deep understanding of Brahms. Not only have I listened to his music but I have read about him and thought deeply about his suffering. In my opinion, the fact of his suffering is underrated as an inspiration for his music, like consider the German Mass. I can bring to him a feeling of understanding not available for many others and also a vivid appreciation of his music.

3. There are many well-defined damages to psychotronics. Among the most dangerous are time-slip and fugue; also depression and fundamental inaccuracy. Many critics of psychotronics think that it is dangerous and no good because change is impossible within the fabric of time. In 2216 Kellermann issued his famous theory that psychotronics was not an objective phenomena at all but an internal one and that everything that went on inside it was a waste of time. Also, it has been thought to create Premature Aging and Internal Organic Damage.

4. What is lacking in Brahms is very hard to say because I do not see too much lacking except for his unhappy romantic life which many people of his time had. He was a great composer. He composed symphonies and concertos and vocal works (like the German Mass) and also music for trios or quartets. Not all were at the highest level but none was less than very good. His problems were perhaps that he should have seen Doctor Freud more than that one time they walked around the lake and maybe he would have had more understanding. And of course he died when he was not too

old but that was a characteristic of that time. Another problem with Johann Sebastian Brahms might have been

Freud feels disgust but consciously represses it, determined to remain professional. One must remain professional at all times; the litter of the subconscious is an ugly sight when strewn before him but the problem is particular to the individual, not generalized (Jung is a charlatan!), and in proper time all can be reassembled. It is this damned Germanic temperament itself that is to blame; this repressive hold when broken leaves for a while no structure at all. "That is perfectly all right," he says to Brahms. "These feelings are very common and are shared by many men in your condition. What did you do after you had completed the act?" He takes out a handkerchief and wipes his brow, relights the cigar, tosses the match into the lake. A distressed swan he had not seen squawks in fury and scurries into deeper water, its eyes blinking. "You should feel at ease," Freud says.

"I don't remember," says Johann Sebastian Brahms. He is sweating too; his forehead gleams with the exertion of pushing all his ugly childhood thoughts to the surface. "It was very dark in the room. I was very tired. Perhaps I kissed her once more. I made apologies. I wiped myself very thoroughly, all parts, and then I disposed of the towel. It must have been storming. The rain hit the windows. I felt the heavens themselves were admonishing me. She was very silent. At some time I must have left."

Freud sighs. "Can you be more specific?"

"No," says Brahms. "I want to be, Doctor, but I cannot. It is all a blur to me. These thoughts, these memories, they pound at my brain and give me no peace but I cannot sort them out." He stumbles over a dangling cuff, stops, looks at Freud intently. "This was a very bad idea," he says. "Discussing all of this, bringing forth these bad recollections. I apologize for taking up your time but I do not think that I should longer proceed. Let us go back and say no more of this. The boat will sail soon."

"No," Freud says, "that is not proper at this time. We must follow through; you are becoming better, don't you see? All these thoughts are coming to the surface where they can be discussed. That is the pathway to release and control." It is not true, of course. He does not believe this at all. The way toward release and control is to contain the thoughts and sometimes to use their hidden energy but he is too far along in this discussion now to stop. Also, like most educated, troubled Viennese, Johann Sebastian Brahms fascinates him. The degree of concentrated energy, shaped toward explosion, is frightening. Freud puffs on his cigar for effect, takes it from his mouth. "Just do the best you can," he says, "beginning with the time you left the room."

Brahms sighs. After a long time, he proceeds. He tells of his uncontrollable lust for Clara Schubert, a lust which he has had for many years and which, at last, seized him on that crucial afternoon. He talks of his guilt, the difficulty of confronting the husband, Robert, in an unassuming fashion. Brahms and Freud walk. They walk the circumference of the lake, about a quarter of a mile, several times. The park is virtually abandoned at this time of day and they attract no attention. This is why Brahms had selected it; he had said that if it were to be known that he was seeking advice from Freud, there would be only one conclusion and that would be scandal. Freud's researches into mental abnormality and distress are well known. Brahms discusses the difficult obligations of his work, the way in which he has become more and more to feel like a performer rather than a composer, the rage which has built within him. Freud listens, saying only enough from time to time to spur on the monologue. It is the theory of his researches that undirected monologue will lead to the truth but sometimes he is not so sure of this. Now, more than ever, as he ages and as his researches continue, he knows doubt. Perhaps it is this which has so infuriated Jung.

Brahms talks of his mother. She was a significant influence in his life, as was Beethoven. Sometimes he feels that he confuses the two of them. Like so many of his patients, Brahms seems to feel it necessary to probe ever more deeply into his history and his motives. Almost alone in such situations Freud sometimes wants to call a halt to this. "Sometimes a cigar is simply a cigar," he wants to say. But there is essentially nothing to be done about this. His reputation has preceded him. That is why Johann Sebastian Brahms sought his counsel. He listens to the composer talk of his stern parent, her uncompromising necessities, her demands, the great sense of obligation which she imposed upon him at all times. Confused swans mutter in counterpoint as they stroll the lake. Their pace has picked up too as they make their fifteenth, now their sixteenth circuit of the stagnant waters, little pieces of shrubbery dangling like familiars. "I tell you," Brahms says, "there is no end to it. There is no end to these humiliations, Doctor. Even Clara cannot take them from me."

Of course, Freud wants to say. Of course your Clara cannot take them from you; she is part of those humiliations, a situation which you have created to replace the stern, admonishing parent, now dead, never dead. But how can he say this to Brahms? How can he possibly point this out, and if he did, what difference would it make? Pain exists like water; it will fill all circumstances. He wheels the cigar in his grasp, casts an arc against the sky. "But of course," he says; "you must proceed."

Brahms proceeds. Open, careless of himself, he has much to say. As if he had never opened himself he goes on and on, a symphony of strife and contradiction. Oh my, Freud thinks. Oh my, oh my. He feels the century itself clamping upon him like a vaginal orifice; soon enough, in only half a decade, it will expel him into the awesome and incomprehensible twentieth. The twentieth awaits him. The twentieth awaits them all, living and dead alike. As if from a near distance, he can smell the fumes, he can feel the superheated fires as that darkness awaits them. Oh, Brahms, he wants to say, your flesh is as grass, your sorrows are as ash; blessed, truly, are the dead against whom your words, your very anguish is merely obbligato.

But he says nothing at all. He merely continues to listen. That is his fate, just as it is his function. He will listen and listen and out of this will come, finally and precisely, the arc of his doom. The twentieth crouches in its passageway, waiting to consume him. The swans grumble.

This is an exit survey. *It is not an examination.* Answer the questions quickly and without attempting to be precise. It is your reaction which is being sought, not explanation. Good luck and thank you for participating in the Psychotronics League First Review.

1. What did you learn about your selected personage from the experiment? What if any characteristics of this personage differed from your preconception?

2. What was the most exciting moment for you?

3. What was the most disturbing moment? Was it the same as (2) above?

4. Would you enter this process again? Would you select the same personage?

5. Do you have any general recommendations about the process as to how it might be improved? Or are you content with the process as it was?

1. I learned that Johann Sebastian Brahms was *real* and that he was a human being just as I am. This differed a little from my preconception

because I was in awe of this famous composer and found it hard to believe that he was a man with the same kind of problems and doubts as all of us. But I was not *very* surprised because I kind of suspected this. I should have researched better, though.

2. The most exciting moment was when Doctor Freud turned on me and said he could not help me because I was a charlatan and a liar who was not being truthful with him and then when he told me to get out of his sight. That was what I meant about not researching.

3. The most disturbing moment was the same as the most exciting moment I have described above. It was disturbing because Doctor Freud was so angry and I did not know what was making him so mad. He said it was all a lie, all of it was lies, and that all the time we were walking around the lake I was thinking I was Brahms and it really was meant to be Mahler only it wasn't because I was so stupid. This made me very upset particularly when he would not stop yelling at me. But it ended soon enough so I guess it wasn't that bad.

4. I would definitely enter this process again but I would not do it as Johann Sebastian Brahms. I would not do it again with anyone unless I had researched him much better. I see now that research is a very important part of psychotronics and that without it things do not really work out very well at all. I also see that one of the purposes of psychotronics might be to *teach* us the value of research for itself so I am not very angry about this but take it as a lesson. I would want to enter the process again but not I think as an important Western figure of music. Maybe I would be a performing figure or royalty instead because they have less problems. King Seville would be a good one to be, for instance.

5. The process was very good and realistic too; I really felt myself at the lake and with the Doctor and so on. It might be improved a little if the research could be done *for* us and like implanted so that we would not have to study. But generally speaking and despite being yelled at I was satisfied with the process and I would recommend it to anyone who wanted a different perspective on themselves or to understand what the past was really like for those who lived through it to make our own times for us.

Stretched on his bed, wracked in his bed, Freud rises at last from the terrible dream and lurches to the window, stares at the moon phosphorescent in the dim, wet night. My God, he thinks, my God. Who was it?

What was it? What has Mahler done to him? He cannot bear these dreams in the wake of analytic encounter; is this the price that his new mental science will extract from him?

It is too high. It is too much. Mahler had mentioned that doomed figure but was it of the tormented Brahms or the dystopic twentieth of which he has so luridly dreamed? Freud unwraps his next cigar with shaking fingers as far beyond, high and filled with song, the dying swan leaps suddenly jagged against the moon.

We are all dying, Freud thinks.

"No," he says aloud, "all flesh is grass. We will be reborn."

The idea of reincarnation goes back in history a very long way and has given rise to many interpretations, including fascinating ones by science fiction and fantasy writers. Here's a story with more thoughts on the matter . . . and its implications.

Mona Clee graduated from the University of Texas at Austin with a degree in law; she now practices in Los Angeles. She attended the Clarion Conference in 1983 and has sold several stories to forthcoming anthologies of fantasy.

ENCOUNTER ON THE LADDER

MONA A. CLEE

It wasn't the kind of place where you'd expect to end up talking about reincarnation. Dividends and Interest was a shiny, fancy, plastic-slick singles bar just off the Loop in Houston, its parking lot full of BMWs and its tables swarming with Yuppies. Normally I hate places like that; I just went there because it was Friday night, I'd had an awful week, and I needed a beer really bad. The Div, as we called it, was the only place within five miles of work where you could hope to get a drink without getting mugged as well.

I hate crowds, and I have an absolute phobia of being jostled. So even though I knew a lot of the people at The Div, I didn't try to mingle with them. I just got my beer and looked around for a place to drink it in peace.

But there wasn't a peaceful spot in the whole bar. The music was turned up loud and grated on my nerves. There were wall-to-wall legal secretaries and junior executive types all hunting at full bore. I could feel myself working up a good case of claustrophobia.

I told myself I could always walk out the door and finish my beer in the parking lot. Braced by that reassurance, I strolled into the back room of The Div, where they had a few tables for people who wanted to eat as well as guzzle. I crossed my fingers, but it seemed I was out of luck there too. Every one of the tables was packed. I was just about to make for the parking lot when I saw Rod, the President of our company, tear out of the room with a look of fury on his face.

Rod is short for Radhakrishnon. Our President is an engineer from M.I.T. who went on to the University of Texas to study petroleum engineering. He used a stake from his father in Calcutta to start up an oil company consulting business, and along the way he branched out into real estate development as well. Today Rod is a very rich man and, so I'm told, very much used to getting his own way.

Apparently he hadn't gotten his way tonight. I saw that there were a number of tables spaced along the far wall of the room, each shaded by a little canopy, and raised above the floor so you had to climb up several steps to get to them. At one of these sat Martha Carvajal, the newest Vice-President of our company, looking as if she'd like to shoot someone. As I watched, she glared at Rod's retreating back, and then polished off the glass of white wine in front of her in one gulp.

I was too tired to care what she thought of me; I just wanted to drink my beer and not be trampled. I went up to her table. "I'm Keith Morrow, Ms. Carvajal," I said, "and I can't seem to find a place to drink my beer. Would you mind if I shared your table? I promise I'm not trying to pick you up."

I thought she was going to say no. Actually, I thought she was going to tell me to get the hell out of there. She frowned—but then seemed to decide that one unpleasant scene a night was enough.

"Go ahead," she said, and looked sullenly at her empty glass.

I thanked her and sat down. I sipped my beer and tried to project an amiable silence. Then the waitress came by, and I ordered another beer. Out of politeness, I looked at our Vice-President. "Ms. Carvajal? Another glass?" I asked.

She hesitated, then nodded. "White wine," she said. There followed a split-second pause, then she made a disgusted face and said, "No, wait. I really loathe white wine, but you're expected to drink it, you know? Bring me a shot of tequila with salt and lime."

She thrust her glass at the waitress and sat back in her chair. When the drink arrived, she dipped the lime in salt, took a king-sized bite of it, and downed half the tequila. I decided I liked her, and that she might even be approachable.

I'd glimpsed her at the company earlier in the day, and had thought her a striking woman. Now, looking at her close up, I was enthralled. It wasn't that she was beautiful. In fact, as I sized her up, I thought she would have been downright plain except for the way she dressed, the way she carried

herself, and something about her eyes. But she was one of those women
for whom the whole is far greater than the sum of its parts.

She had olive skin as smooth as marble, and dark, penetrating eyes. Her
hair was long, dark, expensively streaked, and pulled back in a woman
executive's bun. This set off her high, arched nose, so that the whole effect
was regal, something like a haughty Spanish grande dame who had just
walked straight out of a Velázquez. She was dressed in a dark suit, exqui-
sitely tailored; even my unpracticed eye could see that it was the finest
money could buy. In her ears she wore two diamond studs, and in the
lapel of her suit a diamond stickpin; they were a full carat each if they
were anything. I had no doubt whatsoever they were real.

"What do you think of the company?" I asked. God, I thought to
myself, how banal I sounded.

"I can tell you what I think of its President," she replied. "He's a creep.
Do you know what he did? Here it is, my first day on the job, and he
invited me out for a drink and propositioned me."

"Looked to me like you put him in his place."

"I did," she said. "What does he think I am, stupid or something? Why
should I go to bed with him after I was hired?"

"Hmm," I said.

"I told him it would take one hell of a promotion to get me interested.
If he felt like making me President, I said, perhaps we could discuss it."

"Well. It seemed to shut him up."

She smiled, as if quite proud of herself. When the waitress sailed by, I
ordered us another round. The beer began to warm my toes and loosen me
up a bit, and I fervently hoped the tequila was having a similar effect on
Martha. The more I looked at her, the more I was drawn to her, just like a
fly in a spider's web. She fascinated me. She spoke to forgotten memories
and associations buried deep inside my brain; I wouldn't have left the
table for anything at that point.

She was a hard drinker, with a far greater tolerance than mine. We kept
each other company for another hour, downing beer and tequila, looking
like we were together, so that no one came over to bother us. I sensed that
the day had been hard on her; perhaps it had been some kind of personal
turning point, and she had the shakes, so she wanted to get drunk and
talk. That was fine with me—I wasn't the type to go to singles bars and
pick up women. I was a lot more comfortable, and a lot more interested,

just talking and finding out who they were. Maybe it was my Sixties upbringing, maybe not, but that was my character.

"What do you do at the company?" she asked.

I looked down at my beer. "Nothing exciting. I'm a very minor wheel in the real estate section. I was an English major, you see; my skills are pretty limited."

"Did you start work for the company right after college?"

"No," I said, and sighed in spite of myself. "I got a Master's. William Butler Yeats. Now I'm thirty-three, and I work for a corporation."

"I'm thirty-three also," said Martha.

"And look at you! A Vice-President already. Someday you'll run this company."

Her eyes flashed. "This company, or another. I'll be President."

I felt suddenly uncomfortable, as if a cold wind had entered the bar through an open window. But Martha gave me a quick smile, a most charming smile, and said, "I'd like very much to get out of this city tonight. Will you take me somewhere?"

"What?" I floundered, searching for words. "Where?"

"Out of town." She looked at me, eyes dancing. "Did you go to the University in Austin?"

"Yes, for my Master's."

"Let's go there. Do you remember that little cafe next to campus, the one called Les Frères?"

I nodded.

"It doesn't close until two in the morning. We can be there in three hours. We can sit in the patio under the stars, and look up at the Tower. It will be all lighted up, you know. I think the moon is even out tonight. We can order hot spiced wine and remember how much fun it was to be students."

"You're not talking much like a Vice-President," I said uncertainly.

She smiled. "I'm not a Vice-President again till Monday. Let's go."

"Done," I said. I was a little drunk by then. I pulled out some money, put it on the table, and took her arm. We hurried out to the parking lot, almost perfect strangers, and I led her to my car.

"Oh, my," said Martha when she caught sight of it, "the company's not doing right by you."

"This is Robert," I said. "I will never give him up. He is a 1968 Datsun and he has never once broken down on me. Though I live to afford a

Porsche, I will never forsake Robert. I will restore him, and put him out to pasture in the backyard."

"Executives don't have backyards," she replied; "they have condos."

"But I'm not an executive. At least, not much of one. I'm different." I put her in Robert's passenger seat, got in behind the steering wheel, and fired him up. "Goodbye, Houston," I said, "goodbye, petrochemicals."

"Amen," said Martha.

I turned on the headlights and tore out of the parking lot. "I'm setting the chronometer for 1968, ladies and gentlemen. The voyage will take approximately three hours; please relax and enjoy your trip."

"I haven't heard anyone talk like that since I left school," she said, smiling at me from her side of the car. "You're so much fun."

I felt warm all over. Expansive—here was this compelling woman, sitting beside me in my beat-up old car, drawing words out of me with her smile. I felt wonderful.

"I haven't talked to anyone with imagination since I got my M.B.A.," Martha continued, "and that was eight years ago. I've done nothing but climb the ladder ever since."

"Climb the ladder?" I repeated. "That could be taken a number of ways. What way did you mean it?"

"Why, I meant climbing the corporate ladder, I guess. Getting ahead in life. Achieving. What else could I mean?"

"Climbing the ladder of life. The Ladder."

Martha was silent for a moment. "I can tell we're going to have one of those delightful collegiate conversations," she said at length. "Do go on."

I steered the car onto Highway 290, toward Austin, youth, and adventure. I pushed hard on the accelerator, got old Robert up to sixty, and kept him there.

"Let me tell you a funny story," I said. "One day about twenty years ago my father was browsing through an old thrift shop in Mineral Wells, where I grew up. He came upon a pile of scrapbooks someone had kept, about an eccentric Texas oilman named J. Edgar Davis. He'd been a big gun in the Twenties, and had spent a million dollars to keep a play on Broadway called *The Ladder*. It was about reincarnation."

I heard Martha draw in her breath suddenly. "And?"

The lights of Houston dimmed behind us. I sat back in my seat, wishing Robert had cruise control, and contemplated the next three hours with great relish. "Davis was my kind of guy," I said. "He really believed in that play, even though nobody went to it. It was free, you see—he wanted to get the message across that bad. But even so, hardly anybody went to it."

"Do you believe in reincarnation?" There was a sharp note to Martha's question; she was not just making conversation.

"Oh, it's fun to think about," I said. "Do you?"

"I'm not sure."

I glanced over at her. One thing was very clear: she had said she wasn't sure in the exact tone of voice of one who is very sure—but is afraid to admit it.

"You want to hear a story?" I asked.

"Oh, yes," she said quickly. She flashed those eyes at me again, and I practically fell over myself getting the words out of my mouth.

"This happened to me in college. It just about made me believe in reincarnation—in fact, I think that's the only explanation for what happened."

"Tell," said Martha, her voice soft and caressing, and I launched into my tale.

The story takes place in a town called Burwell. It's in North Texas just a few miles shy of the Oklahoma border, too far from Dallas for much civilization to rub off. At one time, however, it was called "The Athens of Texas."

I went to a little college there, one founded just after the Civil War, named Barker College. It was what passed for snooty in North Texas. Barker was the place rich people sent their kids to keep them from running wild at the University down in Austin. Consequently, if you weren't rich you didn't count at Barker, even if you went there on scholarship the way I did.

I started there in 1970, when we had about a dozen hard-core hippies on campus. They made life bearable to me, since I wasn't about to pledge one of the local frats. My friends and I were very close—we studied together, ate together, did everything together. Outside our group, we had no friends at Barker.

To give you an idea what the place was like, chapel was still mandatory on Sundays when I went there. No alcohol was allowed, and sex on campus was strictly forbidden. If you got caught, the boy was suspended for a week and the girl was expelled for good. Even so, people tried it—once they even caught a couple going at it in the chapel, and after that, some other people in a tree outside the choir robing room. I thought it was pretty repressive, but most of the students were pretty repressed, and didn't find it so unreasonable at all.

There was a rule you had to live on campus, but my friends and I were pretty resourceful. Most of us found sympathetic doctors and told them about the college busting the couple having sex in the tree. After that, the doctors would write the college a letter telling them why we couldn't deal with living on campus in a dorm—for medical reasons, of course. At that point, we pooled our money and looked around town for a house to rent.

We finally lucked into a house just a few blocks from campus. It was the old Cavender house, built around the turn of the century by a man who had been President of the college from 1910 until 1930. He'd left it to his daughter, a maiden lady who had died the past summer, and the house was finally up for rent.

It had fifteen rooms, and we got it for the grand total of one hundred and twenty dollars per month. We got it so cheap for two reasons, one of which was that the real estate management company had no intention of fixing it up, since they wanted to sell it off as quickly as possible. However, the second reason was downright sinister, and we only found out about it after we'd moved into the house.

In 1930, Burwell was the scene of one of the last lynchings in Texas. Even in the Seventies Burwell was a tiny, narrow-minded, shuttered sort of town—you can imagine what it was like in the early part of the century. I never figured out what the hell it was doing in Texas. It wasn't a frontier town; it was southern Gothic, straight out of the backwoods of Louisiana or Alabama. Even by the Sixties, the blacks still lived on one side of town and stayed poor, while the whites lived on the other side and pretended they didn't exist.

Well, in 1930, as I said, there was a lynching in Burwell. It took place May 10, and made the New York *Times* and the London *Daily Mail*. A black man named George Hughes was accused of attacking a white woman and imprisoned in a steel-and-cement vault in the county courthouse while awaiting trial. A rumor got out that he had been spirited away and taken to the county jail, and a mob then formed and attacked the jail. When they found Hughes was not there, they advanced on the courthouse. They dynamited the walls, and used acetylene torches and even more dynamite to shatter the steel vault to get Hughes. This was all in spite of the National Guard, the Texas Rangers, and miscellaneous state troops. Around midnight they got into the vault, tied Hughes up, and put him in the back of a pickup truck. Then they had a parade. They drove all over the town, passed through the Negro quarter, and strung Hughes up in a tree in front of the Cavender house. When he was dead, they returned to the quarter and burned all the stores and homes in a three-block radius.

Why the Cavender house? Well, the local men and women disliked and distrusted the college—that's common enough. But Cavender, the President, was a man with beliefs years ahead of his time. He was a very humane sort of man—liberal, dignified, one of those nineteenth-century Americans who spoke out for his fellow man, in this case his fellow black man. The locals hated Cavender in particular, and so they fixed him, by leaving Hughes's body strung up in his front yard.

"Is this true?" Martha demanded. "I've never heard a whisper of this story, and I've lived in this state all my life."

The lights of a car whizzed past us; I kept Robert going sixty, heading west. "It's all true," I replied. "Now, understand one thing. I'm not saying every white person in Burwell was evil, nor every black man a saint. I'm not even saying that no black man from Burwell ever attacked a white woman. But one thing was true: in those days if you were black, and you got caught in a dubious-looking situation, no one stopped to ask questions. You had to have a death wish to so much as speak ugly to a white woman. In George's case, he was in the wrong place at the wrong time, and with the wrong white man for a friend. I happen to know he didn't do it."

"How?"

"I heard him say so." I stretched, settled back in the car seat, and went on with the story.

So all of us moved into the Cavender house, which we got for cheap because no one local wanted to live in it. There were at least a dozen of us, but the only one of my friends you should know about was Mike Donnell.

Mike was what people meant by white trash—or he should have been. He came from Texarkana, from nowhere, and had no family except for a father who was a drunk. Mike mentioned his father three times in the years I knew him, each time with loathing.

Mike was tall, skinny, and had a chest caved in like a cereal bowl. His face was sort of pinched, and there was a sickly white cast to his skin, as if he'd never gotten much to eat besides biscuits and grits when he was a kid. He came from the kind of people who are bigots because, that way, they have somebody to look down on—otherwise they'd be on the bottom of the heap.

But Mike wasn't like that. He got through high school in Texarkana with pretty decent grades. Right after, he enlisted and went to Vietnam. He survived that, too, and used to make people real mad by saying it was because he didn't get stoned all the time he was over there. When his army time was up, he came back to the States and took his college boards. To everyone's surprise, he scored very high, and when he applied to Barker they accepted him. He got money from the government, as well as a soldier's scholarship from some super-patriotic Barker alum, and so he managed to scrape by and get through college.

Anyone could have predicted he'd join our group, he was so different from the complacent, well-heeled little boys and girls who made up the rest of the student body. He was twenty-three years old by that time, older than the other students, and he had lousy clothes, no car, and no money. But he didn't let it bother him. He was set on being a lawyer, and Barker was famous for getting its pre-laws into good schools. Barker was his ticket out of Texarkana forever, so he just put his head down, worked, and ignored the scornful children around him.

He got approval to live off campus because of his time in 'Nam. He moved into the Cavender house with the rest of us. Months went by, then semesters, then years. You know how it goes. We became best friends, and had endless midnight talks over beer and grass, dreaming, raging, wondering—the way you do when you're young and the world's still fresh.

We talked a lot about reincarnation. Mike had seen some gruesome things in Vietnam, but instead of flipping out over them like some people did, he looked for an explanation. He rejected Christian mythology and began to study the Eastern religions and philosophies. At last he settled on reincarnation as the answer.

He thought it would explain a lot of things, particularly the suffering of innocent people. He also thought it explained his own birth, and his struggles through life. Mike saw the whole of one's existence as a Ladder, each rung representing a life, up which a soul had to climb to reach perfection. He suspected that he had misused money and power in his last life, so that he had fallen many rungs on the Ladder, and was born a poor-white in Texarkana to learn his lesson over.

I didn't buy that at all. Mike was a good man, through and through. I thought he'd done well in his past lives, and that he was undergoing some obscure test of strength and endurance. If there was ever a soul high up on the Ladder, it was Mike.

We used to sit for hours and try to figure out who different people had been in past lives—and, of course, who we were. Mike had a theory that the intervals between successive incarnations were infinitesimal, so that when someone died, the soul passed at once into the body of a child just being born.

We were approaching Brenham. Houston now lay far behind us, and Austin was practically over the hill.

"Are you thirsty?" I asked Martha. "Let's stop at an icehouse and pick up some beer."

"Icehouse," she echoed, and laughed out loud. "That's surely one of your old incarnations speaking."

We pulled into a store beside the highway, bought a six-pack of Shiner longnecks, and drank the first two.

"So," said Martha, "the soul enters a child's body at the moment it's born?" She turned her head and looked at me, her eyes glittering as if the idea had caught hold of her.

I took a swig of my beer. "Yeah," I said, feeling strangely uncomfortable.

Now we come to the strange part of the story. You see, there was a black caretaker named Lamont who literally came with the Cavender house. He had worked for old Miss Cavender all his life, and when she died, it turned out that her will not only gave him a stipend for life, but required that he be kept on as caretaker of the house until his death, if he so desired. That was another reason no one would buy the house.

We always thought of Lamont as old, even though he was only forty when we moved into the house. His hair was already grizzled, and he walked in a slow, stooped-over fashion. He talked to himself all the time he worked in the yard or in the house. You could chat with him for a few minutes, if he was having a good day, but all the while you got the feeling he was distracted. It was as if his mind were somewhere else, as if he were listening to something you couldn't hear.

After Miss Cavender died, various people in the town offered Lamont other jobs, and the current President of the college tried to get him into a job-training program in the next county. But Lamont had no intention of leaving the house. He stayed, and helped perpetrate an amusing spectacle: an old, decaying house full of hippies, surrounded by immaculate grounds and handsome gardens.

The oddest thing of all was how Lamont took tender care of a certain tree in the front yard, a great old bay tree older than the house. You could never speak to him when he was tending the tree. I tried, once, when he was raking leaves underneath it, but he never saw me, he was so busy talking to the tree. He stroked its trunk, mumbling all the while. "It wasn't your fault," he said, again and again. "You couldn't help it. A nice May morning, all pretty and green. You had birds in your branches. You were just standing there, and look what they did to you."

Here's what made it all so weird. Lamont's mother had also worked for the Cavenders her entire life. George Hughes wasn't Lamont's father, now; but the mother was carrying Lamont and was due to deliver that day in 1930 when George was lynched. She saw the mob come up to the house. She stood in the front parlor and saw them string Hughes up to the bay tree, and the sight shocked her so much it sent her into labor. Lamont was born, as far as anyone could tell, at the instant Hughes died.

Of course, the locals blamed Lamont's craziness on the lynching. They said it had marked him in the womb. Mike Donnell, on the other hand, had a different explanation.

He had a theory about crazy people. He said the progression of the soul from one incarnation to another is supposed to be quiet and orderly. The soul is not supposed to keep any of the knowledge and memories of its previous incarnation. If it had learned the lesson of that life and climbed another rung on the Ladder, it was now made of finer fiber than before; for growth in the next incarnation to mean anything, the soul must start life afresh. But sometimes the soul of a dying man is so outraged that it won't let go of the past. It tries to make its next incarnation an extension of the previous one. The result is a kind of madness. The soul cannot develop and grow as it should, under the shadows carried forward from the last incarnation. But neither can it avenge or come to grips with whatever wrong took place then, for when it passed into a new body it was bound to leave all that behind, and broke the laws that govern such passage when it did not do so. The person is split in two; he is forever at war with himself. The madness may in fact be very mild, as in the case of a man who has tormenting dreams that in fact have followed him from an earlier life. Or it may be disabling, as in the case of Lamont.

In short, Mike thought Lamont was really George Hughes. To Mike, the whole thing was as obvious as the result of a laboratory experiment.

We topped a hill, and there, on the horizon, were the lights of Austin. "Almost there," I said to Martha.

"I haven't seen Les Frères in years," she said, and stretched. "With any luck we can park close. Aren't the students all tied up with finals now?"

"I think so."

"It's still cold enough so the cafe won't be crowded—not the patio, at any rate. Only the Marxists with their little beards and heavy coats will be out, smoking cigarettes and drinking that good coffee you can buy at Les Frères. We should have no trouble finding a table."

I nodded. "And now," I said, "for the finale."

Graduation arrived. In a sentimental moment, Mike even telephoned his father in Texarkana and told him about it. I was in the living room when Mike called him, and gathered his father was pretty drunk on the other end of the line; I was flabbergasted, therefore, when his father not only remembered the conversation but showed up at the Cavender house a few days later.

Ray Donnell was sixty-five years old and looked seventy-five. Bloodshot eyes, day-old stubble on his chin, a weathered, suspicious face—he was the picture of backwater trash. He looked mean, too. You could tell from one look at him that he'd spent a lifetime drinking hard and getting in fights. In fact, he'd been drinking by the time he showed up at the house, and it had put him in a surly mood.

He and Mike sat on the porch and talked for about an hour. Ray had a pint bottle in a paper sack and sipped at it steadily the whole time. I was in the front parlor reading in one of the window seats, and since it was May and the windows were open, I could hear them talking. Their conversation was forced and artificial; Mike asked his father stilted questions about people he hadn't seen in ten years, and his father made gibing comments about the college and the students he saw pass by. He had a lot to say about the girls in their bell-bottom jeans and halter tops, more even than about the boys with long hair.

Along about four o'clock I heard the back door slam, and I knew Lamont had come back from shopping. I heard him put packages on the kitchen table; then his footsteps approached and I saw him enter the parlor, an amiable, dreamy look on his face.

Then he came to an abrupt halt. His eyes widened; the strangest look came over his face. I said hello, but he didn't seem to hear me.

He walked to the window seat and looked out at the porch. "Who's that man?" he demanded.

I told him. Lamont didn't reply, but stood staring through the open window as if hypnotized.

Outside, I heard Mike ask his father a question. "Where are you planning on staying, Dad?"

"I thought I'd stay here. I don't have money to throw around like you college kids. What's the matter, ain't I welcome?"

"I can't do that, Dad. All the rooms in the house are taken, even the ones that weren't originally bedrooms."

I heard Ray give a gravelly-sounding laugh. "Just put me in with one of those little college girls. The way they walk around here, I can tell they'd like it."

There was a pause. "You'd better go, Dad," said Mike.

Ray cursed, and there was a shattering sound as he threw his pint bottle on the porch. A chair scraped; I looked out of the window again and saw the older man grab his son and slam him up against the wall of the house. Mike gasped as the breath went out of him. Then I saw him duck, as something bright and shining flashed in Ray's hand.

I froze. "He's got a knife," I said. "He can't use it on Mike—"

Behind me, an unfamiliar voice spoke. "Ray Donnell will do anything," it said.

I whirled. Lamont stood there—or rather, Lamont's body—but someone alien looked out of his dark eyes. The fumbling, distracted creature that was Lamont was gone, and in its place was a cold, inexorable spirit. It crossed to the parlor fireplace and picked up a poker.

"Lamont, what are you doing?" I cried, though I knew perfectly well.

"Get out of my way. I'm going to kill him."

"No, stop. He's drunk—Mike can get away from him."

Lamont stopped, turned, and looked right at me. "Don't you understand? I've got to pay him back for what he did to me. And I can't let Mike get hurt."

With that, he banged open the screen door and stood staring at the father and son. Ray froze. He turned away from Mike and faced Lamont, the beginnings of a grin playing about his lips.

"Well, come on, nigger," he crooned. "Butt in and see what you get."

"Lamont, no!" cried Mike. "He fights dirty. Get away."

"I know how he fights. I saved his neck more than once."

"I've never seen you before in my life," Ray sneered. He waved the knife. "Come on, boy, come and get it."

They fenced. Lamont swung the poker, and Donnell jumped back so that it whistled harmlessly through the air. He laughed, and taunted Lamont.

But whatever possessed Lamont was clever. It forced Donnell to jump away from the poker once more, and then, before Donnell could recover his balance, brought the poker up to connect with his knife hand. Blood sparkled red there as the knife flew onto the front lawn, halfway between the porch and the big bay tree.

"What's this all about?" Donnell's voice was shrill and afraid; that seemed to please the black man.

"We're settling a score," he said.

"What are you talking about?" cried Donnell.

"They strung me up right here," came the answer, "for something you did. You ran away and left me to face it, Donnell."

Donnell looked from Mike to me. "Is he crazy or something?"

"Don't you remember? We picked up a girl downtown, you and me. Or you picked her up, you with that damn fancy roadster. And when she got scared and you hurt her, then she started screaming and ran away— remember? You took off and left me to take the blame. They blew up their own courthouse to get at me. They paraded me all over town like I was some wild animal. When they got tired of that, they strung me up in that tree standing yonder. Don't you remember George Hughes, Donnell? Now I'm going to make you pay for it."

He took a step toward Donnell, who pressed back against the porch railing.

"I didn't do nothing she didn't ask for," said Donnell, talking very fast. "You saw her—just like these college girls with their dugs hanging out. Everybody in town knew what she was."

"Didn't matter," said Lamont. "She was white, and I was black."

"I didn't know it would happen!"

Lamont shrugged. "Now I'm going to kill you," he stated.

He dropped the poker, as if he knew he no longer needed it. He reached out for Donnell, and for a moment his hands closed around the white man's throat. Donnell let out a shriek, and then his legs let go, and he fell to the porch without another sound.

I knew he was dead. Mike stood there for a moment, looking stunned, and then crossed the porch to the black man's side. I looked at the two of them; as I watched, the purpose left Lamont's eyes, the hate flickered, died, and went out, and the old, familiar clouded look crept back into his face. For a moment Lamont seemed to be listening to a voice no one else could hear. Then his face went blank as a sheet of new paper.

"Don't worry," said Mike, putting an arm around him, "I won't let them hurt you. He just dropped dead—his heart was bad, that's what I'll tell them."

Lamont looked down at the body on the floor with a complete lack of recognition. "Who's that?" he asked. "What happened to him?"

Mike and I just looked at Lamont, speechless.

Lamont looked from Mike to me. "Who are you boys?"

The police came, of course, and turned the body over to the county morgue, where it was decided that Donnell had died of heart failure. Mike remained stoic through the rest of the incident; I guessed he was afraid to show any emotion, for fear others would realize how thankful he was his father was dead.

As for Lamont, he had no memory left at all. He could still speak English, of course, and he understood what people said to him, but past that he was like a newborn baby, starting life over. For forty-four years he had lived in the shadow of the wrong done to him in 1930. Now that shadow was gone, and he was free to start living the new life that should have been his so many years before.

We left the freeway, exiting onto the far north end of Guadalupe Street. We headed south toward the University area. There was a chill in the air, as it was getting on toward the end of the year, and the warm yellow streetlights that lined Guadalupe were comforting after our long drive through the black Texas landscape.

I turned onto Twenty-fourth Street and parked the car a few blocks down from the cafe. We walked there and found a table outside with no trouble at all, just as Martha had predicted.

"Hot spiced wine is what I'll have," she said, shivering a little, "with hot tea on the side."

I ordered for both of us.

Martha leaned forward across the table, looking at me intently. "So," she said, "do you believe it all?"

I hesitated; I chose my words carefully. "Let's just say that the whole incident scared me. I stopped thinking about reincarnation so much—I was afraid I really would start to believe in it."

"Didn't you ever wonder who you might be?"

I couldn't keep looking at her eyes. I lowered my face, and toyed with the hot wine the waitress had just placed in front of me. I shrugged, and tried to sound offhand. "Sure."

"Who was Mike?"

"Mike was older than the rest of us, remember, Martha? I was born in '52, but he was born earlier, toward the end of the war. I admit we tried to match up his birth date with certain—deaths—but we never had any luck. A lot of people were dying back then."

"What does he do now?"

"He went on to law school. He worked for Nader's Raiders a while. Now he's an anti-nuke activist in Washington, and from what I hear, pretty influential."

"Still fighting a war," she said softly. The streetlight glinted in her eyes; I knew what she was going to ask. "Who are you?"

"I really don't know," I said, a bit too loudly. It was the truth. I'd tried to find out once, but I got scared and quit. "I've got my quirks, Martha . . . maybe they're holdovers from my last incarnation. I don't know."

"Like what?"

"I hate crowds. Put me downtown in a street full of people and I break out in a cold sweat."

"Claustrophobia."

"No! I love to be inside—the smaller the room, the better. I feel safe there. It's the wide-open spaces I can't stand, not when they're full of people."

She considered. "Have you ever felt drawn to a place, or perhaps a person? Felt like a power outside yourself was pulling you to them?"

I'd had lots to drink. "Yes," I said. "You."

Her eyes bored into mine. "Perhaps our lives were somehow connected —once."

The gooseflesh stood out all over my body, and I could not reply.

She leaned forward. "Tell me, Keith. Are you convinced that the soul passes into a child's body at the moment that child is born—not at the moment of conception? That if you can pinpoint the death of one and the birth of another at a single instant, you can be sure they are the same person?"

I nodded. "That's what Mike thought."

"Because I always suspected it worked that way, Keith. If we're right, then I think I know who I was the last time around."

She seemed to believe every word she was saying, and I felt myself shiver. I was afraid I'd believe it, too. "Who were you?" I asked.

"Evita. Eva Perón."

I gave a start. I almost laughed out loud as relief swept over me. It sounded so grandiose, so pompous, that I couldn't take it seriously. Then I looked into her eyes again. Suddenly everything I had learned about her that night fell into place, suddenly the idea wasn't nearly so preposterous.

"What makes you think so?"

"Why, I was born at the precise moment she died. July 26, 1952, at five thirty-five in the afternoon. Central Standard Time, of course. That's eight-thirty at night in Buenos Aires."

I shivered again. Suddenly I couldn't breathe. I felt as if some smothering realization were about to dawn on me. I wanted to run away.

She opened her purse and put a bill on the table. "Come across the street with me to the library," she said. "It should be open, if it's finals time. I'll show you pictures."

She stood up. "No, let's don't," I said.

"Why not?"

I stood up, too. "I was born just one day after you, Martha. I don't want to find out any more."

She gave me a measuring, penetrating look. "Don't be a coward."

It was an order. I followed her out of the cafe, shamefaced and meek, feeling as if I'd followed along in the wake of her life many times before.

We didn't speak until we reached the library and found, buried in the stacks, bound volumes of magazines from that not so distant time. She pulled out copies of *Life, Time,* and *Newsweek;* as she opened them, I tried not to look but I couldn't help myself.

I'd heard of Eva Perón. I'd seen pictures of her once or twice before, but I really hadn't paid much attention to them. Now as Martha turned page after page, I drank them in. I began to remember; I lost touch with the library around me.

I am standing in a rainstorm in the middle of Buenos Aires, hearing a mass for her recovery. I worship Evita, and she is dying, and I am weeping as I stand there wet and miserable. Every man, woman, and child in the street is joined together in prayer, and I keep hoping that somehow, some way, Our Lord will turn away his hand from her.

Now it is dark. The streets are still filled with rain. Great crowds of her *descamisados*, her beloved peasants, keep vigil around me. Women are weeping, and around me some people are kneeling in prayer on the rain-soaked pavement.

Then we hear, at last, that she is dead. A hush falls over the crowd; some leave the plaza to grieve in solitude at home, others stay through the night to be near her and mourn.

The next day, I hear they have taken her body to the Ministry of Labor to lie in state. They have given her a white mahogany casket with a glass cover, so that we can see her, and put the casket on a bier blanketed with white orchids. They cannot bury her for days; endless lines of mourners come from all over Argentina to file past her, and outside the Ministry of Labor, the street around the statue of Julio Argentino Roca is covered with flowers.

I hear she is to be buried August 10. When the news is announced, the people go wild with grief. They fling themselves onto her casket and try to kiss her through the glass, they scream, they forget themselves.

The army has been called out, for the government fears it cannot maintain order. *Colabore con la policía,* proclaim signs at every street corner, but no one pays attention. They are crazy with grief.

At last I make up my mind to go home. She is dead, and there is no more that I can do. But I cannot move. I am hemmed in on every side by people. Everywhere I turn, there are people and more people.

Someone shoves someone else, and there is a scream. I tense, fearful that the mob will stampede. All around, the police and the army are shouting for order, for quiet, but no one pays attention. It happens then: the mob begins to move like a great animal. I run with it. Ahead of me, an old woman slips and falls; pressed on by the sea of flesh, I cannot stop. I fall, too, and go under. The mob sweeps over us with scarcely a ripple, grinds us under its many feet, and moves on.

I came back to myself. Somehow I was sitting in a library chair, a magazine before me open to a picture of the plaza where I had died. The memories faded as the moments passed—I could no more hold on to them than I could bring back a dream once I had woken. All that remained were the feet crushing me into the Argentine pavement—that, and the cold, sticky sweat that had broken out across my body. I never knew just who I had been; all that stayed with me was my death.

My eyes focused on a paragraph in the middle of the page. "Several persons were trampled to death," it read, "thousands injured in wild demonstrations of grief. The army had to be called out to help the police maintain order. Flowers covered the street, piled up against the walls of the building . . . flowers had to be flown in from as far away as Chile."

But there had been no flowers for me. I closed the volume and got to my feet, sickened. "I believe you," I said to Martha. "Now let's go back to Houston."

She protested, of course. She had hoped I would amuse her that weekend, and she could not really empathize with the feelings that were sweeping through me now.

After what I'd just been through, I couldn't have touched her. We went back to the city. I remained her loyal supporter for the next five years, working for her, loving her always from a distance, putting my department at her disposal.

At last she challenged Rod for control of the company. She lost and was thrown out; in the purge that followed, so was I. You might say that, once again, I was trampled following her demise. But in this incarnation she weathered such setbacks as well as she ever had in Argentina—and this time she did not fall ill and die. She found another, smaller company, rose to the top in a matter of months, and within another five years had swallowed Rod's business whole. He went back to India.

I didn't ask her for a job. I had learned by then that I wasn't cut out for her world at all.

I don't make much money nowadays. I live in Austin and teach a free-lance course in English poetry at a little community college there, and of course I write, too. I try to keep my mind open in the hope I'll remember my life in a certain Latin American country. I always think that if I try hard enough, then someday, somehow, the memories will come back and I will make my peace with them.

Scientists have been among the most enthusiastic readers of science fiction since the genre began, and that's not at all surprising, for sf speculates about the kinds of knowledge we may gain in the future. Non-scientists are fascinated enough to read about such things; scientists themselves actually spend their lives working on new discoveries, so we may assume that their interest is even higher. Here's a story about such a man, a physicist, and the hard choice he had to make because of his passion for knowledge.

Jack McDevitt's stories have been appearing in sf magazines for the past few years, and he has quickly established himself as a writer of great skill: one of his first stories, "Cryptic," was nominated for the Nebula Award in 1984. A novel is forthcoming.

TIDAL EFFECTS

JACK McDEVITT

"I never walk on the beach anymore." The physicist, Gambini, stood near the window, looking out across the illuminated lawns of the Seaside Condo. Rain sparkled in the flood lamps. The Atlantic was hidden by a screen of poplars; but the two men could hear its sullen roar. "During that summer," he continued, "while we waited for the launch, and expected so much, I went out every evening. I was too excited to work."

Harmon rotated his wine between thumb and forefinger, but said nothing.

Headlights flickered across Gambini's rigid features. "I grew up in a small town in Ohio, and I was in high school before I ever saw an ocean. But I can still remember the first time. I've loved the Atlantic ever since." He gazed thoughtfully through the rain-streaked window. "Even now."

Harmon drained his glass and surveyed the room. It was oppressive: heavy, drab furniture; bulging bookcases; neutral, steely colors everywhere. A computer terminal beside a recliner trailed several feet of printout. "I know you're surprised to see me," he said apologetically. "But I had to come."

Gambini moved away from the drapes, back into the yellow light of an ugly seashell table lamp. A shapeless gray sweater hung from his thin shoulders. "I knew that eventually you would," he said.

Harmon held out his glass. Gambini filled it, and his own. They were drinking port, a vintage bottle that the physicist had been saving for a special occasion. "It must be a magnificent time for you," Harmon said, "now that the data has begun to come in. There seems so little that you and your colleagues have not touched. Perhaps, in the end, only the Creation itself will prove elusive."

"Ah," said Gambini, brightening, "we have some ideas about that."

"I'm not surprised. What does Tennyson say? *To pursue knowledge like a sinking star.*"

"Sometimes," observed Gambini, "the price is high."

"You are thinking of the beach again?" He watched the physicist circle the coffee table and settle stiffly into a wingback chair. "You did what you could," he said.

A gust of wind blew the rain hissing against the windows. Outside, somewhere, an automobile engine roared into life. The air smelled of salt and ozone. "How much do you know about Skynet?" Gambini asked.

Harmon shrugged. "Only what I read in the papers."

The lines around Gambini's mouth tightened. "Odd," he remarked. "If it were not for Skynet, you would not be here; there would be no need for this meeting." He laid a peculiar emphasis on the last word. "Skynet," he continued, adapting a professorial tone, "is an array, twenty-two infrared receptors, in Earth orbit. Capable of seeing damn near anything. They were putting it in place last summer. And I was waiting here, as Ryan was at Princeton, Hakluyt at Greenbelt, and others . . ." He set his glass down. It was empty. "We knew that, after it became operational, the world would never be the same again."

"No doubt," said Harmon. "It sounds very important."

Gambini got up and inquired, tolerantly, whether his guest had ever heard of Fred Hoyle.

Harmon's puzzlement was evident. "I don't believe I have," he said impatiently.

Gambini crossed the room and took a thick volume from an upper shelf. "Hoyle," he said, "is best known as a cosmologist, a defender of outworn theories on the nature of the universe itself: what it is, where it came from, where it's going. Trivial matters, really, when contrasted with the question that really absorbed him, that absorbs all of us and knits us together."

"And what," asked Harmon, wondering where all this was leading, "might that be?"

"Simply stated," said Gambini, "it is this: With whom do we share the stars? It is a question with the profoundest philosophical implications. It is the great enigma. Shapley never knew. Nor Lowell. Nor Einstein. They grew old with no hope, and went to their graves with no answer."

"And then we got Skynet." Harmon sounded bored. Irritated. Well, thought Gambini, he has a right to be.

"While they were assembling it, during the late summer, we knew that, by Christmas, we would use it to see other solar systems, planetary bodies out to a distance of more than a hundred light-years. We would be able to perform spectroscopic analyses of their atmospheres. My God, Harmon, we could look for oxygen, the infallible mark of life!"

Harmon nodded.

"I neither ate nor slept during those final weeks. They'd already begun testing the system, and success appeared very likely. I gave up trying to read or work."

Harmon examined the Hoyle volume. It was *Galaxies, Nuclei, and Quasars.* "And you," he said, raising his eyes to Gambini's, "walked the beaches."

"Yes. But only at sunset. When the air was cool."

Harmon leaned forward.

"Each evening there was a group of swimmers. Boys. They were young, thirteen perhaps, no more than that. There were three of them usually, sometimes four, and they were always out beyond the breaker line. One in particular . . ."

"Yes," said Harmon, "he was like that." His voice sounded strange.

Gambini seemed not to have heard. "He was taller than the others. Awkward. With light sandy hair." He got up, slowly, and pushed his fists into the pockets of the gray sweater. "The current can be treacherous, and every night they went farther into the sea. I warned them. They weren't local kids. Locals would have known better."

"We were," said Harmon, "from Alexandria."

"I told them it was dangerous." Gambini hesitated. "But that meant nothing to them, of course. They laughed and, if anything, retreated farther beyond the breakers. The tall one, he was almost as tall as I: the night before we lost him, he stood as close to me as you are now, sun-burned, preoccupied, with all his life before him. He was inspecting tidal pools, for stranded guppies, I suppose. He saw me, and smiled self-consciously as though he'd been caught doing something foolish." Gambini's eyes clouded. He fell silent.

"Did he say anything to you?"

"No. We faced each other for a moment. Then he was gone, up the beach with his friends, snapping towels at each other."

For a long time there was only the sound of the sea, and of water dripping into foliage. Harmon's chair creaked. When Gambini spoke again, he was barely audible. "It happened, as I knew it would. Hakluyt had called me that morning to discuss the latest test results, and I was strolling engrossed across the sand. It was cold and damp, after an all-day rain." He glanced accusingly at his visitor. "They should never have been there. But they were.

"The first indication I had that something was wrong came when a fat middle-aged man ran past me. He hurried along the shoreline to join two of the boys, who were standing hip-deep, anxiously watching the sea; beyond them, desperately far out, a head floated over the top of a swell, and arms thrashed.

"One of the boys turned toward me and screamed (though I could not hear him over the roar of the ocean). I looked along the beach for help: the only other person visible was an elderly woman with two dogs.

"I broke into a run, and was already breathing hard before I even got into the water. The boy sank: he was down a long time while I struggled toward him. Then he came up, coughing and choking. I got through the breakers into calmer water and began to swim. The water was cold, and the drag toward the open sea was very strong.

"Although I was moving quickly (assisted by the current), the distance between us shortened only very gradually. The boy's struggles grew weaker, but whenever I thought he was about to go down, he seemed to find new strength.

"I realized quite suddenly that my own life was in danger. I knew I could reach him, and I also knew that we would probably not get back. It was odd; the possibility of my own drowning raised only a single emotion: the stiletto sensation that it was too soon. *By a few weeks, or a few months, it was too soon!*

"And I hated the child!"

Harmon's mouth tightened, but he said nothing.

"He fought stubbornly for his life. Time after time, the sea rolled over him, but he would not stay down. And though the tide pushed me rapidly in his direction, the distance between us did not grow noticeably shorter. And finally, while I lost headway in a swirl of currents, our eyes locked." Gambini's voice had been rising; but now he stopped to refill his glass. His hand shook so violently that Harmon had to help him. "He must have seen something in my face," he continued, "because I read the sudden, swift terror in his as he realized, I think for the first time, what was going to happen. . . ."

"So you turned back," Harmon said, uncertainly. "No one can blame you for that. No one could expect more."

Gambini threw the full glass of port against a wall. "Who are *you*," he demanded, "to make that judgment? I left him to *drown!*"

"No!" Harmon said desperately. "You tried! His life was not thrown away. . . ."

Gambini's eyes were cold. "I did not abandon him," he said, "because I was afraid. I did it because I was curious. I sold his life for some tracings on a few hundred pieces of paper."

(On the veranda below his apartment, they could hear people talking. Someone laughed.)

"I should not have come," said Harmon.

"Is that all you can say?" snapped Gambini. "You're his father."

Harmon rose. His features were calm, but there was something of the drowning boy in his eyes. "What do you want me to tell you, Gambini?" he asked angrily. "That you too should have drowned? That nothing less is decent?"

Gambini slid his fingers under his bifocals and rubbed his eyes. "Why are you here? After all this time."

"I don't know." Harmon exhaled. "I thought they were safe. Out here, away from Alexandria, I didn't think anything could happen. We were always grateful that you tried. I wrote you a letter."

"I know. I threw it away."

"Yes," said Harmon. "Under the circumstances, it must have been painful."

Gambini stared a long time at his visitor. "He was in your care at the time?"

Harmon nodded.

"You are right to feel guilty," he rasped. "Your son and I, we were both your victims." Gambini's smile trembled on his thin lips. "Do you know what we found when we looked beyond the solar system? (No: don't turn away. This concerns your boy.) We examined several thousand stars, Harmon. Of which about a quarter have planets. Most are Jovian in nature: nothing more, really, than enormous sacks of cold hydrogen. It was, of course, the terrestrial worlds in which we were especially interested: those Earthlike planets orbiting stable suns at temperate distances." A nerve near Gambini's jugular had begun to throb. "I assume I need not tell you that we found no oxygen. Oh, there were traces here and there. But everywhere we looked, among the terrestrial worlds, we saw carbon dioxide. In vast quantities. Do you understand what I'm saying, Harmon?"

Harmon's eyes blazed, but he did not reply.

"No biological processes. Anywhere. We'd always assumed that something had gone wrong on Venus, leaving her sterile under a hothouse atmosphere. Some people have made a career of developing explanations for the phenomenon. But Venus, it turns out, is the norm: it's Earth that is the anomaly.

"I believe, Harmon, that we are quite alone."

"You and I and a few others, Gambini." He threw open the door, and whirled to face the physicist. "Despite everything you've said, I believe you tried. I hope that the day will come when you will realize that you could have done no more."

"If you think that," Gambini said, "I will tell you something to remove all doubt: If it were to do over, with a new universe to know, I would do nothing differently! Do you understand that?"

Harmon's features twisted into a murderous frown, and he wondered (at that moment, and for all his life after) what the physicist was trying to provoke.

But Gambini had already turned away. When the door closed behind Harmon, he was standing at the window. It was raining again, and he was grateful for the cloud cover.

Travel and communications have improved so greatly that anthropologists have noted a trend toward homogeneity among the various peoples of the world: more and more tribes and cultures have adopted the ways of others, so that rituals, customs, even languages are rapidly disappearing from our contemporary world. And what about the specialized knowledge that specific peoples lose when they become assimilated into larger societies? Are techniques and age-old discoveries disappearing too?

Avram Davidson, one of the most original stylists and thinkers in science fiction (among several other genres in which he's written), has won both the Hugo Award and the Edgar Award given by the Mystery Writers of America. His most famous novel is The Phoenix and the Mirror; *the long-awaited sequel to that,* Vergil in Averno, *will be published next year by Doubleday.*

THE SLOVO STOVE

AVRAM DAVIDSON

It would have been a little bit hard for Fred Silberman to have said a completely good word for his hometown; "a bunch of boors and bigots," he once described it; and life had carried him many leagues away. However. In Parlour's Ferry lived Silberman's sole surviving aunt, Tanta Pesha; and of Tanta Pesha (actually a great-aunt by marriage) Silberman had only good memories. Thinking very well of himself for doing so, he paid her a visit; as reward—or punishment—he was recognized on the street and almost immediately offered a very good job. Rather ruefully, he accepted, and before he quite knew what was happening, found himself almost a member of the establishment in the town where he had once felt himself almost an outcast.

Okay, he had a new job in a new business; what was next? A new place to live, that was what next. He knew that if he said to his old aunt, "Tanta, I'm going to live at the Hotel"—Parlour's Ferry had one, count them, *one*—she would say, "That's nice." Or, if he were to say, "Tanta, I'm going to live with you," she would say, "That's nice." However. He rather thought that a roomy apartment with a view of the River was what he wanted. Fred developed a picture of it in his mind and, walking along a once long-familiar street, was scarcely surprised to see it there on the other side: the apartment *house*, that is. He hadn't been imagining, he had been remembering, and there was the landlady, sweeping the steps, just as he had last seen her, fifteen years ago, in 1935. He crossed over. She looked up.

"Mrs. Keeley, do you have an apartment to rent? My name is Fred Silberman."

"Oh," she said. *"Oh.* You must be old Jake Silberman's grandson. I reckernize the face."

"Great-nephew."

"I reckernize the face."

The rent was seventy-five dollars a month, the painters would come right in, and Mrs. Keeley was very glad to have Nice People living there. Which was very interesting, because the last time Silberman had entered the house (Peter Touey, who used to live upstairs, had said, "Come on over after school; I got a book with war pictures in it") Mrs. Keeley had barred the way: *"You* don't live here," said she. Well. Times had changed. Had times changed? *Some*thing had certainly changed.

The building where the new job would be lay behind where the old livery stable had been; Silberman had of course already seen it, but he thought he would go and see it again. The wonderful dignified old blue-gray thick flagstones still paved most of the sidewalks on these unfashionable streets, where modernity in the form of dirty cracked concrete had yet to intrude; admiring them, he heard someone call, "Freddy! Freddy?" and, turning in surprise, almost at once recognized an old schoolmate.

"Aren't you Freddy Silberman? I'm Wesley Brakk. We still live here." They rambled on a while, mentioned where each had been in the War, catalogued some common friends, then Wesley said, "Well, come on into the house, we're holding my father's *gromzil,*" or so it sounded; "you don't know what that means, do you? See, my father passed away it's been three years and three months, so for three days we have like open house, it's a Slovo and Huzzuk custom, and everybody has to come in and eat and drink." So they went in.

There were a lot of people in the big old-fashioned kitchen at the end of the hall; the air was filled with savory smells, the stove was covered with pots—*big* pots, too. One of the older women asked something in a foreign language; im*med*iately a younger man snapped, "Oh for Crise sake! Speak

United States!" He had a dark and glowering face. His name, Fred learned, was *Nick*. And he was a relative.

"This is beef stomach stuffed with salami and hard-boiled eggs," said a woman. "Watch out, I'll pick away the string."

"You gonna *eat* that stuff?" asked Nick. "*You* don't hafta eat that stuff; I'll getcha a hamburger from Ma's Lunch."

Ma's Lunch! And its french-fried grease! And *Ma*, with frowsy pores that tainted the ambient air. "Thanks, Nick, this is fine," said Fred.

Nick shrugged. And the talk flowed on.

By and by a sudden silence fell and there was a tiny sound from forward in the house. "Aintcha gonna feed the *baby*, f'Crise sake?" cried Nick. His wife struggled to rise from a chair crowded behind the table, but "old Mrs. Brakk," who was either Wes's mother or Wes's aunt, gestured her not to; "*I* will do," said she. And produced a baby bottle and a saucepan and filled the pan at the sink. There was a movement as though to take one of the heavy cook pots off the stove to make room to warm the bottle, but the dowager Mrs. Brakk said a word or two, and this was not done. Perhaps only Fred noticed that she moved toward a small pile of baby clothes and diapers in a niche, as though she wanted to bring them with her, but Fred noticed also that her hands were full. So he picked them up and indicated that he would follow.

"Thank you, gentleman," she said. She gave him, next, an odd glance, almost as though she had a secret, of which she was very well aware and he was utterly ignorant. Odd, yes; what was it? Oh well.

In her room, "You never see a Slovo stove," Mrs. Brakk said. It was not a question. It was a fact. Until that moment he had never *heard* of a Slovo stove. Now he gave it a glance, but it was not interesting, so he looked away; then he looked back down at it. Resting on a piece of wood, just an ordinary piece of wood, was a sort of rack cut from a large tin can, evidently not itself brought from Europe by whichever Slovo brought the stove. On top of the rack was something black, about the length and width of a book, but thinner. Stone? Tentatively he touched a finger to it. Stone . . . or some stonelike composition. It felt faintly greasy.

"You got to put the black one on first," Mrs. Brakk said. However glossy black the old woman's hair, wrinkled was her dark face. She put on the saucepan of water and put the baby's nursing bottle in the pan. "Then the pot and water. *Then* you slide, underneath, the blue one." This, "the blue one," was about the size and thickness of a magazine, and a faint pale blue. Both blue and black pieces showed fracture marks. As she slid "the blue one" into the rack, Mrs. Brakk said, "Used to be *bigger*. Both. *Oh* yeah. Used to could cook a whole meal. Now, only room for a liddle sorcepan; sometimes I make a tea when too tired to go in kitchen."

Fred had the impression that the black piece was faintly warm; moving his finger to the lower piece (a few empty inches were between the two), he found that definitely this was cool. And the old woman took up the awakening child and, beaming down, began a series of exotic endearments: "*Yes*, my package; *yes*, my ruby stone; *yes*, my little honey bowl—" A slight vapor seemed to arise from the pan, and old Mrs. Brakk passed into her native language as she crooned on; absolutely, *steam* was coming from the pan. Suddenly Silberman was on his knees, peering at and into the "stove." Moistening a fingertip as he had seen his mother and aunts do with hot irons a million times, he applied it to "the blue piece," below. Mrs. Brakk gave a snort of laughter. The blue piece was still cool. Then he wet the fingertip again and, *very* gingerly, tested the upper "black piece." It was merely warm. *Barely* warm. The *pan?* *Very* warm. But the steam continued to rise, and the air above pan and bottle was . . . well . . . *hot.* Why not?

She said, "You could put, between, some fingers," and, coming over, baby pressed between one arm and bosom, placed the fingers of her free hand in between the upper and lower pieces. He followed her example. It was not hot at all in between; it was not even particularly warm.

Silberman peered here and there, saw nothing more, nothing (certainly) to account for . . . well . . . *any*thing. . . . She, looking at his face, burst out laughing, removed the lower slab of stone (if it was stone), and set it down, seemingly, just anywhere. Then she took the bottle, shook a few drops onto her wrist and a few drops onto Fred *Sil*berman's wrist—oh, it was *warm* all right. And as she fed the baby, calling the grandchild her necklace, her jewel ring, her lovely little sugar bump, he was suddenly aware of two things: one, the bedroom smelled rather like Tanta Pesha's: airless, and echoing faintly with a cuisine owing nothing to either franchised foods or Fanny Farmer's cookbook (even less to *Ma's Lunch!*); two, that his heart was beating very, very fast. He began to speak, heard himself stutter.

"Buh-buh-but h-h-how does it wuh-work? *work?* How—" Old Grandmother Brakk smiled what he would come to think of as her usual faint smile; shrugged. "How do boy and girl love? How does bird fly? How water turn to snow and snow turn to water? How?"

Silberman stuttered, waved his arms and hands; was almost at once in the kitchen; so were two newcomers. He realized that he had long ago seen them a hundred times. And did not know their names, and never had.

"Mr. Grahdy and Mrs. Grahdy," Wesley said. Wes seemed just a bit restless. Mrs. Grahdy had an air of, no other words would do, faded elegance. Mr. Grahdy had an upswept moustache and a grizzled Vandyke beard; he looked as though he had once been a dandy. Not precisely pointing his finger at Fred, but inclining it in Fred's general direction, Mr. Grahdy said, "How I remember your grandfather well! ["Great-uncle."] His horse and wagon! He bought scraps metal and old newspaper. Sometimes sold eggs."

Fred remembered it well, eggs and all. Any other time he would have willingly enough discussed local history and the primeval Silbermans; not now. Gesturing the way he had come, he said, loudly, excitedly, "I never saw anything *like* it before! How does it work, how does it *work?* The—the"—*what* had the old one called it?—*"the Slovo stove?"*

What happened next was more than a surprise; it was an astonishment. The Grahdy couple burst out laughing, and so did the white-haired man in the far corner of the kitchen. *He* called out something in his own language, evidently a question, and even as he spoke he went on chuckling. Mr. and Mrs. Grahdy laughed even harder. One of the Brakk family women tittered. Two of them wore embarrassed smiles. Another let her mouth fall open and her face go blank, and she looked at the ceiling: originally of stamped tin, it had been painted and repainted so many times that the design was almost obscured. There was a hulking man sitting, stooped (had not Fred seen *him,* long ago, with his own horse and wagon —hired, likely, by the day, from the old livery stable—calling out *Ice! Ice!* in the summer, and *Coal! Coal!* in the winter?); he, the tip of his tongue protruding, lowered his head and rolled his eyes around from one person to another. Wesley looked at Silberman expressionlessly. And Nick, his dark face a-smolder, absolutely glared at him. In front of all this, totally unexpected, totally mysterious, Fred felt his excitement flicker and subside.

At length Mr. Grahdy wiped his eyes and said something, was it the same something, was it a different something? was it in Slovo, was it in

Huzzuk? was there a difference, what was the difference? Merry and cheerful, he looked at Fred. Who, having understood nothing, said nothing.

"You don't understand our language, gentleman?"

"No."

"Your grandfather understood our language."

"Yes, but he didn't teach me." Actually, Uncle Jake *had* taught him a few words, but Silberman, on the point of remembering anyway one or two of them, and quoting, decided suddenly not to. Uncle Jake had been of a rather wry and quizzical humor; who knew if the words really meant what Uncle Jake had said they did?

Wes's sister (cousin?) said, perhaps out of politeness, perhaps out of a wish to change the subject, perhaps for some other reason—she said, "Mrs. Grahdy is famous for her reciting. Maybe we can persuade Mrs. Grahdy to recite?"

Mrs. Grahdy was persuaded. First she stood up. She put on a silly face. She put her finger in her mouth. She was a little girl. Her voice was a mimic's voice. She became, successively: hopeful, coy, foolish, lachrymose, cheerful. From the company: a few chuckles, a few titters. Then she stopped playing with her skirts, and, other expressions leaving her face, the corners of her mouth turned down and she looked around the room at everyone. Some exclamations of, supposedly, praise were heard, and a scattered clapping of hands; Mrs. Grahdy silenced all this in a moment. For a second she stood there, poker-faced, stiff. Then she began a rapid recitation in what was obviously verse. Her face was exalted, tragic, outraged, severe: *lots* of things! *How* her arms and hands moved! *How* she peered and scouted! *How* she climbed mountains, swung swords. A voice in Fred's ear said, half whispering, "This is a patriotic poem." Mrs. Grahdy planted the flag on, so to speak, Iwo Jima. Loud cries from the others. *Much* applause. The patriotic poem was evidently over. The downturned mouth was now revealed to be, not the mask of Tragedy, but the disciplined expression of one too polite to grin or smirk at her own success.

After a moment she turned to Silberman. "I know that not one word did you understand, but did the ear inform you the verses were alexandrines?"

He was hardly expecting this, scarcely he knew an alexandrine from an artichoke: and yet. Not pausing to examine his memory or to analyze the reply, he said, "Once I heard a recording of Sarah Bernhardt—" and could have kicked himself; surely she would feel he was taking the mickey out of her? Not at all. All phony "expression" gone, she made him a small curtsy. It was a perfectly done thing, in its little way a very sophisticated thing, an acknowledgment of an acceptable compliment, an exchange between equals. It made him thoughtful.

Grahdy: "So you didn't understand what this Mr. Kabbaltz has asked?" —gesturing to the white-haired man in the far corner. Fred shook his head; if the question dealt with iambic pentameter, he would *plotz*. "This Mr. Kabbaltz has asked, the Slovo stove, you know, 'Did it even get warm yet?' *Hoo, hoo, hoo!*" laughed Mr. Grahdy, Mrs. Grahdy, Mr. Kabbaltz. *Hoo, hoo, hoo!*

Fred decided that ignorance was bliss; he turned his attention to the steaming bowl set before him as the people of the house dished out more food. Soup? Stew? *Pot*tage? He would ask no more questions for the moment. But could he go wrong if he praised the victuals? "Very good. This is very good." He had said, evidently, the right thing. And in the right tone. —It *was* very good.

Mr. Grahdy again: "Your great-grandfather never send you to the Huzzuk-Slovo Center to learn language?"

"No, sir. Not there."

"Then where he did send you?"

"To the Hebrew School, as they called it. To learn the prayers. And the Psalms." Instantly again he saw those massive ancient great thick black letters marching across the page. *Page* after page. A fraction of a second less instantly Mr. Grahdy made the not quite pointing gesture, and declaimed. And paused. And demanded, "What is the second line? Eh?"

Silberman: "Mr. Grahdy, I didn't even understand the *first* line."

Surprise. "What? Not? But it is a *Psalm.*" He pronounced the *p* and he pronounced the *l*. "Of course in Latin. So—?"

"They didn't teach us in Latin."

More surprise. Then, a shake of the head. Silberman thought to cite a Psalm in Hebrew, reviewed the words in his mind, was overcome with doubt. *Was* that a line from a Psalm?—and not, say, the blessing upon seeing an elephant? . . . or something? The Hebrew teacher, a half-mad failed rabbinical student, had not been a man quick with an explanation. "Read," he used to say. *"Read."*

More food was set out: meat, in pastry crust. Then (Mr. Grahdy):

"When you will be here tomorrow? Perhaps I shall bring my *violin*"—he pronounced it vee-*o*-leen—"and play something."

"That would be nice"—Fred, noncommittally; and turning again to the food of the memorial feast, "Delicious!" said Fred.

"Is it warm yet?"—Mr. Grahdy. *Hoo, hoo, hoo!*—Mr. Grahdy, Mrs. Grahdy, Mr. Kabbaltz. People entered, talked, ate, left. Someone: "You're old Jake Silberman's grandson?" "Great-nephew." By and by Fred looked up: Mr. Kabbaltz and the Grahdys were gone. For a moment he heard them just outside the door. Laughing. Footfalls. The gate closed; nobody seemed left but family members. And Fred. Silence. Someone said, "Well, there go the Zunks." Someone else: "Don't call them that. Call them Huzzuks."

Wesley suddenly leaped up, almost toppling his chair. Began to bang his head against the wall. "I can take Chinks!" *Bang.* "I can take Japs!" *Bang.* "I can take Wops, Wasps, Heebs, and Micks!" *Bang. Bang. Bang.*

"Wesley—"

"Wes—"

"Wassyli—"

"Was—"

"I can take Spics and Niggers." *Bang! Bang!* "I can*not* take—Zunks!" *Bang!* Abruptly, he sat down, and held his head.

In Fred's mind: *Question:* So what's a Zunk? *Answer:* A deprecated Huzzuk.

Wes began again. "They can talk Latin. We can hardly grunt. They recite poems. We can barely tell a dirty joke. They have violinists. We are lucky if we got fiddlers. Why did God punish us poor Slovo slobs by putting us in the same country with them, over there in Europe? Why are we still respectful to them, over here in America? Why? Somebody please tell me. *Why?*"

A sister, or maybe a sister-in-law, said, somewhat slowly, "Well . . . they are better educated—"

This set Wes off again. "In *their* dialect, *they* had books, magazines, newspapers. All *we* had was the catechism and the missal, in ours. *They*—"

"*We* had a newspaper. Didn't Papa's brother used to send it to us . . . sometimes? *We*—"

Wesley brushed the invisible ethnic newspaper aside. "The *Patriótsk?* The *Patriótsk.* Came out once a month. One sheet of paper, printed on four pages. What was in it? The new laws, the price of pigs, *some* obituaries, *no* births, and the Saints' Days in both Church calendars: that's *all.* Finish. The *Patriótsk!"* Evidently the invisible newspaper had climbed on the table again, for Wesley swept it off again, and then he trampled on it. Heavily.

"Hey, look at the time. I got to be going. I sure want to thank you for that delicious—"

"We are giving you some to take with you, home," said an aunt. Or was it a niece?

"Oh, I—"

"It's the *cus*tom. And you *liked.*"

"Oh, sure. But my new apartment isn't ready yet, and my aunt is strictly kosher." They didn't say anything ecumenical, neither did they tell him that the Law of Moses was dead and reprobate; they began to put fruit into a paper bag. A *large* paper bag.

But Wes, taking head from hand, was not finished yet. "Why? *Why?* Will someone tell me *why?*"

Someone, surely a sister, too straight-faced to be serious, said, "They are so beautiful; they ride red horses." Wes almost screamed. When had she ever seen a Huzzuk on a horse? When had she ever seen a *red* horse? Nick's wife told Silberman that it was a saying. A proverb.

"Anyway, *you* know, some people say it wasn't the *horse* that was red, but, uh, the things on the horse? What the horse, like, *wore?*" Nick, who had been reading the funny papers with a very unfunny expression, now fired up. Who *gave* a damn? he demanded. Quit *talk*ing about all them old European things, he demanded. Fred announced his thanks for the fruit. Wes asked Nick if he wasn't *in*terested in his rich Old World heritage; Nick, upon whom subtlety was wasted, shouted that *no*, he *was*n't; Wes ceased being subtle and shouted back; Fred Silberman said that he really had to be going. And started out.

Someone came out into the hall and walked along with him: old Mrs. Brakk . . . being very polite, he thought. A dim light was on in her room. She stopped. He paused to say good night. The look she now gave him, had she been forty years younger, would have been an invitation which he knew could not be what she now meant; *what* was it she now meant?

"You want to come in," she said. "You want to see how it works." She moved inside the room. Silberman followed, beginning to breathe heavily, beginning to feel the earlier excitement. He had for*got*ten! How could he have for*got*ten?

"First you put on the black piece, up on here." The book-sized slab slid into its place on the rack. The infant sighed in sleep. "*Yes*, my rope of pearls," she said softly. "Next, you put on the sorcepan with the water in it. Now, I make just a bowl of tea, for me. And so . . . *next* . . . you put in the blue piece," about the size of a magazine, "down . . . *there*. See? This is what we call the Slovo stove. And so now it gets warm. . . ."

What had the old Huzzuks, those quasi-countrymen of the old Slovos, what had they *meant*, "Is it even warm yet?" Silberman forgot the question as he watched the vapors rise, felt the air warm, above; felt the unwarmed space between the two "pieces," the thicker fragment of black stone (if it *was* stone) and the thin fragment of pale blue; saw, astonishingly soon, the size of crabs' eyes, the tiny bubbles form; and, finally, the rolling boil. He was still dazed when she made the tea; he hadn't remembered setting down the bag of fruit, but now he picked it up, set a soft thank-you and good-night, left the house.

He could hear them still shouting in the kitchen.

"That's nice," said Tanta Pesha when he gave her the fruit.

"Tanta, what is it with the Huzzuks and the Slovos?"

Out came the bananas. "The Huzzuks?" She washed the bananas, dried them with a paper towel, dropped it in the garbage. "The Huzzuks. They are all right." Out came the oranges.

"Well, what about the Slovos?"

She washed the oranges. "The Slovos?" She dried the oranges with a paper towel, dropped it in the garbage. "The Slovos? They are very clean. You could eat off their floors. On Saturday night they get drunk," and he waited for more, but no more came: Tanta Pesha was washing the apples. This done, she was overcome by a scruple. "Used to," she said. "Now? I don't know. Since I moved away." How long had she and Uncle Jake lived near the Huzzuks' and Slovos' neighborhood? She began to dry the apples with a paper towel. How long? Forty years, she said.

"Forty years? Forty-two? Let be: forty."

Had she ever heard of the Slovo stove? No . . . she never had.

"Well. Why don't—how come they don't *like* each other?"

Tanta Pesha looked at him a moment. "They *don't?*" she said. She dropped the paper towel in the garbage. Then she put the fruit into a very large bowl and, standing back, looked at it. "That's nice," she said.

The next morning, early, Silberman drove down to the City and made arrangements to be moved, and drove back to "the Ferry." He went to take a look at his apartment-to-be: lo! the painters were actually painting in it. Mrs. Keeley stopped sweeping, to assure him that everything would be ready in a day or two. "Well, a *cup* la days," she amended. "You won't be sorry; this is always been a very nice block, more'n I can say for *some* parts a town, the Element that's moving in nowadays. I give you a very nice icebox, Mr. Silberman."

"Say, thanks, Mrs. Keeley; I really appreciate that. Say, Mrs. Keeley, what's the difference between the Huzzuks and the Slovos?"

Mrs. Keeley shrugged and pursed her lips. "Well, they mostly don't live right around *here*. Mostly they live down around, oh, Tompkins . . . Gerry . . . De Witt. . . . Mostly around there." She adjusted her hairnet.

"But—is there a difference between them? I mean, there's got to be; some are called Huzzuks and some are called Slovos. So there must be a—"

Mrs. Keeley said, well, frankly, she never took no interest in the matter. "Monsignor, up at St. Carol's, that big church on the hill, *he* used ta be a Hozzok, rest his soul. What they tell *me*. Now, your Bosnians, as they call 'um, they mostly live around on Greenville Street, Ashby, St. Lo. The *Lem*kos, whatever the hell *they* are, excuse my French, you find *them* mostly in them liddle streets along by the Creek . . . Ivy, Sumac, Willow, Lily, Rose. Well . . . *use* to. Nowadays . . . nowadays people are moving around, moving *around*," she said, rather fretfully, "and I wish they would-int. I wish people they would stay *put*. So, as t'them people that you ast me about, Hozzoks and Slobos, mostly you find them down around on Tompkins . . . Gerry . . . De Witt . . . *them* streets there. What time is it? Is my program coming on?" She went into her apartment and closed the door behind her. A second later he heard a radio increased in volume. He wandered out into the street.

The streets.

The streets had certainly been wide enough when Uncle Jake's had not been almost the only horse-and-wagon plying for trade along them. But that had been a long time ago. The streets had been full of children then, oh what a merry cheerful sight: you think so? To Fred Silberman as a small child this had been Indian Country, full of hostiles. Oh well. Then, during the Depression, there had been a considerable depopulation. Stores had emptied, and stayed empty, and one of the public schools, "Number Seven," had even closed. However. In the year or two before the War several empty factories had been reopened as Defense Plants, and many new faces had appeared on the streets. Southern Blacks. Island Tans. Mountain Whites. Then Fred had gone off into the Army, and . . . really . . . had only now come back. Coming back out of his revery, he found himself in a time warp.

Gone were the four-story tenements, block after block of them; he was in a neighborhood of wooden houses, *old* wooden houses, old wooden fences, old wooden trees. Right across the street was a store building, a sagging rectangle of boards. Seemingly *just* as he remembered it, even to the raised letters on the glass storefront: SAL DA T A. Untouched by any recent paint was a sign, *Mat. Grahdy, Meats, Groceries.* He went in, knowing that a bell would tinkle, so of course one *did.*

The showcase on one side was large enough to show lots and lots of meats; what it showed now were some scrawny pieces of pig, a hunk of headcheese, a hunk of Swiss cheese, a tray of lilac-colored sausages, and (in a puddle of congealing blood) half of a head of something, cut longitudinally and looking incredibly anatomical. The store seemed vast, and was vastly empty; the smell proclaimed that Coolidge was President; the floor was splintery and clean. Looking up from something on the counter, Mr. Grahdy gazed with absolute amazement. Was he merely amazed that Fred Silberman was coming into his store?—that someone who *looked* like Fred Silberman was coming into his store?—or, simply, that someone, *any*one, was coming into his store?

Then he smiled. Dipped his head to one side. They shook hands. Fred asked for some small item. Grahdy shrugged one shoulder. Fred asked for a different small item. Another shrug. Fred tried to think of some other small item, opened his mouth to name something, said, "Uh—" and named nothing. Grahdy laughed, finger-brushed his long moustaches: *Right! Left!*

"Rice?" he asked. "Sugar? Potatoes?" It was Silberman's turn to laugh. The elder man joined in. A cut of headcheese was his next suggestion; "and a cut of Swiss? a sliced roll? I give mustard for nothing." Somehow they wound up sharing the sandwich. Fred, observing an opened book on a newspaper there atop the counter, asked Mr. Grahdy What was he reading?

The book was turned around. But it was Greek to Fred. "Schiller," said the grocer, turning pages. "Heine. You can read in the original?" He widened his eyes at Fred's headshake. "What great pleasure you are missing. So. But . . . Lermontov? Pushkin? What? 'Nope'?" A look of mild surprise. And mild reproof. A sigh. "So. No wonder you have Slovo friends!" The front of his very clean, very threadbare apron moved in merriment.

This was it. The opening. "Mr. Grahdy—" Mr. Grahdy bowed slightly. His horse, his carriage, were at Fred Silberman's disposal. "Mr. Grahdy . . . what is it with you . . . with you people . . . your people . . . and the Slovo people? Could you tell me that? I would like to know. I would really like to know."

Mr. Grahdy stroked his smile, moustachioes, Vandyke, and all. He looked (Silberman suddenly thought), he would have looked, much like the Kaiser . . . if the Kaiser had ever looked much like having a sense of humor. "Well, I shall tell you. In our old kingdom there back in Europe. In one province lived mainly Huzzuk only. In one province lived mainly Slovo only. In our own province lived we both. How shall I explain? To say that the Slovo were our serfs? Not exact. To say they were our tenants, our servants? Mm . . . but . . . well . . . Our thralls? You see. The kings, they were of foreign origin, a dynasty. We were their feudalists. We Huzzuk. And the Slovo, the Slovo, they were our feudalists!" His smile indicated not so much satisfaction with the subordinate position of the Slovo as satisfaction with his explanation. And, as Silberman stood leaning against the counter digesting this, the old grocer added to it.

The Slovo were not, hm, bad people. They were simple. Very simple people. Had come into Europe long ago following behind the Magyar and the Avar. Had been granted permission to settle down in "empty land" belonging to the Huzzuk. Had become Christianized. Civilized. Gave up their old language. Adopted the language of the Huzzuk. Which they spoke badly. Very badly. —Here, with many chuckles, Grahdy gave examples of the comical Slovo dialect, of which exemplar Fred of course understood nothing whatsoever.

He did take advantage of the old man's laughing himself into a coughing fit and then into smiling silence. "What about their stove, Mr. Grahdy? What's with the Slovo stove? What is it, what is it, how does it *work?"* And here Mr. Grahdy threw back his head and laughed and laughed and coughed and coughed and laughed and coughed and laughed.

It took quite a while for him to recover. And after he had been slapped on the back and had sipped a glass of water and sucked a Life Saver and assured Fred (with many mimes and gestures) that he was now all right, Grahdy spoke in a weakened voice, incomprehensibly; then, rather more clearly, though very husky: *"Did it get warm yet?"* he asked.

Silberman jumped away from the counter. "But what do you *mean* by that? You said it last night and so did Mr. What's-His-Name with the thick white hair and you both laughed and laughed *then*—"

"The woman in the story. The Slovo woman in the story. The famous story anecdote. You know."

But finally Fred got his point across that no, he did *not* know. Grahdy was amused at this. At this, next, Grahdy was incredulous. And finally, persuaded that indeed, famous or never so famous, the story anecdote was absolutely unknown to F. Silberman—"Your great-grandfather did not ever told you? No? *No?"*—Grahdy was absolutely delighted. *God* knows when he had last had an absolutely fresh audience. . . .

A Slovo woman had newly emigrated to the United States. Came to stay with relatives. By and by someone asked that a pot of water be put on for tea. "I will do it," said the greenhorn woman. Did she know how to do it? Of course, of course! What did they think? Of course she knew how! "Shouldn't someone go and show her?" Nonsense; not necessary! Off she went, from the front room into the kitchen to put the water on for the tea. So they talked and they waited and they waited and they waited, and still no call from the kitchen. Had she gone out the back door? So someone went in to see. They found her standing by the stove and looking at it. (Grahdy indicated her perplexed look.) *"Was the water hot yet?"* Here Grahdy indicated that the great punch line was coming; here Grahdy put hands on hips and an expression of annoyance and bewilderment on face.

" 'Was the water hot yet?' "

" *'Hot? Hot? It didn't even get warm!'* "

Neither did Silberman. What the hell. But the story anecdote was not over. The punch line was followed by an explanation. (a) The Slovo greenhorn woman knew nothing about a gas range. (b) The Slovo greenhorn woman assumed that the gas range was, simply, a Slovo stove, American style. (c) So she, seeing that the grate—which to her was, of course, "the black part"—seeing this already in place, she put water in the pot and set it on top. (d) Leaning against the gas stove there happened to be the grease tray, usually placed of course underneath the burners to catch spatters and drips; it had just been cleaned, was why it was where it was. It was enameled, and a pale blue. (e) So, assuming that this was "the blue part," she had slid it into place, underneath the burners. (f) Had *not* turned on the gas, (g) had *not* struck a match, (h) had just waited for this American gas stove to behave like a *Slovo* stove—

—and here came the question and answer together again, as inexorable as Greek tragedy and by now almost as familiar as Weber and Fields or Abbott and Costello:

" '*Was the water hot yet?*' "

" '*Hot? Hot? It didn't even get warm!*' "

This was, evidently, and by now Fred had had lots of evidence, the hottest item there had ever been in Huzzuk humor in the history of the *world:* Joe Miller, Baron Munchausen, Charlie Chaplin, step *way* back. Get ready for something *really* funny: the anecdote story of the greenhorn who thought that by sliding the grease tray underneath the gas burners, and by doing nothing else, she could produce heat!

Hot-cha!

Yocketty-bop-cha!

Why this venerable race joke, certainly worth a chuckle when fresh and crisp, still guffawed its way down the corridors of time, required more consideration than Fred was then prepared to give. But it was a lot, *lot* easier to understand why the Slovos, who had been listening to it for . . . *how* long? forty years? *eighty* years? . . . were beginning to get kind of restless. And—

"And how does it *work*, Mr. Grahdy? I mean . . . scientifically?"

The one-shoulder shrug. "Who knows, my dear young gentleman? Consider the electrical properties of the amber, a great curiosity in the former age; but today, merely we flick a switch."

The local public library was not changed much since Andrew Carnegie had helped endow it; there was nothing in the catalogue under either *Huzzuk, Slovo,* or *Stove* which provided even faint enlightenment. The encyclopedia ran to information about the former dynasty and its innumerable dull rulers; also *The Huzzukya areas have become moderately industrialized* and *The interests of the Slovoya areas remain largely agrarian* and *Exports include duck down, hog bristles, coarse grades of goat hair and wool.* Goody.

In the Reference Room the little librarian with the big eyeglasses listened to his request; said, in her old-time professionally hush-hush voice, "I think there is a pamphlet" . . . and there certainly *was* a pamphlet; it was bound in, and bound in tightly, with a bunch of other pamphlets on a bunch of other subjects. The nameless author-publisher ("Published by the Author") had disguised the fact of not having much to say by saying it in rather large type. Leaning on the volume with both hands to keep it open, Silberman learned that "the Slovoi themselves no longer admit to know just where was or even approximately their ancestral 'Old Home' or 'Old Place' near 'The Big Water.' The latter has been suggested for Caspian Sea or Aral Sea, even fantastically has been suggested 'Lake Baikal.' In Parlour's Ferry are found Huzzuki in many Middle Class professional commercial role and has been correctly suggested Slovoi fulfill labor tasks with commendable toil and honesty." There was nothing about stoves, and Fred felt that unless he wanted eventually to sell photographs of his wrists to Charles Atlas, he might as well let go of the bound volume of pamphlets; he did, and it closed like a bear trap.

The pamphlet probably contained the text of a paper done for a pre-WWI class in Night School, the Author of which, intoxicated by getting a fairly good grade, had rushed it off to a job printer; it was suggested in Fred's mind that he was probably (*prob*ably?) a Huzzuk.

Back at Fred's new apartment-to-be, lo! the painters were no longer painting; the painters were no longer, in fact, there; and neither was the painting finished. Only, in the middle of the drainboard of the kitchen sink sat a white bread and sardine sandwich with a single symmetrical bite missing out of it. Another unsolved mystery of the sea; or had it come there by a fortuitous concourse of the atoms: why not? Down went Fred and rang Mrs. Keeley's bell. By and by the door opened a crack long enough to transmit heavy breathing and the odor of gin and onions; almost at once the door closed shut again and by and by the volume of the radio went up. Mrs. Keeley was not one of your *picky* listeners out there in Radioland who require very fine tuning, and Silberman was unable to say if she was listening to an old recording of the Tasty Yeast Jesters or maybe one of a love song by President Harding. He went away.

A côte chez Brakk, an aunt said, as he came in, "I saved you some fruit stew," and also Wes poured him something powerful-looking. Evidently the conventicle/potlatch was still going on, with Fred's presence still acceptable. Al*though*— A newspaper was lowered; behind it was *Nick.* "Don't make the Old Lady show ya that jee-dee *stove* no more," he said. "She's all wore out."

Fred said, easily, "Okay, Nick. —Who else has got one?" he asked the world at large. There was a thinking pause. Wes said, No one that *he* knew of.

"It's the last of the Mohicans," Wes said.

Nick slapped down the paper. "She better get *rid*da it. Y'hear me? I'm gonna smash it up, I'm gonna throw it offa the bridge; I don' wanna even *hear* about it—no wonder they make funna us all the time!" No one said a word, so Nick said a word, a short and blunt one; and then, as though shocked himself, slammed out of the room. In a moment a car drove rapidly away. Wes was expressionless and, seemingly, emotionless.

Fred sampled the fruit stew. Was it the same as stewed fruit? no it *was*n't. Good, though. As soon as his spoon scraped the bottom, a bowl of something else was set down beside him. And a plate of something else. "Here is beaten-up bean soup with buttermilk and vinegar. This is lamb fritters with fresh dill." Golly, they sounded odd! Golly, they were good!

In a corner across the room an old man and an old woman discordantly sang-sung religious texts from, shared between them, an old wide book in Old Wide Huzzuk or something of the sort. "That's supposed to benefit the soul of the late deceased," said a very young man with a very large and shiny face, in a tentatively contentious tone.

"College boy," said Wes. "Could it hurt?"

Fred Silberman put down his spoon. (Eating fritters with a *spoon?* Sure. Why not? Hurts *you?*) "Listen, where was 'the Old Home Place by the Big Water'?" he asked.

The college boy instantly answered, "Gitche Gumee."

Wes said, with a shrug of his own, far heavier than Mat. Grahdy's, "Who the hell knows? Whoever *knew?* You think they had *maps* in those days? I suppose that one year the crops failed and there was no nourishment in the goat turds, so they all hit the road. *West.* And once they crossed a couple mountains and a couple of rivers, not only didn't they know where they *were,* they didn't even know where they'd *been.*"

Fred said, "Listen. Listen. Nick isn't here, the Huzzuks aren't here, nobody is here but us chickens, *cut*-cut-cut-*cut,* God should strike me dead if I laugh at you: *Where did the stoves come from? The* Slovo *stoves?*"

"Who the hell knows?"

"Well, did they have them when they *left* . . . wherever it was? Lake Ontario, or the Yellow Sea? Did they . . . ?"

Wes just sighed. But his, probably, sister took to answering the question, and the further questions, and, when she didn't know, asked her elders and translated the answers. According to old stories, yes, they *did* have the stoves before they left the Old Place. The black parts they came from the mountain and the blue parts they came from the Big Water. From the *inside* of the mountain, what mountain, nobody knows what mountain, and from the bottom of the Big Water. How did they get the *idea?* Well, Father *Yock*im said that the angels gave it to them. Father *Yock*im said! That's not what the *old* people use to say . . . what *did* the old people used to say? The old people used to say it was the little black and white gods but Father Yockim he thought people would think that meant like devils or something, so he changed it and— Well, there aren't any little black and white *gods,* for God's sake! —Oh, you're so smart, you think you—

"Maybe they were from outer space," said Silberman, to his own surprise as much as anyone else's.

Silence the most profound. Then the "college boy," probably either a nephew or a cousin, said, slowly, "Maybe they *were.*" Another silence. Then they were all off again.

The trouble all began with Count Cazmar. Count Cazmar had, like, a monopoly on all the firewood from the forest. The king gave it to him. Yes, but the king didn't just "give" it to him; he had to *pay* the king. Okay, so he had to *pay* the king. So anybody wanted firewood *they* had to *pay* Count Cazmar. Then he got sore because the Slovo people weren't buying enough firewood, see, because he *still* had to pay the king. Which king? Who the hell knows which king? Who the hell cares? None of them were any damn good anyway. What, old King Joseph wasn't any good, the one who let Yashta Yushta out of the dungeon? Listen, will you for*get* about old King Joseph and get on with the story!

So Count Cazmar sent out all the blacksmiths to go from house to house with their great big sledgehammers to smash up all the Slovo stoves to force the Slovos to buy more firewood and— What? Yeah, that's how Gramma's stove is, like, broken. They *all* got, like, broken. Of *course* you could still use them. But dumb Count Cazmar *he* dint know that. So, what finely happen, what finely happen, everybody had to pay a firewood tax irregardless of how much they used or not. So lotta the Slovo people they figured, ya gotta pay for it anyway? so might as well *use* it. See? Lotta them figure, ya gotta pay for it anyway, so might as well use it. And so, lotta them quit usin' their Slovo stoves. Y'see.

"That's your superior Huzzuk civilization for you," Wes said. Just then the deacon and deaconess in the corner, or whatever they were, lifted their cracked old voices and finished their chant; and everybody said something loudly and they all stamped their feet. "Here, Fred," said Wes, "have some more—have another glass o' mulberry beer." And promptly an aunt set two more bowls down in front of Fred. "In this one is chopped spleen stew with crack buckwheats. And in udder one is cow snout cooked under onions. Wait. I give you pepper."

Eventually Silberman got moved into his new apartment and eventually Silberman got moved into his new job; his new job required (among other things . . . among *many* other things) a trip to the diemakers, a trip to the printers, a trip to the suppliers: *how* convenient that all three were located in a new or newish commercial and industrial complex way out on the outskirts of. As he drove, by and by such landmarks as an aqueduct, a cemetery, an old brick foundry, reminded him that, more or less where the commercial and industrial complex now was, was where old Applebaum used to be. Lo! it seemed: still was! Shabby, but still reading M. APPLEBAUM CASH AND CARRY WHOLESALE GROCERIES. The complicated commerces and industries perhaps didn't *like* shabby Old Applebaum's holding out in their midst? Tough. Let them go back where they came from.

Afterwards, business finished elsewhere, thither: "Freddy. Hel*lo.*"

"Hello, Mr. Applebaum. How are *you?*"

"How should I be? Every week seems like another family grocery bites the dust. Nu. I own a little swamp in Florida and maybe I will close up the gesheft and go live on a houseboat with hot and cold running crocodiles. Ah-ah, here comes an old customer with his ten dollars' worth of business if we are both lucky; Mat. Grahdy."

Sure enough. Beat *him* to the punch. "Hey, Mr. Grahdy, did it get hot yet?"

Grahdy *laughed* and laughed; then gave the counterword: "It didn't even get *warm!* Ho ho ho ho." He gestured to another man. "This is Petey Plazzek, he is a half-breeth. Hey, Petey, did it get hot yet? Ho ho ho ho! —Mosek!"—this to Old Applebaum. "A little sugar I need, a little semolina I need, a little cake flour, licorice candy, marshmallow crackers." M. Applebaum said he could give him a good buy on crackers today. They went inside together.

Petey Plazzek, a worn-looking man in a worn-looking lumber jacket, came right to the point. "If you're driving by the *bus dee*po, you could give me a ride."

"Sure. Get in." Off they went. Silberman's glance observed no Iroquois cheekbones. "Excuse me, but what did he mean, 'A half-breed'? No offense—"

"Naa, naa. Half Huzzuk, half Slovo."

A touch of the excitement. "Well, uh, Mr. Plazzek—"

"Petey. Just Petey."

"Well, uh, Petey, how many people have one of those old Slovo stoves anymore?"

"Nobody. Them stoves are all a thing o' the past nowadays. Watch out for that truck."

"How come, Petey? How come they are?"

Petey rubbed his nose, sighed very deeply. "Well. *You* know. Some greenhorn would come to America—as we used to say, 'He had six goats and he sold five to get the steamship ticket and he gave one to the priest to pray for a good journey.' I'm talking about a *Slovo* now. Huzzuk, that's another thing altogether. So the poor Slovo was wearing high boots with his pants tucked innem and a shirt smock and a sheepskin coat and a fur hat. This was before Ellis Island. Castle *Gar*den in those days. *He* didn't have a steamer trunk, *he* didn't have a grip, he only had a sort of knapsack; so what was *in* it? A clean smock shirt and some clean foot rags, because they didn't use socks, and a little iron pot and some hardtack-type bread and those two stove parts, the black part and the, uh, the, uh—"

"The *blue* part."

"—the *blue* part, right. Watch out for that Chevy. Well, he'd get a job doing the lowest-paid dirtiest work and he'd rent a shack that subsequently you wouldn't dast keep a *dog* in it, y'understand what I'm telling you, young fellow? Lights, he had no lights, he didn't even have no *lamp,* just a tin can with some pork fat and a piece of rag for a wick. And he'd pick up an old brick here and an old brick there and set up his Slovo stove and cook buckwheat in his little iron pot and he'd sleep on the floor in his sheepskin coat."

But by and by things would get better; this was *America,* the land of opportunity. So as soon as he started making a little money he brought his wife over and they moved into a room, a real room, and he'd buy a coal-oil lamp and a pair of shoes for each of them, but, um, people would still laugh attem, partickley the *Zunks* would still be laughing at them because of still using the Slovo *stove,* y'see. So by and by they'd buy a *wood* stove. Or a *coal* stove. And they'd get the gaslight turned on. And they'd even remember not t' blow it out."

"Yes, but, Petey. The wood and coal cost *money.* And the Slovo stove was *free.* So—"

Petey sighed again. "Well. To tell you the truth. It could *cook:* sure. Didn't give out much *heat,* otherwise. Boil up a lotta water, place'd get *steamy.*"

Fred Silberman cried, "Steam heat! Steam *heat!*"

Petey looked startled, then—for the first time—interested. Then the interest ebbed away. He sighed. "None of them people were plumbers. *They* never thought of nothing like that, and neither did anybody else. The Slovo stove, what it come to mean, it come to mean *poverty,* see? It come to mean *rid*icule. And so as soon as they quit being dirt-poor, well, that was *that.*"

Fred asked, eagerly, "But aren't there still a lot of them in the attics? Well . . . *some* of them? In the *cellars?*"

Petey's breath hissed. "Where you *going?* You going to the *bus dee*po, y' shoulda turned *leff!* Oh. Circling the block. Naa . . . they juss, uh, thrown'm *away.* Watch out for that van."

The new job and its new responsibilities occupied and preoccupied most of Silberman's time, but one afternoon as he was checking an invoice with the heating contractor fitting up the plant, lo! the old matter came abruptly to his mind.

"Sudden thought?" said Mr. McMurtry.

"Uh. Yuh. You ever hear of a . . . Slovo stove?"

Promptly: "No. *Should* I have?"

Suppose Fred were to *tell* him. What then? Luddite activity on the part of McMurtry? "Let me ask you a make-believe question, Mac—"

"Fire when ready."

So . . . haltingly, ignorantly . . . Fred (naming no names, no ethnic groups) described matters as well as he could, winding up: "So could you think, Mac, of any scientific explanation as to how such a thing could, or might, maybe, work? At all?"

Mac's brow furrowed, rolling the hairs of his conjoined eyebrows: a *very* odd effect. "Well, obviously the liquid in the container acts as a sort of noncontiguous catalyst, and this amplifies the vortex of the force field created by the juxtaposition of the pizmire and the placebo"—well of *course* McMurtry did not say *that*: but that was what it sounded like to Silberman. And so McMurtry might just as well have said it.

McMurtry said one last word or two. "If these things weren't make-believe it would be interesting to examine them. Even a couple of little pieces might do. What can be analyzed could maybe be duplicated."

Once things got going well at work, Fred thought he would go and ask old Mrs. Brakk . . . go and ask old Mrs. Brakk *what?* Would she let the sole extant Slovo stove be examined by an expert? be looked at in a lab? be scraped to provide samples for electronic microscopic analysis?

???

He might suggest that, if she didn't trust *him*, it might be done through a Brakk Family Trust . . . or something . . . to be set up for that purpose. Via Wes . . . and, say, *Nick*. . . .

Sure he might.

But he waited too long.

Silberman of course knew nothing; how could he have known? The people of the house had just learned themselves. All *he* knew, arriving early one night, was that, as he came up to the house, a tumult began within. Lots of people were yelling. And as he came into the Brakk kitchen, Nick was yelling alone.

"We're Americans, ain't we?" he yelled. "So let's *live* like Americans; bad enough so the Huzzuks make fun of us, I'm *tired* of all them Old Country ways, what next, what else? Fur hats? Boots? A goat in the yard?" He addressed his wife. "A hundred times I told your old lady, 'Throw it away, throw the damned thing *away*, I-am-*tired* they making fun of us, Mamma, you hear?' But she didn't. She didn't. So *I, did.*" He stopped, breathing hard. "And that's all. . . ."

A sick feeling crept into Silberman's chest.

"*Where* did you throw it? *Where?* It wasn't *yours!*"—his wife. Nick pressed his lips together. His wife clapped her hand to her head. "He always used to say, 'I'll throw it off the bridge, I'll throw it off the bridge!'

That's where! Oh, you hoo-*dlóm!*" For a moment his eyes blazed at her. Then he shrugged, lit a cigarette, and began to smoke with an air of elaborately immense unconcern.

Old Mrs. Brakk sat with her faint smile a moment more. Then she began to speak in her native language. Her voice fell into a chant, then her voice broke, then she lifted her apron to her eyes.

"She says, 'All she had to remind her of the old home country. All she wanted to do was sometimes warm the baby's bottle or sometimes make herself a bowl of tea in her own room if she was tired. She's an old lady and she worked hard and she never wanted to bother nobody—' "

Nick threw his cigarette with force onto the linoleum and, heedless of shrieks, stamped on it heavily. Then he was suddenly calm. "All *right.* Listen. Tomorrow I'll buy you a little electric stove, a, a whadda they call it? *A hot plate!* Tomorrow for your own room I'll buy y'a hot plate. O*kay?*"

The effect was great; Nick had never been known—voluntarily—to buy *any*thing for *any*one.

Old Mrs. Brakk exclaimed, in English, "You *will?*"

He gave a solemn nod. "I swear to God." He crossed his heart. "Tomorrow. The best money can buy. Mamma can come with me," he added. His wife kissed him. His older brother-in-law patted him on the back. The old woman began to smile again.

Silberman felt his heart pounding at twice its regular rate. He dared say nothing. Then, by and by, Nick strolling out into the yard and lighting up another cigarette, he strolled out after him.

"Nick."

"Yeah."

"I'm going to ask you something. Don't get mad."

"Gaw head."

"You really threw the stove parts off the bridge?"

"Yeah. Well . . . the *pieces.*"

"Pieces?"

Nick yawned. Nodded. "I took the damn thing to the shop. Where I work. *You* know." Fred knew. "An I runnum through the crusher. And what was *left* . . . I puttum in a bag. An I threw it offa the bridge." He wasn't angry *or* regretful. He let fall his cigarette, stomped it, went back into the house. Fred heard him working the television.

The shop. Sneaky as could be, Fred lurked and skulked and peeked. The light was on, the door was open. Had Nick left them so? No matter; surely *some* crumbles of blue, of black, would be left, and he would zip in, scoop them off the floor by the crusher, and— A long shadow oozed across the floor. The janitor, humping his broom. A real, old-time Slovo, immense moustache and all, of the real, old-time Slovo sort; in a minute he was gone. Fred zipped, all right. But he didn't scoop; there was nothing to scoop. *No* crumbles. There wasn't even *dust.* Tanta Pesha was not physically present but her voice sounded in her great-nephew's ears: *The Slovos? They are very clean . . . you could eat off their floors. . . .*

He drove his car up and down the silent streets. Shouted aloud, "I don't *believe* it! The greatest discovery in thermodynamics since the discovery of *fire!* And it's *gone.* It's *gone!* It can't be gone! It can't be—"

In the days that followed, in the weeks and months, he knocked on doors, he advertised, he offered rewards. Pleaded. Begged. That incredible discovery, mysteriously having come to earth who knew how and who knew how many thousands of years ago or how many thousands of miles away.

It was *gone.*

Fred threw himself into his work. Developed, locally, an active social life. Womanized. Thought of marriage. *Changed.* Other things changed too. Wes Brakk abruptly moved to Idaho, why Idaho? Of all places. "Because he said it was as far away from the Huzzuks as he could get and still wear shoes." Oh. And the rest of the Brakk family, plus Nick—*led* by Nick—almost as suddenly moved to Brownsville, Texas. Why Brownsville, *Texas?* "To get away from the cold." Others might move to Florida, California, Arizona, to get away from the cold: the rest of the Brakk family (plus Nick) moved to *Brownsville, Texas,* to get away from the cold.

It seemed, somehow, a very Slovo sort of thing to do.

They were ripping up Statesman Street again and Fred had to detour. *Had* he to drive along Tompkins, Gerry, and De Witt streets? For one reason or another, he did drive along there: *my,* the neighborhood had changed! The new neighbors glanced at him with unneighborly glances. There was Grahdy's store. But one whole once-glass pane was missing, boarded up. He stopped. Went in. There was Mr. Grahdy, part of his face bandaged, the other part bruised and discolored. His violin was in his hand. He nodded his jaunty nod. "Would you enjoy to hear a little Paganini?" he asked. Began to play.

Silberman felt that he was present at almost the last scene of a very antick drama. Old Mat. Grahdy, with his wife's alexandrines, his violin, Heine, Schiller, Lermontov, Pushkin, Paganini, and the Latin *Psalms*— how long could he last? If he didn't starve to death in his almost empty store, how long before they killed him?

The old man let the violin fall to his side. For an odd, long moment he gazed at Silberman with a very level gaze. Then a smile twitched onto his swollen, battered face. He shrugged one shoulder. He began to laugh. *"It didn't even get warm,"* he chuckled.

TERRY CARR has been awarded eight Nebula citations by the Science Fiction Writers of America, and is one of the most respected editors in the field. In addition to the *Universe* series, he edits the *Best Science Fiction of the Year* compilation and the Ace Science Fiction Specials. His own writing includes the novel *Cirque* and a short story collection, *The Light at the End of the Universe.* He lives in Oakland, California.